ATLANTIS

THE BRINK OF WAR

ATLANTIS

THE BRINK OF WAR

Gregory Mone

AMULET BOOKS • NEW YORK

Cataloging-in-Publication Data has been applied for and
may be obtained from the Library of Congress.

ISBN 978-1-4197-3855-5

Text © 2022 Gregory Mone
Jacket and map illustrations © 2022 Vivienne To
Edited by Howard W. Reeves
Book design by Brenda E. Angelilli

Printed and bound in U.S.A.
10 9 8 7 6 5 4 3 2 1

Amulet Books are available at special discounts when purchased
in quantity for premiums and promotions as well as fundraising or
educational use. Special editions can also be created to specification.
For details, contact specialsales@abramsbooks.com or the address below.

Amulet Books® is a registered
trademark of Harry N. Abrams, Inc.

ABRAMS The Art of Books
195 Broadway, New York, NY 10007
abramsbooks.com

To the Star Sisters and the Ninja

CONTENTS

From: Porter Winfield

Director, National Security Agency

To: President Laura Moffat

The White House

Madam President,

I am pleased to report that we successfully interviewed the
two young people who recently returned from Atlantis. You
will receive a more detailed description of their journey in the
coming days, but we have reason to believe their account is
truthful. The vehicle that carried them is unlike any technology
we've seen, and the girl with them has strangely alien features.
We are convinced she is an Atlantean, but she has thus far
refused to speak with us.

The agency received your note communicating your distaste for
long, unbroken paragraphs, so here is a brief, bulleted summary
of what we know:

- Three individuals, including former professor Richard Gates,
  his son Meriweather Lewis Gates, twelve, and Hanna Barkley,
  fifteen, daughter of Eyetide founder Miriam Barkley and
  investor John Barkley, survived the most recent tsunami in a
  custom-made submarine.

- The crew of three entered Atlantis on July 9.
- The boy, who goes by Lewis, assured us repeatedly that there were no cannibals in Atlantis. We are not sure why he was expecting cannibals, but he asked that we include this in our reports.
- Upon their arrival in Atlantis, they met the Atlantean girl, Kaya, and were mistaken for invaders. With Kaya, they spent several days attempting to evade capture as they traveled through the subsea world.
- Atlantis is much larger than we anticipated. It consists of perhaps one hundred million people and many major cities.
- The technology of the Atlanteans is far more advanced than we realized. They use sound-based, nonlethal weapons and have learned how to control gravity.
- We can confirm that Atlantis is responsible for the devastating tsunamis that have plagued the world's coasts for years.
- The hot sauce in Atlantis is fantastic. I would not have included this point, but Lewis repeated it on numerous occasions. Our code breakers are working to determine if there is some kind of hidden message in this statement, but it may be that Lewis just really liked the hot sauce. Given your fondness for this condiment, we will try to get you some.
- The three travelers were eventually caught and imprisoned in Atlantis. They managed to escape, but Professor Gates risked

his life in the process and remains in Atlantis under the care of a local. We do not know if Gates is alive or dead.

- Hanna, Lewis, and Kaya returned to the surface in a stolen Atlantean warship, destroying a factory in the process. The factory was designed for the mass manufacture of warships.
- The three young people returned on the morning of July 17, and they have remained in quarantine since due to concerns about possible Atlantean viruses.
- Neither Hanna nor Lewis will reveal even the approximate location of Atlantis; we suspect the Atlantean girl has requested this of them. We tried bribing the boy with sneakers from Ambassador Jordan; he accepted the gift but did not return the favor.

Again, we will provide you with a more detailed report in the coming days. As for Professor Gates, I strongly advise against any attempt to rescue him. This situation is far too delicate. Many questions remain about the tsunamis, the intentions of the Atlanteans, and their potential plans for war. Needless to say, we should prepare our armed forces for combat. We hope to have our remaining questions answered soon, and we strongly advise that this journey, and the existence of Atlantis, remain a secret.

Sincerely,

Porter Winfield

1

THE SURPRISE SPY

RIAN sprinted through the dark, narrow tunnels of the sewers beneath the city. The air was hot and thick. His feet splashed through small puddles scattered along the path, and the waterway beside him carried fish scraps, sea greens, and other trash out of the city toward the giant recycling and filtering pools. He stopped and listened. All he heard was the steady rush of the water.

No one was following him.

He ran faster.

When Rian finally neared the basement of Capitol Tower, he was breathing heavily. His heartbeat had accelerated. Was he scared? Maybe. Nervous? Definitely. Rian was a scrawny fourteen-year-old kid with a talent for sneaking around Ridge City. He wasn't a spy.

Not until today, anyway.

He could stop now.

Go home.

That would be the smart choice. The safe one, too.

But would Kaya give up now? Not a chance.

When he came to the rusted steel door to the basement

of Capitol Tower, Rian reached into his pocket and pulled out a small, cylindrical device known as a lock whisperer. The gadget was capable of speeding through endless combinations and sequences of notes. Given enough time, it could find the tune to open any door in Atlantis. He switched it on and listened. The sounds played so quickly and chaotically that he had to cover his ears. Before too long, though, the heavy door slid open, and Rian stepped into the large, high-ceilinged basement.

The sewer water was slightly cleaner here upstream, and it flowed out through small gaps at the base of the walls. After a deep, steadying breath, he tightened his gloves and ankle straps. He checked his chest plate. Everything was powered up. Whistling quietly, he turned on his gravity drive—or Kaya's, really, since he had borrowed her gear—and his feet rose off the ground.

He drifted to the ceiling; it felt like he was swimming through the air.

The vents and trash chutes that snaked down from the building's upper floors all ended here in the basement. Each one was neatly labeled. The lights in the walls were faint but bright enough that he could see the numbers.

A rattling, sliding sound came from one of the openings.

Rian peered up into the dark space, then jerked back.

A clump of trash plummeted down and splashed into the water below.

His instructions were to find chute 14B. With his back to the water, he moved along the ceiling like a spider, his hands and feet pressing lightly against the damp stone, until he found the narrow tunnel, pulled himself inside, and rose. His nose itched. His shoulders brushed the walls as he floated higher and higher. There was no way an adult would ever fit inside. And one of those giant Sun People? Impossible.

Sometimes it wasn't so bad to be small.

The antigravity suit carried him smoothly to the upper floors.

Metallic-tasting air rushed out as he passed vents to other rooms.

Twice he had to scrunch his nose to stifle a sneeze.

Above him, he heard angry, passionate voices that bounced off the tunnel walls.

He drifted toward the source and hovered in the dark, narrow passageway. A faint green light flooded the chute. The same metallic air, too—it was cool against his face. The mouth of the vent was close to the room's ceiling, and given the angle, he wouldn't have been able to see the people inside the room if he'd tried. But he did recognize a few of the voices. He'd heard them on the soundscape.

These were the members of the High Council.

The leaders of Atlantis.

And Rian was spying on them.

He swallowed quietly. Follow the instructions, Rian told himself. Kaya's dad, Heron, had entrusted him with this mission. He'd asked him to record every word in secret, then hurry home and transmit the audio over a specific channel on the soundscape. The whole arrangement was odd—Heron hadn't even asked him in person. Instead, he'd requested Rian's help through a recorded message.

Now Rian reached up and tapped his earpiece. He was late; they were already deep into a debate about the Sun People. Several of the voices were gravelly and tired, and one of the women sounded like she needed to cough. The argument was growing like a wave nearing the shallows.

"They are poisoning our oceans, and our cities are collapsing at a frightening rate!" a woman with a deep voice proclaimed. "We have to find a new home on the surface."

"Our civilization has survived under the sea this long," countered another woman, whose voice was garbled, as if she had an oyster lingering in the back of her throat. "We can manage for a few more centuries."

"How can you be sure?"

A man thumped his fist on the table. "Why should we fight the Sun People? Let them fight each other, as they love to do, and Atlantis can rise from the ashes of their civilizations."

Rian had learned about the existence of the Sun People only a few days before. His whole life, he'd been taught that there was no life on the surface. There were people like Kaya, who believed the government was lying to them, but they never had proof. Based on what he was hearing now, though, it sounded like the High Council had known about the Sun People all along.

They'd been lying to the rest of Atlantis.

The debate turned into a shouting match.

"Their machines are mining and ravaging the seafloor. It won't be long until the Sun People tunnel straight into one of our cities in search of their precious metals and oils. We must act now!"

"The surface was once ours. Let it be ours again!"

"The people of Atlantis deserve to know the truth."

"We should try to negotiate with the Sun People first."

"Negotiate?!" someone yelled. "The last time we tried that, several of our brightest young citizens were killed!"

"Including my son," added another voice.

The room suddenly went quiet. Rian recognized the man's low, forceful growl. He'd heard that voice on the soundscape—Rian's parents always made him listen to the news. But he couldn't remember the man's name. A chair was pushed back from the table; its stone legs ground against the stone floor. The man continued, his voice calm and assured. "We sent that delegation on a peaceful mission, and what did the Sun People do? They blasted a dozen innocent Atlanteans out of the water. So, while I appreciate your opinions and would prefer to live in peace, we cannot ignore the facts. The Sun People poison our oceans, making it ever harder for us to grow and raise enough food for our people. They will not stop, either; their hunger for metals and oil draws them to the depths. Some of you have said we can survive for centuries, but what if you're wrong? What if we have only a few years left? Their submarines have been scouring the seafloor in search of our world, and now they've found it. Their invasion was a success—they stole one of our warships, and I wouldn't be surprised if they are copying it right now, building a fleet of their own. Their next attack will be devastating if they have Atlantean technology."

His voice had risen in intensity. The man paused, breathed. When he resumed, his tone was solemn. "Yes, I lost my son to those heartless creatures from the surface, but I have not let that muddy my judgment on this issue. This is not about my son. This is about Atlantis. We need to stop the Sun People before they invade again. It pains me to say this, but a direct attack is our only choice, my friends. I move to vote."

Rian had to stop himself from interrupting. None of this sounded right. Invaders? He'd met the Sun People. They were kids! And they were completely harmless. Especially the boy, Lewis. If he were a fish, he'd be a minnow. The older one, Hanna—she was different. Smart. Powerful. Strong, too. But neither of them were soldiers. Not even close. Rian wanted to push through the grate and tell the High Council all that he knew, what he'd seen. But he'd been warned not to whisper a word.

One of the women spoke up again, her voice solemn and insistent. "First we must inform the public of the existence of the Sun People."

"No, we must vote now or—"

"Demos, must I remind you again that you are one of twelve equally powerful elected members of the High Council? You are not our leader."

This time, the man said nothing. Rian could practically feel him glaring.

"Agreed," the woman with the oyster voice said, "but I second Demos's motion to vote on war. The invaders he encountered are likely only the first wave."

The argument started up again. Practically everyone was shouting at once. Finally, someone called for order, and the woman with the solemn tone spoke. "An attack on the surface is a very serious matter, but Demos has raised serious concerns.

We all need time to think. I suggest we reconvene in four days to vote for or against this war."

The other members of the High Council agreed. Chairs scraped against the floor as the meeting ended. Pockets of murmurs and whispers broke out. Rian waited until he heard the whoosh of doors opening, the shuffle of footsteps, and then a stretch of unbroken silence after the last of the High Council members exited the room. The green glow of the room's interior lights faded into darkness, and the cramped tunnel felt strangely cold. Rian wanted to get home as fast as possible. Most of all, though, he wanted to talk to Kaya, to tell her what he'd learned and find out what she knew. But he hadn't seen or heard from his friend since she'd hurried off to rescue the Sun People a week before.

He didn't even know if she was alive or dead.

2

ESMERELDA ON THE GRASS

LEWIS studied himself in the mirror hanging from his closet door. His hair was a little long on top, but he liked the flow. His brown eyes weren't that big or small or interesting. Sure, he had a chin, and a nose, too, but neither was very memorable. And his ears? He turned and studied one. Was it weird? Maybe, but all ears were odd. He stood back to inspect more of himself. He wasn't very tall or muscular. Yet he would admit, if pushed, that he was kind of a big deal. He wasn't famous or anything. Not yet. But he had helped discover Atlantis. And he'd sort of helped destroy a fleet of Atlantean warships, too.

For now, this was all a big, giant, annoying secret, but there was no way that could last. A bunch of his neighbors and a few of his friends had been there when they'd cruised into his yard in the Atlantean warship. They'd seen Kaya! She didn't look much like a normal kid. She was human, sure. But her hair was silvery-white, her eyes were unusually large, and her skin was so pale it was almost colorless. Her hands and feet were a little longer than normal—or what Lewis thought was normal—but you kind of had to focus to notice that. Anyway, if you saw Kaya, you'd know she wasn't from the neighborhood.

But all the government and military folks who had swarmed the area had sworn to everyone that the vehicle was just an advanced airship, and Lewis's friend Jet had kind of messed everything up by spreading the rumor that Kaya was from Mars and that Lewis was dating a Martian. Lewis didn't even have a crush on her, though, and if anything, as Hanna pointed out, Kaya was more likely to be from the ocean moon Europa than Mars. Still, the truth about Atlantis would get out eventually, and when it did, Lewis had to be ready for fame. He'd begun carrying a harmonica in his back pocket, because celebrities were always more interesting when they played an instrument.

"Lewis?" his mom asked from his doorway. "Are you okay?"

"I'm fine."

She didn't press. "Okay. Dinner's ready."

The air smelled of grilled meat; he could almost taste the salt and fat. He nodded toward the window. "Is Kaya still out in Esmerelda?"

"Esmerelda?"

"The ship," he reminded her. "You know, the floating, teardrop-shaped glass vehicle in our backyard?" Lewis believed that every unique vehicle needed a good name. His dad's old hovercar, which had been destroyed in the last tsunami, had been named Chet.

"Oh, that Esmerelda," his mom replied.

She pursed her lips and tilted her head. Lewis squinted back at her. "You're looking at me weirdly again," he said.

"That's love," she answered. "I'm still just so happy to see you. Home. Safe. And . . ."

Alive. That was the word she didn't say. He still felt massively guilty about the whole adventure, and it hurt to imagine what those days must have been like for her. His mom and Michael and his stepdad, Roberts, had spent a week thinking he was lost at sea . . . or worse. "I know," he said. "I'm sorry."

"Promise me you won't do that to me again?"

He hesitated. What would he be promising, exactly? He couldn't swear that he'd never return to Atlantis. There was his dad to think about. Plus, he really wanted to go back. There was so much more to see, an entire hidden world they'd barely begun to explore. Next time, though, he'd get her permission.

"I promise," Lewis said. "Really."

His mom nodded toward the ship and Kaya. "Does she tell you how she's feeling?"

Feeling? She was a girl! And he was a boy. So no, they absolutely did not discuss feelings. But she probably did miss home. They hadn't exactly been riding waterslides all day. Since returning to the surface, they'd gone exactly nowhere. "Are we even going to get to show her anything? I'd be bummed if I'd gone to Atlantis and we'd just sat around Kaya's house all day."

"For now, we need to stay here. Speaking of which, do you feel okay?"

"I told you, I'm fine."

"No headaches? No fever or chills?"

When they'd returned from Atlantis a week earlier, Lewis had thought they'd cruise through the streets of the capital in brand-new hovercars—gifts from his corporate sponsors, obviously—as people threw confetti down on them from their apartment windows. Or maybe even money. Small bills would have been fine. Ones and fives. But there had been no parades, no parties. No cash, either. Instead, Lewis, Hanna, and their families had been ordered to keep their adventure a secret and quarantine in their homes for two weeks. Some government agency was worried they might have picked up a weird Atlantean virus.

"I'm healthy, Mom," Lewis said. "They need to let us out of here. Someone needs to go back and get Dad."

She hugged him. He stiffened. Every time he brought up his dad, his mother or another adult either didn't answer or changed the subject. When he pressed them, they always told him the situation was "too complex" or something like that. But to Lewis, it seemed pretty simple. His dad was stuck in Atlantis. He was sick, too, and the doctors down there were probably giving him chopped seaweed instead of real medicine.

They had to rescue him. What was so complicated about that?

"You're different," his mom said, pulling away.

Clearly, she wasn't in the mood; they could talk about his dad later. "Different how?" He straightened his posture. "Taller?"

"No. You just seem . . . different."

"I did kind of go to Atlantis, Mom."

"True."

"And found my way back."

"Also true."

"Plus, I fought off ten heavily armed Atlantean guards."

"Not true."

"Michael believes me."

"Your brother believes everything you say."

"Almost everything." Michael didn't believe Lewis would pay him the twenty dollars he owed him, for example, and he was right.

"Let's go," his mom said. "Dinner's ready. Reinhold's here, and Hanna's joining us."

Before following her, Lewis glanced out his bedroom window. Esmerelda's hull was tinted, so he couldn't see inside. Above the ship, over the tops of the trees bordering their yard, he spotted a single headlight approaching in the sky. Hanna, he guessed. The government allowed Hanna and her parents to visit, so long as they didn't come into contact with anyone else on the way. Hanna came over most nights, and her parents had joined them several times. Her dad was a nice guy. A little formal—the firm-handshake, look-you-in-the-eye type. But Hanna's mom was the sun in their family's solar system. She projected power. Like Hanna, only turned way up.

Their other frequent guest was Lewis's father's scientist friend, Reinhold. The rumpled researcher had to wear a mask when he popped over, but Lewis liked having him around. He was short, round, and bearded, and he wore Hawaiian shirts in all weather, along with wool socks and these weird sandals with two thick straps. But it wasn't his outfits or even the ever-present sprinkling of cheese puff dust on his fingers that made him Lewis's favorite. Reinhold was one of the only scientists who had always stood by his dad; he'd encouraged his father to keep searching for Atlantis even when everyone else had rejected him. He was a true friend.

In the kitchen, Reinhold was already seated at the table, focused on his wristpad, with a light blue mask stretched over his nose and mouth. Tonight's aloha shirt featured surfing Santa Clauses. Lewis's stepfather, Roberts, was piling roasted meats onto an already-full wooden cutting board. The smell of salt and spices and the charred ends of the steak—an uncommon treat—and chicken made Lewis's nostril hairs dance. Sausages were buried under the pile, too. He could hear their insides sizzling. Since he'd returned from Atlantis, the thrill of eating real food, not fish wraps and kelp bars, had not faded. Even the roasted chunks of zucchini and eggplant on a neighboring platter were exciting. There was a bowl of green salad and a mound of pasta with butter and cheese, too, and a pyramid of crusty brown rolls waited on a plate in the middle of the kitchen table. His stomach backflipped and somersaulted.

"Michael?" his mom called out.

Lewis's little brother raced into the room and snagged the seat beside her. Michael was back to wearing two shoes again; last week, Lewis had convinced him that wearing only one was cool. Now Michael was delicately digging something out of his nose with his pinky finger. Their mom yanked at his elbow. "Manners," she muttered.

Reinhold glanced up from his wristpad. He smiled at Lewis, noticing him for the first time. "The adventurer! Still feeling OK?"

"Fine, thank you," he replied. He probably should have asked Reinhold how he was doing, whether he'd had a good day or something like that. But Lewis skipped ahead to the important stuff. "Any word on the plans for rescuing my dad?"

After a quick glance at Lewis's mom, the scientist smiled awkwardly. "Not yet, but my contacts in the government insist that they're working through all kinds of scenarios. They can't just speed down to Atlantis with a battalion and grab him. If they thought the three of you were invaders, then they'll surely see an approaching submarine as an act of war."

The official government guy, Agent Winfield, had said the same thing. But Lewis had a plan. He already had his backpack stowed in the warship, stuffed with plenty of snacks. He'd also jammed in an awesome silver wig that his mom had worn for Halloween the previous year. The Atlanteans had weird hair; the wig would help him fit in. Lewis would lead the rescue team himself, with Hanna as his faithful and unquestioning assistant, and if they did need to bring along a military submarine, they could paint it pink with lime-green polka dots. That way, it would be less threatening. The other members of the team would be highly trained Navy SEALs, but he'd have them dress in actual seal costumes, with whiskers and everything, so they wouldn't terrify the Atlanteans. He'd bring his harmonica, too. If there were any tense moments in Atlantis, Lewis could play, and the SEALs could dance. He wasn't very good yet, but he could always learn on the way.

How could the Atlanteans *not* welcome them?

Lewis noticed a thick envelope tucked under Reinhold's arm. "What's that?"

Since their return, Lewis had received a few gifts. Hanna's mom had given them all awesome new wristpads. Agent Winfield had brought him a very rare and beautiful pair of Jordan 50 high-top sneakers. He wore them constantly, even to bed, and was sporting them now, but Lewis had been hoping that more stuff would follow. A gift a day, maybe, for a few weeks. He had discovered Atlantis, after all. He deserved presents.

The whir of an engine outside distracted them briefly.

Roberts peeked out the window. "Hanna's here," he announced.

Reinhold held out the envelope, leaving a thin layer of orange-yellow cheese puff dust on one corner. "This is for you. It's from the president."

Lewis's mom grabbed the envelope.

"The president of what?" Michael asked.

"Your left nostril," Lewis replied. "She's asking you to cease attacking."

"The president of my left nostril is not a girl!" Michael protested.

"Why not?" their mom replied. "A woman is president of our country. Why couldn't a woman run your nose?"

"Maria," Roberts said, "really?"

His little brother pretended to flick some offending material in Lewis's direction. Lewis snatched the envelope away from his mom, peeled it open carefully under her watchful glare, and removed a single piece of thick white paper, folded twice.

"Well? What does it say?"

"'Congratulations . . . blah, blah, blah . . . you'll be a famous explorer one day . . . blah, blah, blah . . . thanks for keeping the secret for now.' There's nothing in here about Dad, but she does say to call or message her anytime I need anything." Lewis tapped the paper with his index finger. "I'm going to call her."

"Who?"

"The president. I want to give her some ideas for the rescue mission. Plus, I want a pizza."

"And ice cream!" Michael added.

"I don't think that's what she meant, Lewis."

"She says it right here. 'Call or message me if you need anything.' And I have ideas, and we haven't eaten pizza for two days."

"And we need ice cream," Michael added.

"You are absolutely not calling her tonight," their mom replied. Her tone made clear that this was her final answer. Lewis didn't fight; he could always call the president in the morning. His mom moved the letter to a clean spot on the counter.

"Let's eat," Roberts said. "Lewis, can you go get Kaya? I think she's—"

The screen door swung open and banged against the wall

as Hanna stepped into the kitchen with a thick purple sweat-shirt tossed over her shoulder. She was wearing a throwback T-shirt from some nineties band, and she'd touched up the lines shaved into the sides of her hair. They almost looked like racing stripes. Lewis was immediately jealous. In the doorway, Hanna stopped and turned. Then she reached back and grabbed Kaya's hand, pulling her inside. Lewis noticed that Hanna was wearing an old-fashioned wristwatch like the one he'd given away in Atlantis. This stung a little. He'd done the right thing—they'd scored a cruiser in exchange for his watch—but it was kind of annoying that Hanna wore one now.

Standing next to Hanna, broader in the shoulders but a head shorter, with her huge, wide eyes studying the room, Kaya did look almost alien. Lewis studied their interlocked hands, Hanna's brown skin against those ghostly pale Atlantean fingers. Reinhold had pointed out the size of Kaya's hands the moment he'd met her, which had made Kaya self-conscious—she'd taken to keeping them in her pockets.

Kaya blinked. The week on the surface had done some-thing to her, Lewis decided. She was different. Not lost, exactly. Tired, maybe. Or defeated. Like a dog that lacked the energy to bark, or a chicken—actually, no, there wasn't anything remotely chickenlike about her. Maybe there was a simple explanation, Lewis thought. Maybe his mom was right and she was missing home.

"Sorry I'm late," Hanna said, checking her watch. "I had to pass a bunch of security checkpoints. You'd think they'd lighten up a little, given that I've been coming here every night for nearly a week."

A wristpad dinged. Roberts lifted his forearm to read his new message.

"Anything important?" Lewis's mom asked.

Roberts shrugged. "Looks like the radar is down temporarily, but they don't need me." He pulled his sleeve over the screen and looked at Lewis's mom. "I'm here."

Meanwhile, Kaya slunk over to the table. She squinted; the ceiling lights were a little too bright for her eyes. Roberts hurried to dim them.

"I found our friend hiding in her ship again," Hanna joked.

"I wasn't hiding," Kaya replied. Her tone was soft, timid.

Hanna adjusted her belt, and Lewis noticed that she was wearing her favorite new accessory again: a miniature bag with a strap called a fanny pack. Another retro fashion statement. He pointed at it. "Ha."

"Get over it," Hanna said. "You wish you had one. It's waterproof, too."

Roberts nodded his approval. "They're very practical and cool."

Lewis smiled. If Roberts said something was cool, then it was exactly the opposite. This was a minor victory. Hanna sneered at him, then pulled the thick purple sweatshirt off her shoulder. "I forgot. This is for you," she said, handing it to Kaya. "From my mom."

"Your mom got her a sweatshirt?" Lewis asked. He'd scored a wristpad, and Kaya got a hoodie? Apparently he'd won that contest.

"It's not just a sweatshirt," Hanna answered. "It's threaded with electronics and artificial muscles. The sweatshirt compresses around your chest and arms, then guides you through the motions of certain sports or physical activities."

"Why?" Lewis asked.

"My mom was thinking Kaya could use it to learn how to swing a tennis racket or—"

Hanna stopped; Kaya didn't hide her lack of interest. She hung the sweatshirt on the back of a chair. "Thank her for me, please," she mumbled.

"Food's ready," Roberts announced. "Let's eat, shall we?"

Delighted, Reinhold clapped. "I thought you'd never ask!"

The scientist hurried to the counter and filled his plate first. The kids lined up behind him. Hanna took only pasta and salad, but Kaya was too polite to turn down anything Roberts offered. She was heading back to the table with a plate piled high with sausage and grilled chicken when Hanna stopped her. She took the plate and handed it to Lewis, then grabbed Kaya another one, limiting her selection to greens and veggies. Their diet was hard on her stomach. During their first dinner with Kaya, she had politely asked for fish, and Roberts had informed her that the fishing industry had disappeared when the tidal waves had begun pummeling the world's coastlines. The only fish available for eating were farm-raised and probably not up to her standards. He had kind of gone on for a while, and when he'd finished, Kaya had wondered aloud if he was implying that this was her fault, since Atlantis had sent the waves. A massively awkward pause had followed. Lewis had considered dancing to break the tension, even though his mother had imposed strict rules against spontaneous performances at dinner. Then Kaya had asked why the Sun People thought it was okay to dump plastics and pollutants into the sea.

Basically, their first dinner had turned into a big flaming disaster. Lewis's mom and Hanna had worked out a few rules for their dinnertime conversation so it wouldn't happen again. No talk of tidal waves or ocean pollution, plastics, or fishing was allowed. Reinhold had suggested they avoid politics, too, and since then, the dinners had been free of fights.

The table was too crowded, so Lewis grabbed the letter from the president, slipped it into his pocket, shifted his harmonica, and sat up on the counter beside the sink. Reinhold shoved a sausage into his mask accidentally, leaving a giant grease stain. Michael covered his mouth, trying not to laugh, and shot a small piece of macaroni out of his nose. It soared across the table, straight at Hanna's head. At the last instant, she jerked to one side, dodging the projectile like a ninja.

All in all, it was a good start to dinner. For a while, Lewis zoned out, focused on his food. When he tuned into the conversation again, Hanna and the adults were talking about space exploration. Michael was making a bread monster out of his roll. Kaya was quietly pushing roasted broccoli around her plate. The chatter stopped briefly. Lewis guessed that at least five minutes had passed since he'd asked about his dad.

"Now that we're all here," he said, "let's talk about when we're going back."

"You're not going anywhere," his mom replied. "You promised."

"I promised I wouldn't *sneak* back," Lewis clarified.

Before his mom could reply, Kaya noisily set down her fork. She touched her throat, as if checking to make sure her voice translator was working. Staring down at her plate, she announced, "I'm ready now."

Lewis's mom and Roberts glanced at each other. Reinhold stopped chewing. Lewis looked from Kaya to Hanna, who shrugged. Of course Kaya wanted to go home! Even Lewis felt trapped—imprisoned, almost—and he wasn't hundreds of miles and a whole bunch of water away from his family.

"We could go with you," Hanna suggested. "We could try to find the professor."

Lewis sat up straighter. He looked at his mom. "Can I?"

She looked at him sharply. "Are you serious? No."

"What if Kaya and I go?" Hanna suggested.

She was ditching him already? Great friend. He wished Michael would fire another macaroni at her face.

"You'd need to clear it with Agent Winfield," Roberts replied.

"We could sneak away," Hanna suggested.

"Impossible," Roberts answered. "Think about it. How many checkpoints did you have to get through to fly here, Hanna? And there's radar covering this whole area." He looked down at his wristpad. "Well, it's still down at the moment, but they'll get it running again. Before you reach the ocean, you'll have a dozen hovercars blocking your way."

Lewis thought of the letter. "I could call the president."

His mom held up both hands. "No. I already said no. Absolutely not. *N-O*. Capital letters. Bold type."

"Glitter on the outside?" Michael asked.

"Glitter!"

"No to what?" Lewis asked. Maybe she was just talking about the calling-the-president part.

"No to all of this craziness!"

"We made it there and back last time," Hanna noted.

"That's true," Roberts said.

His mom flashed his stepfather a death stare. Roberts stared down at a chunk of zucchini.

"We'd be supersafe," Lewis said, "and triple careful."

His mom studied Lewis quietly for what felt like a year. He said nothing, but in his mind, he repeated the word *please* over and over and over again, like some kind of magical incantation. "Well?" Lewis asked at last.

"Well, what?"

Kaya watched all of this quietly, seriously.

"Are you going to let us go?" Lewis pressed.

"No!" his mom answered. "I'm sorry, but no." The words were a dropkick to the chest. "I thought I'd lost you, Lewis. We're all lucky the two of you made it back safely last time. You know I'm worried about your father. We all want him back. But we need to leave this to the professionals." She turned her attention to Kaya, and her expression softened. "I'm sorry, dear," she continued. She lifted her hand as if she was going to touch Kaya's shoulder, then pulled it back. "I know this hasn't been terribly fun, but . . ."

"Is it my chicken?" Roberts joked.

Their guest was in no mood for humor. Kaya pushed back

from the table and stood. "You've been wonderful hosts," she said. "Thank you for everything. This has been amazing. Truly. But I need to go home."

"You will go home," Roberts said. "But this is an extremely sensitive situation. I'm sure that in a few weeks—"

Kaya's head jerked back. "Weeks?"

Reinhold knocked on the table, then held up one of his stubby fingers, asking them to wait. His eyes were closed. His jaw was working. He finished chewing. "Sorry. I was a touch ambitious with that forkful. I can assure you, Kaya, that meetings are being set up right now. Plans are being made. This is all happening at the highest levels of the government, though, so we can't expect anything to move too quickly."

The girl from Atlantis leaned over the table. She pointed sternly at Reinhold. "Why does your government get to tell me what to do?" she asked.

Startled, Reinhold dropped his fork, and it clanged against the floor. He looked to Roberts, then Hanna. His wristpad pinged. After scanning the message, he replied, "I'm merely the messenger. I am sorry. We're all a little tense right now. Let's discuss this again when we're cooler. Why don't you take a minute outside?"

The scientist hadn't witnessed this side of Kaya before, but Lewis had seen her stand up to soldiers. A small fleet of warships, too. Kaya started to gather her plate; Hanna put her hand on top of Kaya's and told her she'd clear it for her. "Reinhold's right," Hanna said. "Go out and get some air."

Kaya stormed out of the kitchen.

The screen door slammed and rattled.

Hanna paused, then changed her mind and went after her.

"Wait," Reinhold said. "Let's give the Atlantean some time."

"Her name is Kaya," Michael added.

"Let her be, Hanna," Reinhold said again. "She'll be fine."

Ignoring him, Hanna brought her plate over to the sink and signaled for Lewis to come with her. Although Lewis admired her table manners, he left his dish on the counter—it had the magical ability to clean itself—and raced after her, grabbing the purple sweatshirt off the back of Kaya's chair. The fabric was oddly stiff. Heavy, too. The color didn't go well with his freckles, either, but Kaya obviously didn't want it, and Lewis never passed up free gear.

Reinhold leaped to his feet. His legs bumped against the table, knocking over his water glass. "Lewis!" he said. "I think you should stay."

"You spilled your water," Roberts noted.

Michael set his bread monster in the river of Reinhold's spilled drink and roared.

Lewis paused in the doorway. Should he go or not? He waited for his mom's approval.

"Go check on her," she said.

Outside, the moon was bright in the cloudless sky. Hanna's long, narrow airbike rested on the lawn. The body was tastefully scratched and dented—she didn't like anything that looked too new. Lewis wouldn't have been surprised if she'd dinged it up on purpose.

The door to the warship was open. At least Kaya hadn't shut them out. Most of the hull was transparent, too, so they could see her sitting in the pilot's seat, her feet propped on the dashboard. A light breeze curled into the cabin as they climbed up into the ship. Kaya whistled, closing the door behind them. The slightest wind chilled her. How would she even deal with January? Or snow?

Lewis studied her, trying to imagine what she was thinking. He failed.

Hanna leaned back against the dashboard, careful to avoid the control pads and dials, and stared up and out. The glass hull of the warship was perfectly clear. Pinpricks of light shined in the night sky.

"It's like a sea of stars," Kaya said, following Hanna's stare. "And they all have planets like ours?"

Hanna had said something about this a few nights earlier. "Well, not exactly like this one, but yes, those stars are basically distant suns, and each one is probably surrounded by multiple planets. We've already found more than five thousand of them that are like Earth."

Kaya was silent for a moment. Hanna, too. She was always doing all the teaching, so Lewis grabbed this rare opportunity. "We don't know if any aliens live on them, though," he explained. "Or even what they'd look like. Most people think they're green, with really big eyes and heads. I think they're probably shaped more like hot dogs. They wouldn't taste like hot dogs, though. If they did, they'd all eat each other because they'd be so delicious."

"That's not a common view," Hanna said.

"Your world is amazing," Kaya said. She swung her feet off the dashboard. "Really. It's more fantastic than I could have imagined." She turned her huge eyes on Lewis, then Hanna. "Thank you both so much," she added, "but I can't stay. I don't care who is going to try to stop me. I want to go home. I need to go home."

Had she not understood? Lewis wanted to return to Atlantis as much as anyone, but Roberts had said they'd be turned back right away. Lewis hated that he was even going to suggest it, but if he could just convince her to wait a few more days—

He felt a faint pressure under his seat.

Hanna stepped away from the dashboard and held on to the back of the copilot's chair.

The warship was rising off the ground.

"Kaya?"

"This is not me!" Kaya said. "I'm not doing this."

"Then who is?" Hanna asked.

"I don't know."

The warship was rising faster now, nearing the top of the huge oak tree. Through the glass, Lewis saw his mom dash out into the yard. His little brother followed, then his stepfather and Reinhold. All of them watched as the warship rose higher and higher. Lewis focused on his mom. He'd promised her. He'd said he wouldn't do anything like this again. And now it looked like he'd flat-out lied. Yes, Lewis sometimes exaggerated. He occasionally fabricated. He withheld the odd detail.

But he wasn't a liar.

"Can you stop it, Kaya?" Lewis asked. "You have to stop it!"

Kaya moved to the dashboard, pressed her hands to the control pads. "I'm trying," she said, "but nothing's working."

Esmerelda was higher than his family's wind turbine now.

The bottom of the ship was metallic, so he couldn't see his family. He hurried to the back so he could look out through the glass. His mom was still watching in shock. He pounded on the walls of the ship. He yelled, trying to tell her that this wasn't his doing. That they weren't in control.

Then the warship rocketed away into the darkness, leaving what remained of his family staring up into a suddenly empty night sky.

3

ALL RIVERS RUN TO THE SEA

KAYA squeezed the armrests and tried to stay calm. She breathed. Checked the controls again. And again. But she had absolutely no idea why the ship was moving. Or where they were going. Where did she want to go? Well, that much she knew. Kaya wanted to return to Atlantis. Desperately, and as soon as possible. The surface was too different. The sun was painfully bright. The "fresh air" they all bragged about clogged her nose—every time she stepped outside onto the grass, she started sneezing. Their food was too heavy. Their greens were rubbery. And this stuff they called meat? Ugh. Every time she swallowed a bite, she felt like there was a stone in her stomach. Chocolate? Sure. Ice cream? Absolutely. Her stomach ached after eating it, but the pain was worth it.

The people were all so tall; they made her feel tiny. Insignificant, almost. Their music was weird. The smells inside the house were sickening, and her friends had carried them into the ship. Lewis stood beside her now, leaning over the control panel, and his sausage breath was intolerable. A thin film of grease covered a few of his fingers. Kaya was ready to grab his wrist if he tried to touch one of the pads or dials. She didn't want that nastiness on her dashboard.

Lewis was staring at her now. Blinking. That look on his face made her forget his greasy fingers. He was harmless. Helpless, really. "You can't stop the ship?" he asked.

He'd already asked the question three times, and each time, Kaya had given him the same answer. "No."

"And you swear you don't know what's happening?" Hanna asked.

Kaya jerked back. Hanna's eyes were narrow with skepticism. Seriously? Kaya couldn't believe that Hanna didn't trust her. "You really think I'd lie to you?" Kaya asked.

Silence. Hanna waited way too long to respond.

"No," Hanna said at last. "I trust you."

But did she?

Kaya leaned forward, looking toward the horizon. Soon, she hoped, she'd see the ocean. The ship cruised forward at a steady pace, high above the houses and trees.

Kaya didn't belong here on the surface.

She belonged in Atlantis.

"Someone else is obviously controlling the ship," Hanna said.

"Who?" Lewis asked.

Again, they looked at her. The two of them waited, watching her with their little eyes.

Kaya didn't bother masking her frustration when she replied, "I don't know."

Yet she had an idea. Or maybe a hope? When Kaya had

last spoken with her father, she and Lewis and Hanna had been escaping from Atlantis in the stolen ship. The Erasers had sent a small squad of warships to stop them. And they probably would have blasted them into seadust if her father hadn't appeared in a warship of his own and fought the Erasers so the three kids could escape. At least one of the agents' ships had been crushed in the fight. The warship factory had collapsed under the weight of miles of ocean. But the kids had survived. Her dad, too. He'd talked to them over the soundscape, promising to find Lewis's father.

That was the last she'd heard from him.

And now their stolen warship was moving on its own.

What if her dad had found Naxos, the brilliant engineer who'd taken care of Lewis's father? What if they were working together? Her dad and Naxos probably knew the warship better than anyone. Naxos had designed the vehicle, and her dad had been in charge of manufacturing it. She wondered if they'd discovered a way to control Esmerelda remotely—if they were the ones bringing her back to Atlantis.

Whoa. Wait.

Now she was calling the ship Esmerelda, too? And assigning it a gender? Kaya needed to clear her head. She didn't know if it was the sunlight or the food, but Lewis was infecting her thinking. No way could she let that happen.

Kaya gritted her teeth, closed her eyes tightly, and breathed in and out.

She could still smell the grilled meat. Had the scent seeped into their clothes?

Another unsettling thought occurred to her. If it was

possible for her dad and Naxos to steer the ship, then Kaya had to consider a frightening possibility.

What if the Erasers were controlling the ship?

What if Demos was pulling them back to his prison?

The warship sped forward.

Hanna tapped her wristpad. "I'm not getting reception."

Lewis was sitting on one of the benches behind them, typing frantically on his own device. "Me neither. I'm trying to tell my mom that this isn't my fault, that we're not controlling the ship, but my messages aren't going through. What's happening?"

Hanna studied the interior of the ship. She squinted, scratched her chin. "Something's blocking the signal."

Should she try one more time? Sure. Kaya placed her hands on the control pads, entered a set of commands. The pad pulsed against her palms. She felt the same error message she'd received every other time she'd tried to steer. "I'm totally locked out," she said. "I'm not getting any messages or communications, either, but I guess we're going back to Atlantis."

"No," Hanna said. "We're definitely not."

Her friend's response shocked her. Hanna had said it with such certainty, too. "What do you mean?" Kaya asked.

Lewis joined them at the front of the ship. The meat smell was finally gone. He was rubbing his hands together, and the inside of Kaya's nose briefly burned with a different smell. He saw her recoil, then nodded. "Hand sanitizer," he explained, pointing to his backpack. "I've got everything in there."

Ignoring him, Kaya faced Hanna. "Okay, if we're not going back to Atlantis, then where are we going?"

"Well, my wristpad might not be getting reception," Hanna explained, "but the compass still works, and it says we're heading west."

"So?" Kaya asked.

"If we're going to Atlantis," Hanna said, "we're going the long way around the planet. The ocean is east. The west is all mountains."

Kaya tensed. She studied the two Sun People. Were they lying to her? Was this some kind of trick? Lewis looked genuinely surprised, even confused. But that wasn't unusual; he seemed to exist in a constant state of bewilderment. More importantly, they were her friends. She had to trust them. Right? Kaya wasn't sure anymore. The only person she truly knew she could trust was herself.

"Weird," Lewis said. He leaned over the dashboard, looking left and right. Kaya watched him peer up through the roof of the ship. "Where is everyone?" he asked.

A good question. Roberts said they'd be followed. Where were all the hovercars?

"The radar's down," Hanna reminded them. "But I'm still surprised no one followed us."

"So what do we do?" Lewis asked.

Hanna leaned back in the copilot's seat and shrugged. "We wait."

The sky was clear all around them. A single dark gray cloud drifted overhead like a huge wide-winged ray, and the warship cruised faster and faster, away from the ocean, toward the foothills of a long, wide spread of mountains. Kaya felt herself calming. Why, though? They were going in the wrong direction.

Everything was out of her control.

She was just . . . waiting. And she despised waiting.

Yet a strange sense of clarity and focus grew within her.

She was going to get back to Atlantis. Soon.

Nothing and no one was going to stop her.

Miles of darkness stretched between the clusters of lights below. Kaya didn't know how long they'd been traveling; Lewis said it must be at least eight thousand years. The scene below changed. The *landscape*, they called it. This was the forest Lewis had told her about, and beyond it, the mountains. He said it was too bad that Kaya couldn't see it during the day, but she preferred the night. The moon was bright enough. While gnawing nervously on her fingernails, Hanna explained the science behind how the mountains had formed.

The peaks and crags stretching out before them mirrored the undersea ridges that hid Atlantis from the rest of the ocean. Lewis had bragged about the beauty of these mountains, but to Kaya, they weren't all that impressive. The mountains on the surface were covered with tall trees, while hers were blanketed in sea life and muck, but the real difference, of course, was what lay above them. Miles of ocean washed across the top of Atlantis.

Here, the sky was their sea, the roof of their world.

She preferred the cold, dark water.

A waterfall poured down from between two of the peaks.

The sight of the glimmering silver sheet reminded Kaya of home.

Esmerelda was aiming straight at the water.

Not over the peak. Directly into the center of the mountain.

"Are those windows?" Hanna asked.

To the right of the waterfall, a single row of five narrow windows were embedded in the otherwise rocky mountainside. What was this place? Kaya wondered.

"That's totally an evil lair," Lewis said.

"A what?" Kaya asked.

"An evil lair," he repeated. "The headquarters of a supervillain. They love hiding behind waterfalls."

"Isn't it Batman who does that?" Hanna asked. "He's not evil."

Lewis was briefly quiet. Then he said, "But he does have villainous tendencies. Or this could be Area 51. Or what if they have a special one for Atlanteans? Area 52! Then Area 53 would have talking cats."

Kaya ignored him. She touched the twin pads again, trying one last time to control the ship. She pulled her hands back, hoping to steer higher, up over the mountain face, but Esmerelda held her line. "It's still not working."

"Strap in," Hanna ordered. "This could get ugly."

The three of them buckled up.

The ship slowed almost to a stop.

Kaya glanced back at Lewis. He was squeezing his eyes shut and hugging the purple sweatshirt to his chest. She spun around and stared out at the rippled, waving sheet of water in front of them. The nose of the ship moved through it slowly, like a swimmer testing the temperature of a darkwater pool with her toe.

The thick film of water washed over the sides of the ship.

Hanna grabbed Lewis by the arm, urging him to look. He leaned forward between them, squinting through the glass.

The front of the ship passed into some kind of cave. Bright white lights filled the space.

The last of the water flowed off the hull. The view cleared, and Kaya discovered that they were in a room larger than any she'd yet seen on the surface. The floor, walls, and ceiling were perfectly smooth and flat, and the space was shaped like a giant cube. The surface of a deep pool rippled faintly to her left. There were no signs of sea greens or farmed fish, unfortunately. Several unusual and identical vehicles were moored at the edge. They were spherical in shape and surrounded by steel cages. This had to be some kind of test facility. A primitive version of Naxos's lab. The watercraft were clearly supposed to be submarines. Kaya almost wanted to laugh. She knew Atlantean kids who'd built better subs.

The rest of the room was filled with workstations and those bright, multicolored screens the Sun People loved so much. Two large machines with long, metallic arms rolled across the room. Robots? Yes, that's what Hanna had called them.

"What is this place?" Kaya asked.

"I have no idea," Hanna admitted.

Lewis nodded with certainty. "I'm telling you, it's Area 52."

There was no point sitting at the controls any longer, so Kaya stood near the door as the warship slowed to a stop, hovered, then descended to the floor. Across the room, a group of men and women, several of them in matching gray uniforms, stood waiting. Two of them held weapons—not the sonic blasters they used in Atlantis, though. These were narrow, short, and small enough to fit in your hand. Hanna and Lewis started backing away from the door. Lewis was clutching that sweatshirt and looking at Hanna, probably hoping she'd know what to do. Hanna looked more curious than frightened—eyebrows scrunched together, mouth tightly closed.

Kaya glanced at her pack, propped on one of the benches.

She still had a sonic blaster hidden inside.

"No," Hanna said, reading her thoughts. "That's not going to help."

The door to the warship opened.

The uniformed group moved no closer.

They were scared, too, Kaya realized.

She jumped down to the ground.

One of the men in gray gasped.

A woman wearing a thin, knee-length white coat kicked him lightly. "Be normal," the woman muttered.

"Who are you?" Kaya asked.

"Amazing," the woman said.

"Your name is Amazing?" Lewis asked.

He was in the doorway now, just barely leaning out.

"What? No. I'm Dr. Lin," the woman answered. Then she pointed at Kaya. "You're amazing. Are you really from Atlantis?"

Kaya sneered. Generally, she didn't like it when people pointed at her. But she *really* didn't like it when they hijacked her ship and pointed at her. And that question! She was so, so tired of that ridiculous question. A few days earlier, after one of the government agents had asked Kaya that, Lewis's mother had suggested what she said would be a funny response. Kaya didn't really understand the humor, but she tried it out anyway. "No," she said, "New Jersey."

Not even a chuckle. Except from Lewis.

"What are we supposed to do now?" one of the men asked.

As Kaya studied the space, the people, and the exits, Hanna started firing off questions. Then she warned that her parents were very influential people who would get them all in serious trouble if they didn't let the kids go free. Lewis added that his parents were important, too, just in a different way.

A man with a gray moustache answered. "You're not even supposed to be here," he said, motioning to Lewis and Hanna. His voice was deep and rough; the sound of it hurt Kaya's ears. "We just want the Atlantean."

The Atlantean? "I have a name," Kaya pointed out.

Lewis breathed out dramatically. "Stand back, or you might get Atlantean germs."

The mustached man and a few of the others retreated, but the woman in the white coat stood anchored in place. "There are no viruses," she said. "We tested the air in your house."

Lewis jerked his head back slightly. "You did?"

"Your saliva, too," the woman added.

Kaya recoiled. That was vile. "You sampled our spit?" she asked.

"Of course we did," the mustached man responded.

"That's gross," Lewis noted.

"Smart, though," Hanna conceded.

Enough conversation, Kaya decided. She wasn't in the mood to stand there all night. "Could someone please explain what is happening? How did you control my ship?"

The woman clapped once, then rubbed her hands together. "Yes, someone can explain, but she's not here yet." She turned to her colleagues. "These three are resourceful. Split them up until she gets here."

"Until who gets here?" Hanna asked.

"We're not splitting up," Lewis said.

The two uniformed figures raised their weapons.

Immediately, Lewis sidestepped away from Hanna and Kaya. "Or we could split up! No problem. Whatever works for you guys."

The pistols were smaller than sonic blasters, and each one had a small round hole at the front. What did these weapons do? Did they even blast out sound at all? Kaya couldn't be certain, but she figured it wouldn't be smart to test their power. She decided to go where the men with the weapons told her to go, and they led her down a long, cold hallway and into a small room. "You'll wait in here," Dr. Lin said. "Make yourself comfortable."

Comfortable? The space looked more like an office than a place to rest. "Where are we? Why are we here?"

"All your questions will be answered soon," the woman replied. She backed into the hall and started to close the door, then paused as she scanned the inside of the room again. "I'm sorry," she said, "but we don't often have guests."

The door shut with a click.

A high-pitched beep followed.

There was a handle affixed to the door. A button flicked from grccn to red.

That surprising feeling of calm hadn't left her.

She was frustrated, sure. Annoyed? Absolutely.

Yet her heartbeat was slow and relaxed.

Kaya waited a few minutes before testing the door. Locked, naturally.

You didn't lock guests in their rooms.

You locked prisoners in their rooms.

So she was a prisoner. For now, anyway.

The nearest window opened easily. Apparently, these people didn't jail their visitors very often, either. She leaned her head outside. The cool night air pushed against her face. She could smell the waterfall, hear its familiar rush and roar. The moon glowed. The trees stretched out below her like a blanket of deep dark green.

If she'd had her gravity suit, she could've jumped off this ledge and drifted back to safety. But she'd left her suit with Rian, back in Atlantis.

The thought of him stirred up a wave of guilt. The last time she'd seen him, he was leaping out of her window to draw the Erasers away from her. Had it worked? Was he safe? Or had they caught him?

Was he now trapped in that terrible underwater prison?

Kaya clenched her teeth, as if she could crush the thought.

She allowed herself a few long, slow breaths.

She had a million questions. About Rian, her father, this strange prison.

One thing was clear, however. She had to get home, and to do that, she had to get out of this room. She couldn't even control the ship anymore, so there was no point trying to sneak back to Esmerelda. There was water below her, though, and she knew from one of Hanna's mother's dinnertime talks that most water eventually flowed to the sea.

If she couldn't drift home through the sky, she'd swim the rivers and streams.

Hanna would be fine. Lewis, too, because Hanna would protect him.

Plus, Kaya had returned them safely to the surface. She'd done her part.

The wall outside her window was jagged and nearly vertical, but there was a ledge just wide enough to stand on. Carefully, she climbed out and stood with her back and palms pressed against the damp stone. There were trees below her and to the left, and the waterfall spilled down into a natural pool to her right.

Slowly, Kaya shuffled toward it. No gravity drive would save her if she lost her balance. The trees did look pretty, but she guessed they wouldn't feel too lovely if you were crashing through them on your way to the ground.

If she could get closer to the waterfall, though, she could jump into the pool.

Her toes curled over the ledge.

The drop wouldn't be short. Ten body lengths at least.

She edged closer and felt the mist on her face. The thick sheet of water poured down to her right, splashing into the pool, which fed a wide, winding river.

Soon the most dangerous part was over; there was water below her now, not trees and solid ground. But that water was really, really, really far away. She closed her eyes.

What had happened to that powerful feeling of calm?

Enough, she told herself.

Enough fear.

Enough worry.

Kaya read the churning water below. The rush and flow were sensible. Predictable. None of the boils or bowls on the surface or swirls and currents suggested hidden rocks. Beyond the pool, the water calmed, coursing smoothly ahead into what Lewis and Hanna had called a forest. This water would lead her home, or at least closer to Atlantis. She lifted her hands off the wall, leaned forward.

And leaped.

Turned in midair.

Flung her arms over her head.

Squeezed them together tight.

Sucked in as much oxygen as her chest would hold.

Prayed that she'd read it right, that the water was safe and clear.

Then she knifed through the wild, churning surface and into the darkness.

The water enveloped her. Immediately, she felt the calm return.

She let herself hang there in the cold, churning dark, relaxing in its embrace. But only for a moment. Then she swam down, along the bottom and away from the water-fall, until she felt the pull of the river. There was no need to surface. Not yet. She could hold her breath for another two minutes at least, and she was going to let the river pull her as far away as possible. With her arms at her sides, she turned her palms skyward and sculled, pushing upward to keep herself down. In Atlantis, they rarely swam in rivers, reserving them for ferries and boats. But it was wonderful, being carried along this way.

The river slowed and widened.

The surface stilled.

Kaya's chest ached slightly; her brain was telling her to breathe. Had it been that long already? The bottom had changed from rocks and stones to silt and sand and tiny, unhealthy, scraggly water weeds. Could you even eat them? She didn't think so. The river itself was beautiful, though. Moonlight shined through the surface, turning the water a silvery gray.

Her lungs were really starting to ache now.

Slowly, she lifted her head out of the river and breathed, extending her arms up in front of her shoulders. The water was calmer at the surface, but still moving with energy and purpose. Gravity, she realized. In Atlantis, the water moved where they wanted it to move. Here, gravity decided every-thing. The moonlight sneaked through gaps in the forest ceiling. Trees of all sizes and shapes stretched up from both banks, their branches winding, reaching higher. Were they growing toward the moon? Or was it the sun? She hadn't quite understood when Hanna's mom had tried to explain it to her; all the Sun People had crammed so many facts and ideas into her head that her brain was overstuffed.

The forest thinned, and ahead of her, down the river, the lights of a house sitting close to the water shined across a stretch of green. The soft yellow light reminded her of Atlantis. The grassy lawn rolled down from the house to the riverbank. She stopped and listened.

Sounds in the distance, upriver.

An unfamiliar buzzing.

Lights appeared on the water behind her.

Two small flying machines were cruising side by side.

Looking for her? Maybe. Kaya hurried to the shore.

Her feet sank into thick, cool mud. She crawled up onto the soft riverbank.

The tiny vehicles were getting closer. The trees across the lawn might provide cover. She could hide there in the darkness until the lights were gone. Kaya sprinted for them.

A sound ahead of her—footsteps crunching against dry leaves.

A figure emerged from behind a tree. A woman, with a man standing beside her, half a step back. His right hand was on his hip. "Are you lost, sweetheart?" the woman asked.

Her tone was wrong, dripping with fake friendliness. The woman stepped into the moonlight. She was older than Lewis's mother, Kaya guessed. Her hair was short, brown, and weirdly shiny. Her skin seemed to glimmer, too, and her smile seemed practiced. But what had she called Kaya? *Sweetheart?* The Atlantean word for *sweet* meant something delicious. Something you ate. And the heart was the machine that kept you alive, pumping your blood. Did the woman want to eat her heart? Or was Kaya's translator failing? She tapped her ear.

"What's wrong?" the woman asked. "You can trust me."

"I can't trust anyone right now," Kaya muttered.

The woman chuckled a bit. "Yes, well, that's probably smarter. I stopped trusting people decades ago, and I've been far more successful ever since."

"You just told me to trust you."

"Yes, well, don't listen to me, Kaya."

"But I—"

She froze.

Her name.

The woman knew her name.

"Ah, realization! Awareness! Even in this light, I can see it on your face. I'm honored. I was on my way to meet you when I heard you'd, well, jumped."

Kaya backed up.

The buzzing was louder now.

The flying machines were directly behind her, hovering.

"I don't understand."

The woman pointed up at the stars. "There's too much to understand! Dark matter, for example. Most of the stuff in the universe is invisible. Amazing. And now we find that Atlantis is real, and you discover you've been lied to about what's happening up here on the surface? It's all too much! I don't envy you, Kaya. I really don't. But you weren't thinking of swimming back to Atlantis, were you?" The woman paused, studying her. She bit her lip. "Oh, you were! How precious. Well, you never would have made it alive. So why don't you quit trying to escape and let me explain everything back at the office?"

"The office?"

"Yes, my office. The lovely little enclave behind the water-fall. You're probably wondering why I'd build a research lab behind a waterfall. I'd ask you, why not? That's the fun of being a billionaire. Wait—I'm sorry, you don't know who I am."

"No," Kaya said. "I don't."

"I'm not used to that," the woman replied. "But I forgive you. My name is Susan Silver, and I am many things. Founder of the Sunshine Corporation. Philanthropist. Thought leader. Two-time captain of the Harvard swim team. But enough of my resume! I want to make a deal with you, Kaya."

"What sort of deal?" Kaya asked.

"I'd like to help you get back to Atlantis."

4

THE FLOODED CITY

RIAN rolled out of bed, exhausted. He had barely slept; his mind had been swimming with questions about Kaya, the meeting, and the upcoming vote on the war. The night was always noisy, as he lived in Ridge City. But now every sound seemed threatening. At the slightest creak, he imagined an Eraser sneaking into his room or landing on his balcony. Thankfully, though, he was safe, and his mission had been a success. He'd followed Heron's instructions and transmitted the recording through the special channel. Maybe he had a future as a spy.

"Have you seen my favorite goggles?" his dad called out.

"Where did you hide my suitcase?" his mom replied.

Why were they packing? They hadn't told Rian anything about a trip. He yawned, stretched, and found them in their room, stuffing bags with clothes, swim gear, and their beloved crystals. The sight of the rocks made him wince. His parents had joined some weird new religion recently. Couldn't they just worship whale spirits like normal Atlanteans? The whole thing was super embarrassing.

"What's going on?" he asked.

"Good morning, Rian!" his mom replied. Her hair was pulled back, and her face was radiating excitement. She glanced at his dad, who couldn't hide his smile, either.

Rian motioned to their bags. "Are we going somewhere?"

"Yes and no," his dad said.

"What does that mean?"

They paused. His parents had some kind of weird, silent conversation. "I'm very sorry," his dad said, "but your mother and I won a trip to Pella—"

"For a whole week!" his mom added.

"We'd love for you to come with us, but . . ."

"Adults only," his mom explained.

Rian blinked. "That's . . ."

"Amazing, right?"

Terrible would be a better word. *Unfair. Tragic.* Maybe even *criminal?* Pella was supposed to be gorgeous. The best food, cleanest water, and most amazing wave pools in Atlantis. A girl at his school had gone last year with her family, and she'd bragged about it for a week. And now his parents were going. Without him. And they thought he'd be happy for them? No way. Not a chance.

He crossed his arms over his chest and sneered. "What am I supposed to do while you're on vacation?"

"Oh, come on, you'll figure something out! Hang out with your friends."

"You could have a sleepover . . . and make a fort!"

A *fort?* Were they serious? Fourteen-year-old kids didn't build forts.

"We're really sorry you can't come."

"So sorry," his dad added.

Rian couldn't even respond. They weren't sorry. They were thrilled. His parents had never gone on vacation without him before. They'd barely gone away at all! Normally, a getaway for their family was a night at his grandparents' house on the other side of Ridge City. "How did you even win a trip?" Rian asked.

"How?" his father repeated. His eyes widened. His lower lip rose. He glanced over at Rian's mom. She shrugged, equally clueless. "I don't know! But does it matter? When you win a free vacation to Pella, you don't ask questions!"

"But what about me?" Rian asked again.

"We found you a babysitter."

"A babysitter? Are you serious? I'm not a baby."

His mom paused her frantic packing. "We know you're not a baby, Rian, but we can't leave you home alone for this long, and we were very, very lucky to find someone on short notice."

"We're both sorry," his dad added, "but this is all very last-minute, and it's a once-in-a-lifetime chance—" A knock at the door interrupted his father. "Good," he said, "she's here."

"Who?" Rian asked.

His parents made no effort to answer his question or the door. Instead, they used the knock as an excuse to go right back to packing. They were infuriating. Were they going to ask him to pack lunches for them before they left? If they did, he'd squirt soap into his dad's salad.

Another knock.

Rian whistled. The front door slid open.

A woman with short blond hair and a small, unsmiling mouth stood waiting. After a moment, she asked, "Aren't you going to invite me in?"

"No."

"Why not?"

"I don't know who you are," Rian answered. Normally, guests had to ring up from the entrance to be let into the building. "How did you get up to our floor?"

The woman glanced back toward the stairwell, then up at the hallway's ceiling. "I'm resourceful."

Behind him, his dad clapped as he peered out of his room. "Oh, good," he said, "you're here! Rian, this is your babysitter."

His mom invited the woman inside, and the light in the room changed, darkening briefly, as a cruiser passed by the main window. The babysitter stood close to the doorway and held her flattened hand over her eyes. She said the light bothered her and asked if they wouldn't mind pulling down the window shades. Rian complied, but this wasn't a good sign. What kind of person had his parents hired?

They didn't have long until the train left, his mom explained, so she sped through the emergency details. Rian stopped his mom when she started talking about what he liked to eat. He reminded everyone again that he could take care of himself. His mom deposited a small stack of coins on the kitchen counter, and then his parents dropped their bags and pulled him into a kind of huddle. He recoiled. Sometimes his parents got weird, and this was one of those moments. His mom removed her necklace, turned the green stone around in her hands, bowed her head, and whispered something.

Meanwhile, his dad lifted a jagged blue gem to his mouth, as if he were breathing in its mystical energy, and they began to mutter some kind of prayer.

When they were finished, his mom looped the necklace over Rian's head. The green crystal felt heavy against his chest. Cold, too. Both his parents held their hands out and whispered another one of their prayers: "May the Earth spirit and rockglow lead you safely through the waters." His dad held his fingers to the jagged crystal and added, "And may the waters bring you the peace of a stone."

Rockglow? Rian had no idea what they were talking about. He'd been doing everything in his power to avoid learning about their religion, but he thanked his parents anyway. For now, he tucked the necklace under his shirt—he could toss it later.

"Don't worry, dear," his mom said. "You'll be fine."

His dad squeezed Rian's shoulder briefly, adding, "We'll be back before you know it."

And with that, they rushed out the door and down the stairs.

Rian moved to the window, pulled aside the shade, and watched as they burst out onto the street and hurried south, toward the train station.

His dad was literally skipping.

Great. His parents were happy.

Rian? He was stuck at home with a stranger.

The babysitter settled into his mom's favorite chair. She placed a black bag on the living room table, removed a cube the size of her fist, and whistled. The device emitted a low hum.

"Right," she said, her voice low but clear. "Now that we've gotten that out of the way, let's move on to more important matters. Good work sending the recording. We were impressed."

Rian stiffened. How did this woman know about the recording? He'd never even seen her before. "I don't know what you're talking about."

"Good answer," she said. The woman pointed to the cube. "As you've probably guessed, the Erasers are listening. They have been ever since you helped Kaya escape."

"You know about that?" Rian asked.

"Yes, and more," the woman answered. She pointed to the cube. "This device will block the sounds of our conversation, but after a few minutes, the Erasers will become suspicious. I need to be gone before they arrive. Understood?"

"No. Not really."

"You're probably wondering who I am, too."

"Yes."

"I'm not going to tell you."

"Thanks."

"What I will tell you is that Heron sent me. Oh, and sorry about knocking you down."

Slowly, this was starting to make sense. Rian flopped down onto the couch across from her. The day before, he had been walking home from the neighborhood wave pool after bodysurfing for a few hours when someone had slammed him to the ground. He hadn't seen the woman's face, only heard her whisper, "From a friend." Then she'd disappeared into the crowd, leaving Rian with a slightly bruised elbow and a small bag in his hands. When he'd stood and brushed himself off, he'd looked inside and found the lock whisperer. He'd been so excited about the gadget that he'd almost ditched the bag, but then he'd felt something else and pulled out a new earpiece. He had turned, studied the crowd, but the woman was gone.

The device was unused, from the looks of it, and an expensive model, too. He had snaked through the crowd to a quiet spot against a wall, between a diving equipment store and a tea shop, and popped it into this ear. A message had played, and he'd recognized the voice of Kaya's father immediately. In a stern tone, Heron had told Rian that he was entrusting him with a critical mission, then gave him instructions for how to sneak into Capitol Tower, drift to the fourteenth floor, record the meeting of the High Council, and send the file back. Heron had said the future of Atlantis was at stake. Yet it wasn't until he'd mentioned Kaya—*If you don't do this for me or for Atlantis, then do it for your friend*—that Rian had decided to accept the task.

The annoying part was that her dad hadn't even said whether Kaya was okay or not. Maybe Heron didn't know himself.

But Rian had done exactly as he'd been asked, and now this stranger was sitting in his mom's favorite chair, masquerading as a babysitter. He pointed toward the street. "My parents aren't in trouble, are they?"

"No, they really are going on a wonderful vacation. I should know—I paid for it. The contest was a ruse."

"You paid for their vacation so you could babysit me? I mean, I'm flattered, but—"

"No."

"No?"

The babysitter pointed to the bag she'd brought. "I paid for their trip so you can go to Evenor."

"The flooded city?"

"That's the one." She leaned forward and pushed the bag toward him. "Inside, you'll find the address of your destination, your train tickets from here to Cleito, and enough coins to pay for your passage from Cleito to Evenor. I threw in a new breather and a good pair of goggles, too. You'll need them both. You still have the lock whisperer?"

"Yes." And he was planning on keeping it, too. "What about Kaya?" he asked. "Has Heron been in contact with her?"

"That's what the transmitter is for," she said, pointing to the bag.

"What about snacks?" he asked. He was trying to be funny. She didn't laugh.

Rian reached forward and started searching through the bag. The woman wasn't lying; she really had stashed gold inside. The breather looked pretty sweet, too—one of those models that allowed you stay underwater for hours at a time. But where was this transmitter she was talking about? He pulled out a spherical contraption covered in panels and folded-down antennas. "This thing?"

The woman lowered her voice. "Yes. Heron is in Evenor, and he needs that transmitter to contact your friend Kaya. I can't bring it myself. The Erasers will track me. If you can get that device to Heron, he might be able to summon Kaya—and our ship—back to Atlantis." She stopped and stared at the buzzing cube. Then she glanced out the window. "That's all I should say. The less you know, the better."

The less he knew the better? Rian didn't agree. "I have a bunch of questions," he said.

She held her hand to her earpiece. Her brow furrowed. Rian hadn't thought it was possible, but somehow, the woman turned even more serious and stern. She stood. "I have to go."

"One question," Rian pleaded.

"Make it quick," the woman said.

Rian paused, then asked, "Why me?"

He was hoping she'd say something uplifting. Something about him being brave, bold, resourceful. Intelligent, even.

Instead, she was brutally honest.

"We don't have any other options, Rian. You're the only one Heron trusts."

"That's not very inspiring."

"I don't aim to inspire. If you don't think you can do this . . ." She was eyeing the bag now, as if she was ready to take it back.

Rian glanced down at the transmitter, felt the weight of the gold. He'd have to lose the Erasers on his way to Cleito, make sure they didn't track him. And then he'd be traveling from one strange city to another all on his own. But if going to Evenor would help Kaya, the decision was pretty simple.

"No," Rian said. "I'm in."

A not-so-gentle nudge woke Rian from a trance. He'd been staring at the mist-covered, jagged stone walls of the tunnel forever. Blue light from the clusters of glowworms living in the crevices shined through the mist. His driver, a small, muscular woman with deep green eyes, had poked him with the end of an oar; he swatted away the second jab.

"We're almost there," she said. Then she pointed to her earpiece. "Are you listening to the news?"

The trip had been a blur so far. The blond woman had given him only about a minute to pack a small bag. Then she'd made him sneak out of his home through the garbage chute, arguing that the Erasers would be watching and might follow him if he used the door. Rian had raced through the tunnels below the city, ridden the train to Cleito, then paid for a ferry ride to Evenor. He'd just missed a boat full of a few dozen tourists heading there for a visit, so he'd been forced to hire a small ferryboat for himself. Naturally, the driver had wondered why a kid his age was traveling alone, and he'd offered to pay her extra if she would forget she'd asked.

The craft looked like it had been patched and rebuilt a dozen times. The seats were painfully uncomfortable. The hull leaked, too, and Rian had spent the whole ride with his feet in a puddle of water, so he was thrilled to hear they were finally close. But what was she saying about the news? He sat up straighter. His back ached. "What station?"

"Every station," she answered.

Rian adjusted his earpiece and tuned in to the soundscape. She was right—the stations were all playing the same program, an exclusive announcement from one of the most well-known journalists in Atlantis, Glandor Thrall. Rian knew her voice well; he and his parents listened to Thrall's stories about the

58

latest happenings in Atlantis on a nightly basis. This was no ordinary news, though. Someone on the High Council had shared secret information with Thrall. There was no mention of Kaya, or of Rian himself, but Thrall called out Heron by name. She reported that sources inside the High Council had told her Heron was a traitor to Atlantis and that anyone who knew anything about his whereabouts should relay the information immediately.

The bigger news, though? Thrall announced that the Sun People were real. She knew they had been to Atlantis. And she was telling everyone that their visit had been an invasion.

Atlantis, she announced, was on the brink of war.

The driver's eyebrows rose and fell. "That's something, isn't it? All these years, I thought those stories were made up."

Rian was stunned. He couldn't think of what to say.

"Are you even listening, kid? The Sun People are real!"

"Right," Rian said. "That's amazing. Totally."

"Amazing? It's terrifying! We ought to strike back, I think," his driver continued. "We should show them what Atlantis can do! That way, they won't get any more ideas about swimming straight in through our front gates."

Rian didn't respond.

The tunnel walls narrowed.

Ahead of them, the light changed. A dull yellow glow soon filled the space, and Rian heard the sounds of a large and open cave.

His driver nodded ahead. "Welcome to Evenor."

The ferryboat rode the water out of the tunnel and into a wide lake. The air was damp and warm and tasted slightly metallic. He licked his lips—the distinct tang of iron. Several cruisers and scattered drifters in gravity suits passed overhead. Boats sped across the water, kicking up waves in their wakes, and the surface roiled in spots as bubbles rose up from below. There were docks and floating fish markets between small island gardens lush with seagrasses and colorful plants. A bunch of them had odd-looking mounds in their centers that were blanketed with flowering plants and vines but also had doors and windows. "What are those?" Rian asked.

The woman pointed to one of the mounds. "Those ones there are homes," she said. "The locals rent them out to tourists, too. Not a bad business, I've heard. The rest"—she pointed to a few of the empty islands—"are small parks. Lovely spots for picnics. Visitors adore them."

An open-top ferry packed with thirty or forty Atlanteans motored lazily across the lake as the driver detailed the scene for his riders through a loudspeaker. The sound carried over the water to Rian, and he listened to the guide talk about Evenor's preflood days. Rian had learned about Evenor in school. The place was thriving once, as busy and popular as Ridge City. Then the outer walls had begun to collapse, and water forced its way through cracks in the cave. Much of the city was crushed, and the part that remained was completely flooded. Usually, when something like this happened, the surviving residents fled to another part of Atlantis. Yet the people of Evenor had remained. They'd drained and strengthened what was left of their buildings, waterproofed the windows and walls, and rebuilt their newly soaked metropolis. That had been decades ago, though. Now Evenor was a popular tourist destination. Atlanteans who liked adventurous vacations came here to swim and explore. Rian had never heard about the picnics, though.

"You have a breather and goggles?" his driver asked.

He reached into his backpack, checked for the fiftieth time to make sure the spherical transmitter was stashed away inside, then removed his swimming gear, sealed up his bag, and slipped his arms through the straps. He pressed a few buttons to tighten and streamline his clothes and pack, then tried on the goggles. The lenses were wide and clear, and the fit was perfect. He pressed the breather over his mouth and nose. The device suctioned itself to his face. The air that came through the filters was fresh and clean. Even that slight metallic taste was gone.

"You've never been to Evenor, have you?" his driver asked.

"No," he confessed.

His driver pointed into the distance. "You should swim a little ways before you descend, find a section of the water that's free of bubbles." She eyed a calm stretch between a few islands. "That spot there looks perfect. That's closer to the center of the city, too. Do you know where you're going?"

"I have an address."

"That'll work. There are maps all over the city for the swimming tourists. You seem like a resourceful kid. I suspect you'll find your way." She glanced back at the spot she'd chosen for him, then smiled wide. "You're in for a treat, young man. Now get going."

He needed no more encouragement. Rian thanked her and dropped backward off the side of the boat. The water was warm and dark. He could feel its great depth. He swam at the surface first, toward the middle of the cave, then dove. The breather, which pulled oxygen out of the water like the gills of a fish, worked beautifully; he inhaled and exhaled almost as easily as if he were walking the streets of Ridge City. His goggles fogged, but a quick tap of a button on the side cleared them, and he swam down through a torrent of bubbles into a calm expanse of water.

What he saw next stunned him. He'd heard about Evenor, but nothing had prepared him for the eerily beautiful world below. Towering rock and metal spires stretched up from the seafloor. They were dotted with windows casting blue and green light into the water. Streams of bubbles rose from between the buildings. Fish swam along the bottom. No, not fish—people! They were so far away they looked like minnows, and the tall buildings and domed structures were enormous. The largest buildings in Ridge City had fifteen floors. These had to be twenty or thirty stories high, and they twisted and thinned as they rose, more like coral that had grown in the water naturally than something that had been built. Yet it wasn't all blissful and perfect. In the distance, he could see the top of a small mountain of fallen rock where a wall had caved in.

A submarine crossed below him. Yellow light shined out through its windows. Rian swam deeper. Passing the tops of the towers, he noticed people crossing from one building to another. A long, straight line of smaller figures stretched between two towers. Kids, he guessed, following an adult.

This was probably a swim team, not a field trip, because school didn't start for another month. Evenor was swarming with fish, too—great thick schools and solitary wanderers. Rian had always been terrible at naming them; biology was his worst subject in school. But he recognized the blue-and-gray-and-silver creatures, most about the length of his arm, and thick. The ones with the huge lower jaws and snaggleteeth—barracudas. There were flat, wide fish, too, and beautiful, dark manta rays spreading their waving wings.

The pressure was building in his ears. He swallowed, clicked his jaw.

The air filtering through the breather was actually slightly tinny, he decided, but still clean. He felt like he could stay underwater forever.

Down on the city floor, he spotted narrow alleys and watery tunnels snaking into the walls. The water was brighter down here—a beautiful, radiant blue. Wide windows wrapped around the lower floors of the buildings. Yellow-green light shined out of restaurants and shops. There were crowds inside, eating and drinking. He circled the base of one tower and passed an unusually large stretch of windows. He swam close to the glass to peer inside. A huge, open amphitheater stretched back into the building. He wished Kaya could see this place.

The alleyways were all named after fish and other sea creatures. He was looking for 42 Squid Way.

Ahead of him, Rian noticed two swimmers in brand-new gear lingering in front of a wall, studying one of the maps his driver had mentioned. When they kicked away, he hurried to take their place and studied the map to figure out where he needed to go. Thankfully, he wasn't far.

The names of the alleys were carved into signs or etched into the stone walls.

He swam around several corners.

A woman dolphin-kicked into a passageway to his left—a round opening in the cave wall large enough for one person, maybe two. Rian swam closer and spotted the sign—Squid Way. Water was flowing into the tunnel like some kind of undersea river. He drifted, letting it pull him inside. There were holes in the rock walls on either side and numbers etched into the stone beside each one. The numbers had slightly different designs. Some were done in large, fanciful fonts. Others were simple, small, and clean.

Number 42 had a slightly askew circular door. Rian grasped an iron handle beside the entryway to remain in place as the current tried to tug him onward. Through a window in the center of the door, he could see that the water on the other side was dark.

He knocked.

The door, after a few long moments, slid open.

Water rushed in, filling the space, and Rian slipped into the dark, narrow tunnel.

He was hundreds of miles from home, in a foreign city, looking for the most wanted man in Atlantis. The green crystal his parents had given him bumped against his chest. He patted it briefly for courage.

The tunnel was five meters long at most, and then it

curved upward and ended. Light shined from above him. Rian pressed his hands and feet against the walls, stopping himself. He could see up through the water into some kind of room, and he could make out the rippled faces of people leaning over and staring down into the hole. He tapped the crystal again, then swam up out of the water. Strong hands grabbed his forearms and dragged him onto a stone floor like a hooked fish.

He removed his goggles, then the breather, and found himself in a room about the size of his family's apartment. Dull green plants grew along one wall. There was a low couch to his left, a table and benches to his right. In a kitchen directly ahead of him, water trickled down a rough rock wall into a large sink. He rubbed his eyes. Naxos, the Atlantean inventor who'd turned up at Kaya's house and helped her rescue the Sun People, stood nearby. The last time Rian had seen him, the man had looked like he'd been in a fistfight, then bathed in a sewer. Now he appeared rested and restored. But he seemed nervous, too, and he was frantically wringing his hands.

Kaya's father, Heron, was waiting beside him. He crouched on the floor in front of Rian. His eyes were bloodshot and puffy, and there were dark half circles below them. Heron was holding his hair at the back of his head with both hands. A week earlier, Rian would've been relieved to see him.

Now?

Not so much.

He was pretty much a criminal.

Heron reached out and clasped Rian's hands. "You're okay?" Heron asked. "No injuries?"

Rian paused. Systems check? Yes, he was okay. Tense, but okay. "Sure, I'm—"

"Good. We got your message, the recording from the meeting."

"Very brave work," Naxos added.

At least someone appreciated him. "Well, thank you, I—"

"Did you bring the transmitter?" Heron asked.

Quickly, Rian loosened his clothes, removed his backpack. He pulled out the small, spherical contraption the woman had given him. Nothing looked broken, and Heron breathed a deep sigh of relief as he took the device in his hands. Carefully, Kaya's dad passed the transmitter to Naxos. Then he glanced at one of the closed doors across the small room.

"We may still have time to reach her," Heron said. "I just hope she's listening."

5
THE BILLIONAIRE
OF AREA 52

AT LEAST the last time Lewis was in jail, he hadn't been alone. Plus, the prison in Atlantis had beds, couches, multiple rooms, watery gardens, even exercise equipment. This place? Terrible! They'd locked him in some kind of conference room. Alone. And he hated being alone.

He sat at a long, wide oval table surrounded by low chairs. Lewis imagined he was a superhero. No, he'd forgotten—he was a spy, code name Lefty. Once a year, he met here with other young spies from around the world to discuss upcoming missions. One of the agents was from Belarus. Another was from Japan. Operatives from Australia and Egypt were coming, too, along with a highly intelligent talking penguin from Antarctica. This spy, Chilly, was their leader. She decided their missions, and she was paid in fish.

Lewis shook his head.

He had to focus.

He inspected the room. No phones. No computers.

And the jerks had grabbed their wristpads, too. He couldn't even play a game, let alone message someone.

There wasn't anything to eat, either. Or was there? Two rows of cabinets stared back at him from the opposite wall. He scrambled over the table and opened one of the doors. Notepads, pencils, pens. Was this a room for poets or something? The next cabinet was packed with hats. They were cool hats, though, with the familiar logo of a rising sun right in the center, above the bill, and mesh backs. He knew the brand: the Sunshine Corporation. They made all kinds of vehicles, including really, really sweet hovercars. He tried on a hat, slipped one of the notepads into his back pocket, then opened the final door and uncovered a glorious cache of potato chips, cashews, almonds, and those little squeeze packs of peanut butter. And on the bottom row? Cereal! All different kinds. Not the healthy stuff, either. These colorful treats were dusted with marvelous sugar. Lewis stuffed his already-crowded pockets, grabbed a box of Happy Unicorns, then dropped into one of the comfortable rolling chairs and started to eat.

The door opened.

He searched for a weapon.

Fortunately, it was Hanna. "Let's go," she whispered. She paused, squinted, frowned. "Why are you pointing a packet of peanut butter at me?"

He was aiming it as if it were some kind of Atlantean blaster. "Never mind that. How'd you get out?"

"The locks are electronic," she explained. "I reprogrammed mine. Not that hard, actually."

For her, anyway. He followed Hanna into the hallway.

One of the men and the woman in the white lab coat from earlier turned the corner ahead, walking toward them. Neither held a weapon. Lewis raised the peanut butter packet. "Make one move, and I'll use this!"

The woman backed away. "Please, no, I'm highly allergic."

"Me too," the man added. His voice quivered slightly. His face was colorless.

"Lower the squeeze pack," Hanna said.

Lewis did as he was told. He didn't really like weapons, anyway. Even delicious ones.

Hanna pointed at the woman. "You can't hold us here. We're minors. Especially him," she added, gesturing to Lewis.

Especially him? What was that supposed to mean?

"Please," the man answered, his voice still weak. "This is all a misunderstanding. We didn't think you'd be in the ship with her."

"We're more than happy to get you all home as soon as possible," the woman added.

"All of us?" Hanna asked. "Including Kaya?"

Now the woman smiled. "Especially Kaya. But you need to meet someone first."

An announcement blasted through a loudspeaker near the ceiling, calling Lin and Marvel to the aqua lab. "That's us," the woman explained. "I'm Helen Lin."

"Which makes you Mike Marvel," Lewis guessed.

"Frank, actually," the man replied.

"You should switch to Mike. It sounds cooler."

Marvel paused long enough to convince Lewis he must be considering the change. Then he led them through a maze of gray hallways with polished cement floors. The air was tinny. Chlorinated, too. The pool smell intensified as they neared the same room they'd been in an hour or so earlier— the aqua lab, apparently. At least a dozen people were crowded around Esmerelda. They'd draped some kind of glimmering electronic fabric over the vehicle.

"What's that?" Lewis asked.

"Where's Kaya?" Hanna asked. "What are you doing to her ship?"

Lin winked and pointed toward the small crowd.

A woman turned and smiled when she saw Lewis and Hanna. She walked toward them with long strides. "What are we doing with the ship?" she asked. "We're giving it an upgrade!"

"Wow," Hanna said. "You're Susan Silver."

"Who?" Lewis asked.

Hanna pointed at the logo on Lewis's new hat. "She started the Sunshine Corporation. She's one of the wealthiest women in the world."

"The wealthiest!" the woman replied, walking toward them with long strides. "That other pretender inherited her money in a divorce. I earned mine. You may call me Silver. Not Susan. I utterly despise how children address adults by their first names these days. It erodes generational respect. Also, I just had my ears operated on, so don't bother whispering. My hearing is amazing. I'm trained to read facial expressions, too, so I can guess what you're thinking." She paused. "Actually, I take that back. I have no idea what you're thinking, young man, but I do like your hat."

Lin moved to the woman's left and a step behind her. Marvel flanked her on her right, and he stood a little straighter, as if being around this woman gave him confidence. If he changed his name to Mike, Lewis thought, he'd be able to stand that way all the time.

"Where's Kaya?" Hanna asked. "If you hurt her—"

"Hurt her? We wouldn't dare harm the Atlantean. Kaya? Where are you, sweetheart?"

Their friend stepped into view from behind the ship. Her arms were crossed over her chest. Her hair was wet. She pointed to Esmerelda. The engineers were attaching the odd sheet underneath the vehicle now, as if they were wrapping it in a second skin. "Did you know about this, Hanna?" Kaya asked.

There was frustration in her voice. Anger, almost. Roberts had used the same tone the last time Lewis had stretched plastic wrap over the toilet. He understood why Roberts had gotten angry, even if the trick was hilarious. But why didn't Kaya believe they were on her side?

"We've told you we don't know anything," Hanna insisted.

"Honestly," Lewis added.

Silver changed the subject. "You're the Barkley girl, aren't you? I know your parents. Or rather, they know me. That makes you Lewis, correct? Son of the delightfully stubborn and utterly brilliant Richard Gates?"

She'd called his dad brilliant! He was starting to like this lady, even if she was holding them captive. "That's me," Lewis said. Then, thinking of the letter in his pocket, he added, "I'm also pretty good friends with the president."

"I've been following your father's work since the beginning,

Lewis. His theory on the source of the waves was so unusual, so outlandish, and yet so grounded in beautiful science that I suspected it might be true. One merely had to look beyond the expected." Thin lips pressed lightly together, Silver breathed in through her nose, looked at Kaya, then at Lewis and Hanna. "So."

"Are you going to explain what's happening here?" Hanna asked. "Why are you holding us captive? And what are you doing to the ship?"

Lin bit her lip and made a nearly inaudible noise. Without looking back, Silver told her to go ahead and explain. "That fabric is one of our latest innovations," Lin began. "It's covered with high-resolution video screens and miniature camera lenses. Once it's stretched into place, it will shrink around the vehicle like . . ." she looked at Lewis and squinted briefly ". . . a giant computerized gym sock. And then when we activate it, the cameras on one side will feed pictures to the screens on the opposite side, so no matter where you stand . . ."

"You don't see the ship," Silver said. "Only what's on the other side of it."

This made almost no sense to Lewis. Plus, he was stuck on the idea of a computerized sock. Would it let you search the Internet with your toes? If it started to smell, would it automatically order deodorant online?

"So it's like an electronic invisibility cloak," Hanna noted.

"Precisely! It's capable of absorbing sound waves, too."

An invisibility cloak? That he understood. Smart people were so annoying. Why didn't they just say that the first time? He'd always wanted an invisibility cloak. Not to do illegal things, though. Or at least not in a breaking-the-law kind of way. He might cheat in soccer a little, for example, and use it to ditch his defenders. A prank or two would be fun. Lewis could sneak into Jet's house and hold one of his little sister's toys in the air in front of his friend to trick him into thinking the doll was possessed. Jet was terrified of haunted toys. Then again, so was Lewis. He shivered as he thought of a mysterious floating doll, even if he'd be the one holding it, and decided he didn't want an invisibility cloak anymore.

"That sounds really cool and all," Lewis said, "but why are we here? And why's your hair wet, Kaya?"

"Your friend thought she could swim back to Atlantis," Silver explained. "Cute, right?"

Lewis eyed Kaya. She looked away. "You tried to leave without us? Really?"

"You ditched us?" Hanna added.

This time, Kaya didn't answer. So it was true. And it stung. Emotionally, that is—not like a hornet. Lewis wouldn't have left her behind in some random Atlantean evil lair. Plus, they'd been so nice to her. His mom and Roberts had hosted Kaya. They'd tried to feed her great meals—expensive ones, too. Even Lewis knew you weren't supposed to sneak out of a sleepover without saying thank you. He'd only ever done that once, and he'd had a really good reason: Kwan's pug, James Bond, had peed all over Lewis's sleeping bag in the middle of the night.

Hanna turned away from Kaya and faced Silver. "Wait. *You* were controlling the ship?"

Silver drew a short breath in past her lower teeth, then held up one hand, palm facing out. "Confession! Yes, that was us, but we had no choice. Not with such a fabulous deal before us!"

"I don't understand," Lewis said. "What deal?"

"She wants our technology," Kaya said.

"Oh," Hanna replied.

Lewis still didn't understand. He caught Kaya glancing into the ship. Was she going to try to escape?

Silver noticed his friend's glance, too, and uttered a smug little noise in response. She reached into her shoulder bag and dramatically removed Kaya's sonic blaster. "You're not looking for this, are you, Kaya? We didn't think you could be trusted with it." The billionaire handed the weapon to one of her guards. Then she clapped excitedly. "Let's get back to the technology. If you were to ask the average child what super-power they'd want, do you know what they'd say?"

"Smell," Lewis answered.

"What?"

"Not supersmell, as in a stronger sense," he said. "I'm thinking of skunks. Imagine if you could make yourself smell so bad that—"

"Flight," Hanna answered, cutting him off.

Silver squinted at Lewis. "You truly are perplexing! Your answer, Hanna, is what I had in mind. The power to fly, to cast off gravity's yoke and soar through the air!" She waved dismissively at Esmerelda. "Never mind giant, cumbersome vehicles like this one. Imagine if the tools we needed to fly were installed in formfitting gear and strapped to our bodies! Imagine hundreds of millions, even billions, of humans flying around the world without these silly vehicles!"

This wasn't actually that hard to imagine. Not the technology, anyway. Lewis had seen suits like that in Atlantis. Their antigravity cruisers were amazing, too, but watching people float through the sky on their own was light-years beyond awesome.

"Some hovercars still burn fossil fuels," added Marvel. "We could replace all those climate-killing engines. We could literally save the planet."

"Marvel? You interrupted me."

"I'm so sorry."

The poor engineer looked ready to faint. Lewis felt bad for the guy. "In his defense, you did pause," he noted.

"That was a dramatic pause!" Silver explained. "Go clean the executive toilet, Marvel."

"But I—"

"Clean the bowl, or I'll send you back to that midlevel lab where I found you."

The defeated scientist slunk away.

Lin took a cautious step back and another to the side.

"So," Silver resumed. "I want the gravity suits."

Lewis glanced at Kaya; she was sneering. Apparently, she didn't like this idea.

"How do you know about the gravity suits?" Hanna asked.

"Did you tell her, Lewis?" Kaya asked.

What? Him? Did Kaya really not trust him after all they'd been through? "No!" he said.

"No, he didn't tell me," Silver replied. "I've been watching and listening to everything that's been going on at your house, Lewis. Such fascinating discussions at your dinner table. And this Roberts fellow? He seems to be quite the chef! I'd love to join you one night."

"You listened to our conversations?" Lewis asked. "Those were private."

"Private? There is no such thing as privacy. How cute of you to hold on to that idea! I almost want to pet you. But you probably don't even wash your hair, do you? Ick. Children. Such an unfortunate way to perpetuate a species. It would be so much better if people like me could just live forever, or make adult copies of ourselves. Where was I, Lin?"

"The deal," her associate answered.

"Yes! I'm having trouble convincing Kaya, but as I explained, if she hurries back to Atlantis and returns with one or two of those wonderful gravity suits I've heard so much about, we will compensate you all handsomely."

"Huh?" Lewis asked.

"She's saying we'd get paid," Hanna replied.

"How much?"

Hanna elbowed him. "Lewis!"

"A substantial share of the profits would be appropriate. We can negotiate precise terms later. I can assure you I'm generous, though. Generally speaking, without getting into dollars and percentages, what do you think?"

Lewis would probably buy a small mountain. Maybe one with a ski slope and an indoor water park and a five-story mansion with a race car track in the basement for high-powered electric scooters. The second floor would have a basketball court that would spread apart and reveal an indoor pool. He'd probably need a laser tag arena and a trampoline park, too. Plus, he could get a new house for his mom, Michael, and Roberts—whatever kind of house they wanted. Maybe he'd give some money to charity, too. He could help feed kids.

All that would be incredible. Totally.

But there was also another piece of the plan that appealed to him. A part that meant more than millions and mansions.

If they went back to Atlantis, they could find his dad.

"Let's do it," he said.

"It's not your decision," Kaya snapped. She practically spat the words at him.

Hanna pointed to Esmerelda. "You have a gravity drive right there in that vehicle. Why do you need the suit?"

Now Lin intervened. She looked to Silver for permission first before explaining their reasoning. "It would take years to figure out how to miniaturize the warship's gravity drive enough to fit into a suit."

"Or we can wait a few days," Silver said, "and simply copy what you bring back."

"I already told you," Kaya said. "I don't care about your money, and you can't have our technology."

Sure, Lewis thought. She could insist all she wanted, but Kaya didn't know the woman's money. He'd always been taught not to judge people until you got to know them. Why not treat money the same way? What if they all spent a little time with some of Silver's money before rejecting her offer? A few days, maybe, or a week. He was sure Kaya would grow to love it.

"I'm not sure you understand how much money we're

talking about," Silver replied. "Hanna, maybe you could explain what ten million dollars means here on the surface—"

Holding up her hand, Kaya cut her off. "What's that?"

Lewis pointed to Silver. "I'm sorry, did you say ten million?"

"What's what?" Hanna asked, turning to Kaya.

Had no one else heard that number? Lewis could almost see the figure and its seven delightful zeroes floating in the air over Silver's head. The digits sparkled and glowed.

"Quiet," Kaya said. "I hear something."

"I do detect a faint pinging," Silver noted.

The engineers had just finished vacuum sealing the new skin around the warship. Now they backed away, and Lin and a few others followed Kaya and Hanna into Esmerelda. Lewis started after them, but Silver gently grabbed his arm above the elbow. Her fingers were thin and cold. Her grip was tight, and she smelled like lavender.

"Listen to me for a minute," she whispered. She moved between him and the ship. "This is life-changing money, Lewis. I know what you've been through with your father. I know how your mother has suffered. I've seen your tiny little house. Your two friends don't understand. Hanna doesn't care about money because she *has* money. Go back to Atlantis with them and bring me back one gravity suit, Lewis. That's all I ask!"

"I'm not a thief," he said.

She tapped the brim of his new hat. "You stole that," she replied. "That looks like one of our notepads, too."

He tried to give both back, but she recoiled. "Fine," he said. "I'll keep them. But I'm not a thief."

"I know that, Lewis!" she said reassuringly. "Of course you're not! And this wouldn't be stealing. You can pay for the suit in Atlantis. They use gold, right? I'll give you the coins you'll need. Write your mom a nice little note explaining what you're doing and where you're going, and I'll make absolutely sure that she gets it as soon as possible. You'd be helping your family, Lewis. In exchange for the suit, I'll make sure you enjoy the kind of wealth that will change your life, your mother's life, your little brother's life. You could fund monuments, scholarships, entire research departments in your father's name, to honor his legacy!"

Why was Silver talking about monuments? "My father's alive."

She paused. "Sure. Of course he is."

"He *is* alive," Lewis insisted. "I know it."

Before Silver could respond, Hanna called to him from the ship. "Lewis, come here!"

The billionaire leaned close. Her breath was chilly. Slightly minty, too. "Think about it, Lewis. One little gravity suit in exchange for life-changing wealth."

Across the floor, Hanna leaned out the open warship door. "You're going to want to listen to this," she said. "We picked up an emergency message."

Roberts, he guessed. Or his mother. "Tell my mom we'll be back soon," Lewis said.

"It's not your mom," Hanna said. "The message is coming from Atlantis."

6

GENEROUS ELF

KAYA could barely concentrate with all of them crowded around her. Hanna, Lewis, Silver, Lin, Marvel, and two of those uniformed men were all inside the ship. *Her* ship. They smelled—that odd, musty, Sun Person odor she could barely tolerate. And they wouldn't stop talking. The speakers hissed. Static masked the words of the message. Silver asked what was going wrong. Hanna suggested tuning the frequency. Lewis said he was scribbling a letter to his mom, but he was half listening, too, and telling Kaya to increase the volume. Why would making it louder help?

Kaya closed her eyes. Clenched her teeth.

Ignore them—she needed to ignore them.

She placed her palm on the control pad, tuned the soundscape scanner. The static softened. Another slight adjustment and . . . clarity.

Kaya restarted the message and turned up the volume.

A familiar voice emerged.

She jerked back, surprised. "That's my dad," she said.

Silver shrugged her thin shoulders. "He's speaking gibberish," she said.

"That's their language," Hanna replied. She pointed to her ear. "Amazing tech," she said to Silver. "These little earpieces automatically translate Atlantean speech to English, so we can understand it as well as Kaya."

"How intriguing," Silver replied. "That could be very profitable. But tell me, Kaya, what does the message say?"

The woman's hand was on her shoulder. A chill coursed down Kaya's arm.

Kaya removed her hand from the pad.

Shook her shoulder free.

Crossed her arms over her chest.

Her father's message was odd, but the main point was clear enough. "He says we have to get this ship back within two days or Atlantis will attack the surface."

All seven Sun People were silent. Stunned. Yet Kaya knew what she had to do. She sprang to her feet. "I need to leave. Now."

Hanna checked her old-fashioned wristwatch. "It's Thursday night now. So we need to get this ship to Atlantis by Saturday night, or Saturday afternoon, to be safe. Can we do that, Kaya?"

We? No way was she letting the Sun People come with her. They'd anchor her down. She'd never get back in time.

Silver clapped her hands. "My last trip to the moon took only thirty-six hours. A day and a half to get to Atlantis? That should be easy."

Why was this woman interfering? Kaya addressed Hanna and Lewis directly. She hoped they'd understand. "I have to go back alone."

"No way," Hanna said. "I'm going with you."

Lewis looked up from his note. "What about my dad? I'm going, too!"

Okay, so maybe they wouldn't understand. Kaya pressed her hands to her eyes. Then, quickly, she studied each of her friends. Hanna stood with her jaw firmly set. She was clearly determined. Meanwhile, Lewis reminded her of one of those strangely cute puppy creatures he'd shown her so many pictures of back at his house—his wide, plaintive eyes made it impossible for her to reject his plea. Even if they might slow her down, there was no way she was getting rid of her friends.

"Fine," Kaya said. "Let's go."

The entire group immediately kicked into action. Lin talked Kaya and Hanna through a few technical details relating to the electronic skin. Lewis finished and folded up his note, then handed it to Silver, who huddled with him in the back of the ship, talking seriously about something. His mom, probably. Or his dad? Either way, it was helpful—Kaya and Hanna could work faster with Lewis occupied. Marvel and two other men returned with armfuls of snacks, including a dozen small boxes of the stuff Lewis called cereal. One of the cardboard containers had a picture of what looked like a four-legged narwhal. Kaya stared at the image for a moment—their world was so odd.

Once they'd finished preparing, the goodbyes were brief and uninspiring. All three of them were very happy to leave Silver.

Soon, the warship was rising off the floor. Kaya pushed

Esmerelda forward through the falling water and out into the night air.

Inside the cabin, the Sun People were quiet. Upset with her, Kaya guessed. She had tried to ditch them. Twice. She'd probably be annoyed, too, if she were in their position.

The tops of the trees below were a blur.

The sky was clear, the gray moonlight bright.

And she was finally free.

A break in the tree cover revealed the winding river below. Kaya remembered her attempted escape from earlier and laughed a little. This certainly was easier than swimming to Atlantis. Plus, if she hadn't been caught and brought back to the lab, she never would've received the message from her dad.

Everything was flowing her way now.

She was swimming with the current, not fighting against it.

Hanna started working through their schedule. "The last time, it took us six hours to get from Atlantis back to the coast," she explained. "So if we fly most of the way instead of going through the water, we can probably make it that quickly again. Then we'll still have almost two full days to get the warship back to Ridge City."

Kaya considered her math. Technically, that was true.

But there was more to it than that.

How were they even going to get into Atlantis? She didn't entirely understand the instructions in the message.

There was a crunching sound behind her—Lewis was eating cereal. He stood between their seats. "Should we test the skin?"

Hanna nodded. "Definitely."

Lewis clapped and rubbed his hands together. He lowered his voice, stared ahead of them seriously. "Stealth mode, activate!"

That was definitely not how the system worked.

You didn't whistle, either, but of course he tried that, too.

This was Sun People technology, which meant Kaya herself wasn't even sure how to operate it. Hanna reached forward and tapped a small square device Lin had added to the control panel. She'd stuck it to the surface with some kind of black, bristly patch. Hanna peeled it off and noticed Kaya watching her. "Velcro," she explained. "Invented when we went to the moon for the first time." The device's screen brightened. Shapes and images appeared. Hanna tapped one. "Ready?"

Again, Lewis stared ahead. "Stealth mode, activate," he said.

Kaya nodded to Hanna, who switched on the skin.

"Poooooooofffff," Lewis whispered.

And then . . . everything seemed normal. Had it worked? She wasn't sure. But she had a test in mind. Edging forward in her seat, Kaya slid her hands over the control pads, pushing the vehicle faster. Below them and far ahead, a hovercar cruised slowly. Kaya steered so they were alongside the vehicle, then slowed to its pace. Carefully, she swerved closer. The warship was only a few meters away. Kaya could have jumped the gap between them.

Two women sat in the cabin of the hovercar. Neither one noticed the Atlantean warship.

"Amazing," Kaya muttered.

Lewis slapped the back of her seat. "Ha! You admit it!"

"Admit what?"

"That we're not totally useless! We can build cool technology, too."

Kaya slid her hands forward on the control pads again, steered the ship higher and faster. "I didn't say you Sun People were totally useless."

Hanna shrugged. "You've been a little harsh."

She paused. She didn't want to apologize. But she had been critical. Hopefully they could understand. "This has been . . . hard," Kaya admitted.

Hanna responded with a sympathetic smile. She understood, at least. Kaya could see that. "Let's get you home," Hanna said. "Why don't you show us how fast this ship can fly?"

Now that was a plan she could follow.

Maybe she should have told Lewis to sit down. Warned him, at least. But Hanna wanted to see what Esmerelda could really do. So Kaya would show her.

She pushed the warship to its top speed.

The force pressed her back against her seat.

The trees below transformed into a dark green blur.

Standing between them, Lewis shifted one of his feet forward and let out a long, low, moderately hilarious cheer. "Let's gooooooooo!"

Through clenched teeth, Hanna muttered, "Higher."

Kaya angled them higher. Good advice, too—a cluster

of taller-than-average buildings rose up out of the darkness. The warship skimmed over the structures, missing them by a few meters.

That was a little closer than Kaya would have liked.

The last thing she wanted to do was crash.

She slowed the ship.

Hanna sighed. "How long can the batteries last?" she asked.

Not forever—Kaya understood that much. She checked the power reserves. She didn't fully know how this part of the warship worked, but she didn't want to admit that to Hanna, or even Lewis. "Long enough to get us back home," she guessed.

Hopefully she was right.

The ship cruised over scattered towns; their lights glowed like the radiant bugs in a dark cave. Before long, the wide expanse of the ocean stretched out across the horizon. Finally. Kaya pulled back slightly, slowing the ship, conserving power. She exhaled. The wind had died.

The ocean was glassy, almost silver in the moonlight.

That feeling of calm returned. She wasn't home, but she was getting closer.

Then Lewis started asking about their plan to rescue his father. Hanna wondered aloud how they'd sneak into Atlantis unnoticed. Wouldn't the Erasers be looking for them? Wouldn't they be scanning the sea? These were good questions, and Kaya had only a vague plan. But she did know that they wouldn't be able to waste time looking for the professor. They had an attack to stop. Kaya couldn't tell Lewis that, though.

But he kept asking about the professor and their rescue plans.

He was making Kaya's already-impossible task even harder.

Could she still get rid of them? If she dropped them in the ocean, the Coastal Patrol Roberts had talked about would rescue them, and Lewis and Hanna would be returned home safely. In a roundabout way, if she dumped them out here, not too far from the shore, she'd almost be helping them.

Right?

No!

That was a terrible idea. Kaya shook her head as if she could throw off the thought. How could she even consider leaving them out here? She had to bring them with her.

"Why's it doing that?" Hanna asked.

She was pointing to the control panel. One of the pads was shaking.

An alarm. Kaya looked back and up over her shoulder.

Two vehicles were flying high overhead, following them.

Kaya explained as Hanna returned to the copilot's seat. "Must be jets," Hanna guessed. "The cloak is still active, so I guess Silver's antiradar system doesn't work as well as she thought."

Lewis deepened his voice again. "Antiradar, full power!"

Hanna sighed. "It doesn't work like that."

These jets were faster than the Sun People's whining hovercars.

Kaya pushed the warship to its top speed, and the flying machines still kept pace. What now? she asked herself. She couldn't allow them to follow her all the way out to the ridge. Then they'd know, or at least suspect, that Atlantis was nearby. Lewis and Hanna had promised they hadn't told anyone on the surface the location of Atlantis. Her world was safe mostly because its location was still a secret. Her dad wouldn't be too proud if she showed the Sun People their front door.

She turned to Hanna, then Lewis. "Can they swim?" she asked.

"Who?" Lewis replied.

"Your jets," Kaya said. "Are they fast in the water, too?"

"Nope."

If the jets couldn't swim, then she'd dive. The trip would take longer, but not much more than half a day. That left them more than a day in Atlantis. Kaya explained her thinking.

"That works," Hanna replied.

"As long as we have time to find my dad," Lewis added.

Again with the professor! Kaya ignored the comment. She slowed the ship to a drift and steered downward. The jets turned and swooped toward them. Despite the calm surface, there was energy in the water. The swells were long and large. Tens of meters separated one from the next. She aimed for the trough of one of the rolling waves. The jets sped closer, shining painfully bright spotlights at them. Kaya squinted and shielded her eyes—the Sun People complained, too. She pushed the ship down and into an oncoming wave. The whale-like nose of Esmerelda slipped through the roof of the ocean. The seat belts dug into her chest and shoulders as the ship recoiled from the shock. The white light dimmed. The watery darkness wrapped around them, and the cabin turned silent as she steered them down into the comforting embrace of the sea.

Finally, she was going home.

Seeing the water was one thing. Having it cover them so completely, and shield them, was positively fantastic.

"So what's the plan?" Lewis asked.

His voice was odd. Garbled. Was it her earplugs? She wriggled them both, then realized he was just eating again—a pungent meat stick—and chewing with his mouth open. Gross. "The plan?" Kaya asked.

"Yeah, the plan," Hanna added. "Lewis, close your mouth." She checked her wristwatch. "I figure the trip will take a solid twelve hours through the water, which gets us to Atlantis"—she paused, rocking her head back and forth, calculating quickly—"sometime in the early afternoon. That gives us at least a day to figure out where we need to take the ship, exactly. We're not storming back into Atlantis, right? I don't feel like getting knocked unconscious again. Oh, and I'm not wearing anyone's weird clothes like last time, either." She lifted her forearm to her nose and sniffed. "I'm still struggling to scrub the stink off my skin."

Lewis slipped between their seats, turned, and sat on the control panel. The speaker switched on; he'd accidentally started to play the message again. He apologized, but this was probably as good a time as any to review it. After all, it was a little odd, and they hadn't completely deciphered its meaning the first time. Kaya turned up the volume.

In two days, the High Council is voting on whether to launch a full-scale attack on the surface. If you return the warship to Ridge City before then and show that the Sun People are not invaders, we may have a chance to stop the vote. The Erasers will be looking for you, so we will meet you in Edgeland. Enter Atlantis like the generous elf. Do not delay. The future of Atlantis depends on you.

She played the message again.

And again.

After the fourth time through, Lewis slapped the dashboard. "Topeka!" he exclaimed. "I figured it out!"

"You mean eureka," Hanna said.

Lewis paused. "Nope, I mean Topeka. Famous Greek scientist. Loved bathtubs. Discovered Kansas. Check Wikipedia."

"Topeka, eureka, I don't care," Kaya said. "What did you figure out?"

"Play it once more."

He held up both index fingers as her father said the most confusing line:

Enter Atlantis like the generous elf.

Lewis stretched his arms out wide. His eyes bulged. Did he think it was obvious? Well, it wasn't—or not to Kaya, at least. He placed one foot on each of their armrests. He licked his thumb, then reached down and rubbed a smudge off the top of one of his precious sneakers. Kaya still didn't understand why the Sun People wore clothes on their feet, but his obsession with this particular model—what had he called them? Jordans?—was truly bewildering. It wasn't like the shoes countered gravity.

"The generous elf!" he said. "Don't you get it?"

Hanna jumped in before Kaya could respond. "Never mind the elf, Lewis. Are we sure it's a good idea to go back to Edgeland? That place was dangerous."

And completely awesome, Kaya thought. The grime, the

stench, the noise and chaos of Edgeland were pure excitement. She'd go back the first chance she had. But not now—not with the warship. That piece, Kaya guessed, was misdirection. "He knew the Erasers would be listening to the soundscape," Kaya explained, "so the last place we should go is Edgeland."

Hanna stood and paced between the bench seats on either side of the ship. "Naxos said he was taking the professor to that Evenor place, right? Your father said he was going to meet them there, Kaya." She stopped. With certainty, she announced, "We're going to Evenor."

Really? The last time Kaya checked, they were cruising in an Atlantean ship.

And she was the only Atlantean onboard.

She was going to decide on their destination. Not Hanna.

But there was some logic to the idea. They definitely couldn't go straight to Ridge. The city was hidden beneath a mountainous layer of solid rock. The nearest outlet to the open sea was a hundred miles away. Getting to Evenor wouldn't be easy either, though.

Lewis interrupted her thinking. "Excuse me? Can we talk about the elf now?"

Kaya closed her eyes briefly. Fine. She'd humor him. "The word doesn't translate. What's an elf?"

"Magical creatures," Hanna said. "As in, not real."

"That's not very helpful."

Kaya swung her seat around as Lewis slid down off the control panel. He waved Hanna out of his way, then started to pace the cabin with his hands behind his back, as if he were a teacher. "Elves have pointy ears, but they're not Vulcans, and

Vulcans are not elves," he began. "Vulcans are very logical. Some elves are good with bows and arrows. Others live in tree houses and make delicious cookies. Actually, the cookies are a little dry. You really need to dip them in milk to make them work—"

"Lewis?" Hanna interrupted. "Focus."

"Right. So the best elves, and the ones we need to think about, are generous. They give you stuff."

What was he talking about? What stuff? This was getting frustrating. No, infuriating.

"What's your point?" Kaya asked.

"Well, these particular elves make toys, and then this big bearded guy named Santa Claus gets into a sleigh and delivers the gifts all around the world, except Atlantis, I guess, since his sleigh isn't a submarine . . ."

"Lewis," Hanna said, her voice sharp.

"You're veering off course again," Kaya added.

"Right," Lewis replied. "My point is that he's an elf!"

"Who?" Kaya asked.

"I'm super confused right now, Lewis," Hanna admitted. "Kaya's dad is an elf?"

"No, Santa Claus! He's the generous elf."

This was what happened when they let Lewis lead a discussion. "Hanna," Kaya said, "can you please explain?"

"Not really, no. We don't do Christmas in my house. Instead of presents, we make donations to educational foundations."

Lewis winced. "Ouch. That's brutal."

"Fulfilling, actually," Hanna replied. "Lewis, would you mind explaining to both of us what in the world you're talking about?"

He nodded seriously. He clasped his hands behind his back and started pacing again. Did he really need to savor and enjoy this moment so much?

Yes, Kaya realized. Yes, he did.

"Santa Claus," Lewis began, "is described in the famous poem 'The Night Before Christmas' as a jolly old elf."

Hanna covered her face with her hands. "Please tell me you're not going to rely on Santa Claus to get us back to Atlantis."

"No! I already told you, his sleigh doesn't go underwater." Lewis waved his hands above his head. "It's a convertible. There's no roof. Otherwise, maybe. But think about it. That message says to sneak into Edgeland like the generous elf. And how does Santa Claus get into homes? You've got to know this."

"Through the chimney," Hanna said. "That never made sense to me, though."

"Exactly! The chimney, which is on the roof. Maybe we're supposed to enter Evenor through a chimney in the roof of Atlantis."

The word didn't translate. "What's a chimney?" Kaya asked.

"Part of a house," Lewis explained with a shrug. "You make a fire downstairs to keep the house warm, and the smoke passes up and out through the chimney."

A thought occurred to Kaya. "That sounds like a vent."

"A what?" Lewis asked.

Now Hanna was nodding. "A hydrothermal vent. They release heat and superhot minerals from the Earth's interior into the ocean."

"Exactly," Kaya said. Hanna was looking at her strangely; Kaya guessed she wasn't entirely following her reasoning yet. But there was a slim chance Lewis was right.

Kaya closed her eyes and held up her hands, silently asking them to let her think. What did she know about Evenor? That it was flooded and supposedly a really interesting place to visit. But she'd learned something else in one of her science classes. Something about heat. Yes! Before it was ruined, the city was one of the hottest in Atlantis, so engineers built pipes that pumped the heat out into the surrounding ocean through vents in the ridge.

They were basically artificial versions of hydrothermal vents.

Or Atlantean versions of these chimneys Lewis was talking about.

Could that be it? Were they supposed to slip in through one of those vents?

She explained her theory. Lewis agreed immediately.

Hanna wasn't so sure. "Chimneys aren't a great way in or out of a house, no matter what Lewis tells you."

"What if there are tunnels near the chimney-vent things?" Lewis asked. "You showed us those secret routes in and out of Edgeland. Maybe Evenor has them, too. Or maybe we could just drive down through one of the vents. Esmerelda's pretty tough."

He was right. The ship was resilient.

Kaya stared through the glass into the darkness of the water. The ship had incredibly powerful sensors. She'd taught herself how to use them during the past week. "If there are tunnels, I should be able to find them," she said.

"That's a big if," Hanna noted.

"With other ifs crowded around it," Lewis added. "Like a giant, sloppy if sandwich with pickles and tomatoes. But who doesn't love sandwiches?"

Kaya ignored him—she was beginning to think this was the only way to think straight around Lewis. One important piece of his theory didn't float. "What I don't get, Lewis," Kaya said, "is that my dad is the one speaking in the message, and he has never heard of elves or this bearded chimney crawler."

Lewis's eyes lit up. "That's exactly my point!"

"It is?" Hanna asked.

"Yes! That's how I know this is what we have to do, where we have to go. Don't you get it? Your father didn't come up with that part of the message," Lewis said. "My dad did!"

7

Into the Darkness

LEWIS couldn't sit still, and Hanna wouldn't let him dance out his energy. They'd forgotten to get their wristpads back from the Sunshine people, too, which meant he still didn't have any games to play. So he paced around the small ship. He did jumping jacks. He tried push-ups, too, but his wrists started to hurt during the third one, and he gave up halfway through the fifth. Afterward, he did feel stronger, though, and nothing could exhaust his enthusiasm. They were pretty much on a mission to save the world, and his dad was alive! Not only that, but his father had sent a message only Lewis would be able to decipher.

That meant he expected Lewis to return to Atlantis.

So his father actually believed in him.

Lewis felt fifteen feet tall. Or maybe half that. The ceiling inside Esmerelda was only about eight feet high, so if he were any taller, he'd have to bend over, and his neck and back would hurt. Never mind his imagined height, though—his secret scheme was far more impressive. When Lewis told his dad about the deal with Susan Silver, he'd be amazed. His father would be able to use some of the money to build a new lab.

And get a new hovercar, too. And a new house. Someplace closer to Lewis, so they could hang out more.

Unexpectedly, Lewis yawned. None of them had slept, and they'd been plowing through the ocean for hours and hours. He didn't know if it was night or day. Sunlight didn't reach down this far, so they were surrounded by darkness.

Hanna and Kaya were working at the instrument panel. Kaya said she was learning more about how the ship worked, and she was also teaching Hanna how to read and control the sensors with her hands. Hanna was proving to be a slow learner, which was kind of awesome, because she learned everything else so quickly.

All the downtime was a little boring, but it did give him time to think. Was it wrong, what he was planning to do? He'd be helping his family. Plus, as Susan Silver had explained it to him, he wouldn't really be stealing. She'd given him a bunch of gold coins to buy a suit. So he'd be paying for the gear, fair and square. He definitely wasn't doing anything wrong. But if that was true, then why wasn't he sharing his plan with Kaya?

Why was he keeping it a secret from Hanna, too?

He yawned again.

He didn't want to be the first one to fall asleep. That would be a sign of weakness, and he had already shown far too many of those. He reached into his backpack, pulled the president's letter from a side pocket, unfolded it, and read it through once more. The paper was creased in way too many places from all the folding and stained in one spot. The signature was smudged. His mom was going to be furious about that, but he could blame it on Kaya. The phone number was difficult to read, too, and he wanted to remember it in case he felt like calling the president sometime. He stared at each digit, imagined etching it into his mind, then folded the letter and slipped it into his pocket.

"What are you doing back there?" Hanna called out to him.

"Thinking," he said.

"Be careful," she replied.

Kaya laughed.

He yawned again. More jumping jacks? No. He tried on the purple hoodie Dr. Barkley had made for Kaya. The fit was a little loose, even for him, but Hanna came around behind him and adjusted something. The sweatshirt compressed. The arms and chest were suddenly tight, and Hanna patiently explained how the hoodie worked. In addition to normal threads, the sweatshirt had these things called actuators that could flex and bend like human muscles. A miniature computer in the cuff of the sleeve controlled everything. She showed him a little touch screen control panel in the waistband, too. Her mom had programmed the hoodie to teach Kaya how to properly swing a tennis racket, but you could also set it to teach you a bunch of other sports and activities. Lewis didn't get a chance to scroll through them all before Hanna set it to basketball and stepped back.

Immediately, Lewis lost control of his upper body.

The sleeves were moving on their own.

He was shooting an imaginary basketball over and over.

At first it was kind of funny.

He imagined game-winning three-pointers swishing through the net.

Crowds cheering and chanting his name.

Hanna was chuckling. Kaya, too.

But after about ten seconds, it started getting weird.

He couldn't actually stop his arms—the sleeves were too strong. "Help?" he pleaded.

Kaya hurried back and grabbed him from behind, pinning his arms. He could hear the tiny motors whining as the sweatshirt tried to move. Hanna managed to reach the touchscreen and shut it down. Then Lewis ripped off the sweatshirt and tossed it into the far corner. "That thing is haunted!"

Hanna shrugged. "It's pretty cool, though, right?"

"You can keep it," Kaya replied. "But tell your mom I said thank you, Hanna."

The ship moved unexpectedly; Lewis reached out and grabbed the wall to balance himself. "What was that?"

Back at the control panel, Kaya shrugged. "A shift in the current," she said.

"How far out are we?" he asked.

"A ways still," Kaya answered. "Five or six hours at least."

"Try to sleep, Lewis," Hanna suggested. "We'll need it."

Lewis wasn't a baby. He didn't need her telling him when to take a nap. But he was definitely tired. He lay down on the floor, using his backpack as a pillow, and after a series of ever deeper, louder yawns, he drifted off. All his grand thoughts about saving the world leaked into his sleep, and he dreamed he was floating along a wide river as a horde of alien spaceships descended. All of the aliens inside looked exactly like sparrows, only with little fingers at the tops of their wings. They had unfamiliar but sophisticated accents, too, and they flew out of the ships in swarms, shouting indecipherable insults. He was wrestling dozens of them in the shallows of the river, engulfed in a cloud of feathers, when Kaya shook him by the shoulder. Startled, he chirped.

"What was that?" she asked.

"Nothing."

Hanna was just stirring from a nap, too, stretched out on one of the benches. She rolled her head. Her neck cracked.

Kaya rubbed her eyes. "We're almost there."

"No one's shooting at us?" Hanna asked.

"Not yet," Kaya replied.

Lewis's mind was still tethered to the dreamworld when he realized the copilot's seat was empty. He dashed toward the front of the ship, tripped, rolled, then staggered over to the seat, grabbed the back, and flung himself down. As Kaya moved to the pilot's seat, Hanna stood between them, watching. The water was less crowded with sea stuff down here, but the darkness was almost complete, and Kaya didn't want to turn on their lights. She was worried they'd attract attention. Instead, she explained, they were pinging the seascape in front of them with sound waves, then reading them as they bounced back to map the distance to the ridge and its shape. All of which kind of made sense in a sciencey sort of way, but Lewis still wished they'd just crank up the headlights.

Kaya started wringing her hands. Lewis noticed she was squinting, too. "Everything okay?" he asked.

"We're in range of Atlantean sensors now," she said, lowering her voice.

The last time he and Hanna had been in this situation, a giant robotic submarine had knocked them all unconscious with a weird subsonic pulse. He wondered aloud whether they were in for the same fate today.

"No, we should be able to get past the sensors since we're using a really narrow soundbeam," Kaya said, her voice still quiet. "You three were bouncing sound all over the place when you turned up last time."

Okay, sure, that made sense. But the tension was unsettling. He was thinking about dancing a little or maybe playing a few notes on his harmonica. He had another question first, though. "Is that why we're whispering, too?"

Kaya shrugged. "Hey, I haven't snuck into Atlantis before," she noted. "I figure the less noise, the better."

Subtly, Lewis slipped his harmonica back into his pocket.

"They said the skin could absorb sound, too," Hanna noted. "Maybe that's helping."

"We're getting close," Kaya said.

Lewis looked out through the glass at the darkness. He didn't see anything. "How do you know?" he asked.

Kaya lifted her hands off the pads. "The ship's sensors," she said. "Plus, you can see the heat from the vents." She pointed out through the glass. "Notice the way the water ripples?"

Lewis watched. The dark water near the glass moved in waves that reminded him of the air near the grill when Roberts was cooking. The thought made him think of home. His mom was going to be worried, but once she read his note, she'd understand. He was relieved that Susan Silver had offered to give her his message. The billionaire wasn't so bad after all.

"Wow," Hanna said. "Does that mean we're near a vent?"

"I think so," Kaya said. "According to the ship's maps, Evenor should be right below us."

Lewis watched as Kaya moved her hand around on one of the tablets. This part still amazed him. Or maybe it confused him; sometimes the line was so blurry. A few days ago, in his backyard, Kaya had explained that the maps were stored inside the device. She'd shown him how she read with her fingers, feeling the shifting lines, bumps, and ridges. Now he watched as she lifted one hand off the surface, tapped the pad aggressively several times, swiped right, and traced a circle. Seconds later, she jolted upright. She bit her lower lip.

"Did you find something?" Hanna asked.

"There's a hole in the ridge ahead," she said.

"A hole?"

"Or an abandoned vent converted into a tunnel, maybe."

The complete darkness, the tension in the submarine, the fact that they were now miles below the surface—Lewis was feeling increasingly uneasy. "Or it could be a hiding place for a giant monster waiting to swim out and swallow us."

Hanna sighed. "That was a movie, Lewis. There are no giant monsters!"

The best movie of all time, to be exact. The one movie he and his dad both loved. The one they could watch together over and over without either of them falling asleep. They always argued about their favorite parts, too. Was it when the giant worm popped out of the asteroid? Or when Han sliced open the tauntaun to save Luke and its steaming innards spilled into the snow? His dad preferred the latter. Lewis was partial to the space rock monster. As for Hanna's protest . . . well, what did she know about monsters? Quietly, he replied, "There wasn't supposed to be an Atlantis, either."

Hanna squeezed her lips shut and nodded.

Then Kaya flicked on the lights. The seafloor was blanketed with gray sludge, like a mud-covered plateau atop a huge mountain range. The bottom of a weed-encrusted plastic bottle jutted out of the mess. Other scraps of surface trash were scattered all around: more plastic fragments and bits of netting and rope. Hanna gasped. "Did we do this?" she asked.

"That's not Atlantean trash," Kaya said.

"This is terrible," Hanna answered. "People need to see this. Any chance you packed a camera, Lewis?"

He pulled out his harmonica. "No, but I could play something. Maybe break the tension?"

Hanna took a quick breath, as if she were about to say something, then stopped herself. "We're trying to be quiet, remember?"

Next to him, Kaya pulled back on the control pads, slowing the warship almost to a stop.

A brownish-gray cloud billowed all around them.

As it settled, a wide, gaping hole in the seafloor came into view.

Lewis leaned over the control panel. "Are we really going in there?" he asked.

The water cleared, then swirled suddenly. A brown, rusted jumble of fused metal and glass popped out of the opening and rolled away from them in the opposite direction. Quickly, Kaya switched off the lights, but the vehicle was already disappearing in a cloud of muck and sludge.

"Did they spot us?" Hanna asked.

"No," Kaya whispered. "That's a driverless trawler. A bottom fisher. We're lucky—if someone had seen my lights . . ."

"Well, they didn't," Hanna noted.

"Where are we?" Lewis asked.

He watched Kaya feel the pads again. Double-checking, he guessed. "If the maps and scanners are correct," Kaya said, "we're here."

Lewis leaned forward and slapped the dashboard. "So let's gooooo!"

Kaya glared at him.

Hanna, too.

He winced and dropped his voice a few decibels. "Quietly," he added.

In silence, Kaya steered Esmerelda toward the opening, then down and into the tunnel. Lewis was surprised when she switched their lights on again. Thankful, too, because he saw no slimy evidence that they were traveling down some giant sea creature's throat.

Hanna put her hand on his shoulder. "See, Lewis? Just a tunnel. Not a monster."

"Did you just read my mind?"

"No," Hanna said. She shivered briefly, as if she'd swallowed something bitter or disgusting. "I don't think anyone would want to read your mind, Lewis. That would be dangerous."

Kaya laughed softly. "It would probably be filled with pictures of . . . what were they called?" She paused. Then her face brightened. "Sandwiches."

Lewis did love sandwiches. Especially with pickles.

Esmerelda pitched back, pressing him into his seat. Hanna stumbled but stayed on her feet as the ship rose up out of the water and into a huge cave.

No, not a cave. Another tunnel, Lewis realized. Blue lights shined to the right. There was a greenish glow in the distance. Esmerelda floated in place as seawater rushed down the outside of the glass hull.

"We're here," Kaya whispered, as much to herself as to them. "We actually made it."

Hanna grabbed Lewis's shoulder hard. She was smiling; he beamed back up at her. His father had been searching for this world for years. He had given up everything to find Atlantis. And sure, he had found it eventually. But now Lewis had made it to Atlantis *twice* in less than a month. Yes, Hanna had done it, too. She was brilliant, though, and resourceful and strong. Lewis had made it on dance skills, charm, and a decent reserve of bravery he hadn't known he possessed. What was next? Would he go to Mars for winter break?

He deserved a little bit of recognition. At home, he liked to make certificates of accomplishment for himself and stick them to his bedroom door. But he didn't have the right paper with him, so he just reached over his shoulder and patted himself on the back.

That wasn't quite enough, though, so he jumped out of the copilot's seat and danced to a silent tune. Quickly, Hanna snaked his scat.

As Lewis finished his celebratory shuffle, Kaya steered their craft toward the green lights and into a cave that could have held several soccer stadiums. A thick layer of mist hovered below the ceiling. Dozens of cruisers drifted through the air, and a vast lake dotted with small islands and docks stretched out before them. Boats and ferries sped between the islands, which were carpeted in green vines and blue and yellow flowers. Some of them looked deserted, but others had small dome-shaped buildings in their centers. The structures reminded Lewis of igloos, only without the ice. Or, given that they were covered in greenery, tree forts without the trees. He decided to call them treegloos and imagined that furry, Ewok-like people lived inside. They'd play xylophones, and he'd dance to their music, and they'd all become best friends.

Hanna nudged him and pointed to two lines of people, maybe twenty in all, drifting over the scene in gravity gear. "What are they doing?" she asked Kaya.

"Probably a tour," Kaya guessed. "Evenor gets loads of visitors."

Sure, the place was sort of interesting. Lewis liked the treegloos. But Evenor definitely didn't compare to the rest of Atlantis. He had seen massive aquafarms. A filtering pool surrounded by waterfalls. He'd been to Edgeland and Ridge City! He'd even spent a little time in an underwater prison and visited what was pretty much the coolest factory he could imagine—even if it was operated by evil agents. So, while it was exciting to be back, if he were to rank all the Atlantean places he'd visited on a scale of one to awesome, Evenor would earn a C at best.

Still, he reminded himself, his dad was here somewhere.

That earned the place a few points.

Hanna held out her wristwatch, showing him the time. "Four o'clock at home," she said. "I was only off by a few hours."

The word *home* was like kryptonite—even the slightest reminder of his family sucked all the energy out of Lewis. But his mom would understand. Once Silver brought her the note, and his mom learned about the deal, she'd understand.

Kaya steered them close to an island with a large treegloo in the center. A man with the long gray hair of an old musician stomped out. He stood, stretched, glanced in the direction of their warship. He looked nothing like an Ewok.

Lewis waved. The man did not wave back.

"Not very friendly here," Lewis noted.

"He can't see us," Hanna reminded him.

"What?"

"The skin is still active," she said. "You never switched it off, did you, Kaya?" Their pilot shook her head. "Incredible!" Hanna added. "We're fully invisible!"

Kaya piloted Esmerelda into a clearing. The island itself was a little larger than Lewis's backyard. Large crates were stacked up against the side of the treegloo. Once the ship settled to a stop, Kaya whistled, and the doors slid open. Cautiously, she stepped out first, and Hanna followed. The man remained out of view on the other side of the treegloo, oblivious to their presence. Lewis slipped on his mom's silver wig, then jumped out after his friends. The ground was squishy. He felt like he was stepping on a huge clump of seaweed. Water leaked into his Jordans. He wondered if he should have removed them, since Atlanteans didn't wear shoes, but the kicks were just too beautiful to take off. Every time he spotted them on his feet, he felt a little faster, stronger, more awesome.

Behind him, the door to the ship was still open. This was super weird, though, because the outside of the ship was invisible, yet you could see the interior through the doorway. It looked like a portal to another world. They needed to disguise Esmerelda, not leave it out in the open for any Atlantean to spot.

Lewis whistled, attempting to close the door.

His first attempt failed.

So did his next seven.

Finally, Kaya returned to his side. "Listen carefully," she said.

She whistled three distinct, clear notes.

The door sealed shut. The ship disappeared from view.

He told himself to record the notes in his mind. Unfortunately, his brain was more of a filter than a bowl. Most stuff washed right through and down the drain.

Kaya was watching him. Those huge eyes of hers were like mental microscopes. He felt like she was reading his mind. He shrugged. She smiled and laughed. "What?" he asked.

Kaya reached out and flicked a few silvery strands of his wig. "Nice hair," she said.

"Very Atlantean," added Hanna.

"The foot clothes, too," Kaya added, pointing to the Jordans.

Near the island's edge, Lewis noticed a collection of odd stones, each one about the size of a soccer ball, but with handles on top. He really hoped they wouldn't have to lift weights. His arms were still tired from his push-ups. Thankfully, instead of calling for an impromptu exercise class, Kaya guided them around the treegloo to the far side of the island. The man stood at the edge, holding a fishing rod. Lewis had been thinking about Atlanteans and their fish- and seaweed-heavy diet, and he was convinced they could be taught to like sausages. Forget Kaya's revulsion. She was only one person. He was sure that if he opened a restaurant down here, or even just a food cart, it would eventually be a smash hit. This dude with the wild gray hair looked like he'd be open to grilled meats.

Kaya lifted her fist to her mouth and coughed.

The man didn't react.

She coughed louder.

The man swung around and immediately dropped his rod. His mouth opened in astonishment. His teeth were yellow, crooked, and sharp. His hair could have been torn off an old mop, and even from ten paces away, Lewis detected the odor of a forgotten wet dish towel. He wasn't sure he wanted this man in his restaurant anymore—the other patrons would probably flee. The man's wide gray eyes were jumping between Lewis and Hanna. He was mostly looking at Hanna, though. The silver wig was that convincing.

Kaya addressed the mop-haired Atlantean. "Is this Evenor?"

The man shook his head. "Not really."

"What do you mean, 'not really'?" Hanna asked.

Kaya pointed into the water. "It's down there."

Lewis tried to peer over the edge of the island, but he didn't see any city hiding below. Unless it was really small and he and Hanna and Kaya had to miniaturize themselves. Which would be terrible. He'd seen enough movies about people turning tiny to know it wasn't fun. All the bugs would become giant monsters. Even goldfish would be terrifying. Those giant, vacant eyes! He shivered. "Don't tell me we're going to need a shrink ray."

"What are you talking about?" Hanna asked him. "The city's underwater."

Lewis kicked himself. Most people didn't actually kick themselves when they kicked themselves, but Lewis had always thought it was important to follow through, the same way he liked to literally pat himself on the back. So he struck himself forcefully in the back of the leg with the toe of his Jordans. It hurt, but only a little.

"Do you have any breathers?" Kaya asked.

The man shrugged. "Do you have any coins?"

Hanna dug through her fanny pack and pulled out a shiny gold piece.

Surprised, Kaya turned toward Hanna. "Where did you get that?"

"Lewis packed snacks. I packed currency," Hanna explained. "I wanted to be ready in case we came back. This is my only gold piece, though. The rest of the stuff in here is mostly old electronics. I figured if that watch of yours bought us a cruiser last time, Lewis, then these gadgets might score a few things, too."

Okay, but where did she even get a gold coin? "Do you just have gold lying around your house?" Lewis asked.

"No, not lying around," Hanna said. "We keep it in little drawers."

Of course they did. Next to the diamonds, probably. Sure, he had some gold in his own pockets, but it belonged to Susan Silver, and he had to save that for the suit. Life wasn't fair. Why did Hanna get to be rich? Why did his friend Kwan get to have a robotic kitchen? Why did his buddy Jet get a new wristpad whenever he broke his? Everybody had money except Lewis and his family. But he was going to fix that. He'd make sure his mom had little drawers full of gold, too. He'd buy Michael an unlimited supply of candy. He'd order Roberts special razors to shave his gleaming head. Lewis would buy himself a different pair of Jordans for every day of the month and a special closet to store them all and keep them safe. The room would have a large, comfortable chair in the middle with a straw that connected to an unlimited pool of ice-cold apple juice, and the shelves would rotate so he could relax in place while his Jordans carouseled before his eyes.

Hanna elbowed him.

Right—Atlantis.

Saving his dad, and the world.

"May I see that?" the man asked, pointing a crooked finger toward the gold piece. There was a greedy, almost hungry look in his eyes. Hanna flipped him the coin. The man inspected the gold closely, then glared at the passing cruisers and boats. Next, he scratched at the surface with long finger nails, smiled, and performed a little jig that reminded Lewis of Irish step dancing.

Although he'd never done this sort of dancing himself, Lewis had studied videos and thought he could use some of the steps in his own new routine. The chicken dance was getting a little old. Tiresome, Hanna had called it. And it wasn't like he'd invented it, either. Perfected it? Sure. He'd humbly admit that much. But his new routine—the raptor dance—would be all his own. There were still some kinks to work out, but the basics were in place. You needed to tuck your elbows in tight, for example, to make it look like you had really short little dinosaur arms. The hands needed to hang down slightly; the wrists had to be soft and relaxed. Leaning your whole body forward was key, too. The posture he had mastered. But the moves? Those he was still honing. Yet he was confident that people would be raptoring soon enough, and that they'd talk about the mustached explorer who'd pioneered the dance in celebration of his many brave and fantastic accomplishments. For now, though, he was still learning, and he could probably borrow a bit from the Atlantean. "Could you do that again?" Lewis asked the man.

Kaya grabbed his shoulder; her grip was insanely strong. "No dancing, please. And you, sir, have been paid. How about those breathers?"

The man turned left and right, scanning their surroundings again. He studied Lewis and Hanna. "It's dangerous for us to stay too long out here in the open. Let's get the three of you inside."

"Dangerous? Why?" Kaya asked.

"Because all of Atlantis is looking for these two."

8
TRUST IN TRIPLETS

KAYA followed the man around the green, flowering building to a door made of thick dried kelp. This detour was already turning into a disaster. She should have left Hanna and Lewis on the surface. Not out in the ocean, necessarily, but back on the shore. Then they would've been safe, at least. Now they were in danger. And her friends were totally ruining her chances of sneaking back to Ridge City unnoticed. The very first person they'd met knew exactly who they were! And he'd said all of Atlantis was looking for them.

How were they supposed to hide now?

Still, she couldn't abandon them.

Kaya had to protect them.

Forcing herself to smile, she waved her friends inside.

The air in the small, strange home was warm, wet, and heavy. Hanna pinched her nose. Lewis lifted his chin slightly, tilting his head back. He said the space smelled like something called beef jerky. Three chairs were arranged around an overly warm vent in the center of the room. Against the walls, three beds were crammed between stacks of rusting gadgets and piles of dishes. The steam-fogged windows let in very little light, and an old woman with a curved back studied them through narrowed eyes. A man who stood a head taller than the other two and wore his hair in a ponytail grabbed several mugs from a cluttered cabinet. "That's my brother, Argon," the first man said. "This is my sister, Fenitia. I am Rass. We're triplets."

"You don't look alike," Lewis noted.

Rass agreed. "I'm the handsome one."

"Really?" Lewis responded.

Kaya noticed Hanna kick the side of one of his precious shoes.

"Welcome," Fenitia said.

Her voice was surprisingly soothing, almost pretty. Kaya didn't like it. Or her.

This place made her uncomfortable.

But they still needed the breathers.

"I can't believe it! Sun People," Rass said.

"We were amazed when we heard the news," Fenitia added, "and now you're here in our home. Will you have tea?"

"Not if it's made out of seaweed," Lewis replied.

"What else would it be made from?" Fenitia asked.

The last thing Kaya wanted to do was sit around talking. "We should be going—"

"We have time," Hanna said, interrupting her. "We'd love some tea."

Kaya nearly protested, but Hanna was right. They needed to be polite. They couldn't afford to make more enemies.

And they could wait a few minutes, maybe, but no more. She nodded toward Fenitia. "You mentioned hearing the news. What news?"

"The news about the Sun People," Fenitia replied.

"The High Council announced it officially," Rass added. "The Sun People are real, the surface is crowded with life, and a group of warriors recently invaded Atlantis, stole one of our newest ships, and destroyed a government factory, with the help of a traitorous engineer and his rebellious daughter."

Kaya felt Hanna's hand on her arm.

Her father was not a traitor. He was a hero for what he'd done. He'd saved their lives. But the rebellious daughter bit? Sure. That was true enough.

Rass leaned forward, lowered his voice. "Are you the invaders?" he asked.

Fenitia pointed at Lewis. "Not this one. He's no soldier."

Adjusting his ridiculous silver wig, Lewis stood and puffed out his chest. "In fact, I am a very famous warrior. Most of the Sun People call me Steelheart because I'm so cold and menacing."

"Settle down, Steelheart," Hanna said.

The other brother, Argon, chuckled as he prepared their tea. Fenitia dragged one of the three beds over to the vent and instructed them to sit. She and Rass dropped into well-worn chairs as Argon quietly spooned clumps of green powder into each of the cups, then poured in the hot water. "He makes the best tea in Evenor," Fenitia said.

Kaya forced a smile, but none of this felt right. They

needed to move, not sit around. After Argon handed her a cup, she leaned toward Rass. "The breathers?" she whispered.

"Tea first," he said. "It's our custom."

"We're fine, Kaya," Hanna said.

As Lewis leaned forward to drink, Hanna subtly elbowed him. He stopped, smiled, and lowered the mug. A smart decision. One should never take tea from strangers. Kaya set down her mug as well.

"Relax," Fenitia said to Kaya.

Her voice was kind and soothing.

Kaya didn't like it.

"So, you three," Hanna asked, "how long have you lived in Evenor?"

"Seventy years," Fenitia replied. "We were raised here in Evenor before she flooded."

Now they were telling stories? Ugh.

Kaya moved to the door, pulled apart the kelp strands and peered out.

Cruisers drifted past without stopping or slowing. Several boats veered by as well. No one was steering any closer to their island, though. Kaya crossed the room, wiped the fog from one of the windows. Outside, Esmerelda remained invisible.

"Relax," Fenitia said again.

Kaya breathed in through her nose. "You were saying?"

"We've lived in this house for fifty years," Rass added.

"Just the three of you?" Lewis asked.

In a low grumble, Rass replied, "Just the three of us."

"Wow," Lewis said. "I can't imagine living with my brother

for the next fifty years. He already smells like cheddar. When we're in our fifties or sixties, he'll probably reek of gorgonzola, and I bet he'll still be picking his nose, only he'll have those long old-people hairs winding out of his nostrils." Lewis stopped. Then, to Argon, he added, "Like yours."

The quiet brother covered his nose.

"Our parents didn't survive the flood," Rass continued, "but the three of us were tending our aquafarm when it happened."

Now Kaya listened closely. She'd heard stories about collapses before. The firsthand accounts from the people who'd been there were often terrifying.

"The water burst through the walls of the city like they were made of mud," Fenitia recalled. "The whole western wall turned to rubble, and the water rose until everything was covered."

"The government gave up on us," Rass continued. "Wrote our city off as one of the lost ones. But the people of Evenor are stubborn and tough. Ingenious, too. We developed methods of sealing and draining the buildings. We built new homes in the walls designed for underwater living."

"That's impressive," Hanna noted. "You must have worked fast!"

He waved his hands in the air. "We learned to prevent the water from rising farther up here, too," Rass added. "We saved our city."

"These days, it's quite the vacation destination," Fenitia noted. "They call it adventure tourism."

Edging forward, Hanna clasped her hands and rested

her elbows on her knees. "How do you maintain the right air pressure up here?"

The three Evenorians acted like they hadn't even heard her question. Kaya almost felt bad for Hanna; no one was ever able to explain things in as much detail as she wanted. But Kaya was glad they wouldn't be subjected to a lecture. There was no time for that.

"So," she said, "how about those breathers?"

Rass glanced at Fenitia. "Right," he said. "I'll get them now."

"Why the rush?" Fenitia asked. "You haven't even touched your tea."

Her brother moved to the far side of the room and began rummaging through a cabinet. High on a nearby shelf, Kaya spotted a dozen metal spheres of varying sizes. Some were gleaming and polished, others dented and rusting. "Isn't that them?"

"Ah, right," Rass said, stepping back. "There they are."

"We're always misplacing things," Fenitia added.

"Did you seriously forget they were there?"

"Yes?" Rass answered.

Kaya sprang to her feet and spun to face Rass. "You're stalling! You're waiting for someone. Who? The Erasers?"

Fenitia shrugged and bit her lip. "They're offering quite a reward."

Lewis pointed to one of his shoes. "If you were looking for a reward, I would've given you one of my Jordans!"

Hanna hurried to the door and leaned out. "What now, Kaya?" she asked.

Before Kaya could respond, the previously quiet brother, Argon, spoke up. "Relax," he growled. "No one's coming."

"What do you mean, no one's coming?" Fenitia replied. "I told you to message the emergency line!"

Argon stomped his foot. "For fifty years, you've been telling me what to do! Now there are Sun People here in our house, and you want to give them to the Erasers for a few coins?"

"More than a few!" Rass said. He leaned toward his brother and whispered the amount.

Argon's eyes widened briefly. Then he closed them tight, as if he were squeezing a thought down to nothing. "No! It's still not enough. I don't care how much they're offering. These are real, living Sun People, and they are clearly not soldiers!" He held up what Kaya guessed was a transmitter. "I'm not sending that message."

"We could be rich, Argon!" Rass added, pleading. "I could finally get my own place. Maybe even find a girlfriend!"

"It's a little late for that," Lewis replied.

Backing against the wall, Argon climbed up onto one of the beds and held the transmitter higher. "We're being lied to. We should be helping these kids, not handing them over to those despicable agents! I don't care what you say or how much they'll pay. I'm not letting you send the alert!"

Rass joined his sister, both of them pleading with their stubborn brother.

Hanna started for the exit. "Kaya? What now?"

Kaya picked three breathers from the shelf and tossed one each to Lewis and Hanna. She found a few pairs of goggles hanging from a hook—they'd need those, too. "We're leaving," she announced, "and we're taking this stuff with us. Tell the Erasers to pay you back if the gold we gave you isn't enough." Then, to Argon, she added, "Thank you."

Desperately, Rass lunged for Argon. The ponytailed brother leaped aside, trying to dodge the attack, then crashed to the floor. With unexpected quickness, Fenitia pounced on him. As the triplets wrestled, Kaya held aside the thick strands of kelp and waved her friends through the door. Lewis raced around the house toward the still-invisible ship. "We're not taking that," Kaya called to him. "We have to leave it here for now."

"What? Why?" Lewis asked.

Kaya had taught herself all about the ship's power system during the trip back to Atlantis, reading nearly every page of the operations manual. The warship had an onboard generator that charged its batteries when the vehicle was stationary. They'd been plowing through the open ocean for half a day, and the power was depleted. So Esmerelda needed to remain still for a while—at least an hour. Hanna had understood all of this when Kaya had explained it to her earlier. But Hanna learned just about everything instantly. Lewis wasn't nearly as quick. Should she use an example that related to dancing? Or was there a way to relate it to his precious footwear?

"I don't know how to explain—"

"I've got this one," Hanna said. "You see, Lewis, Esmerelda's like a little kid who's been running around all morning. She needs to take a nap."

"Right," Kaya said, holding up a breather. "So she's staying here, and we're going swimming."

Excited, Lewis begged her to open the door anyway, insisting that he needed his own goggles. Atlantean gear wasn't good enough for him, apparently.

Back inside the house, Fenitia shouted in triumph.

Rass yelled something about how they were going to be rich.

Argon cried out, "Go, Sun People! If you're still here, go!"

Kaya hurried to the edge of the island and found several old-fashioned diving weights. The ones in Ridge City were made of advanced metal with comfortable handles that molded to your grip. These were simple, carved from rough stone, but they'd work.

Lewis returned with his goggles and a pocket full of what she guessed were his precious snacks. Kaya whistled over her shoulder, shutting the door, then showed Lewis and Hanna how to use their breathers. The devices were simple, really, but the Sun People looked at them like they were some kind of superadvanced technology. You basically twisted the sphere, separating the two halves, then twisted again so you could fit one half over your mouth, the other over your nose. The device molded and suctioned itself to your face.

A muffled shout came from Lewis as he attached his breather.

Kaya sat at the edge, grabbed one of the weights, and placed it between her legs. She waited until each of them had done the same. Lewis adjusted his goggles. Kaya pressed hers against her face, ensuring they were tight, and watched Hanna test the dark water with her bare feet. Her ankles were more flexible than his; at least she knew how to kick. Thankfully,

Hanna had ditched her foot clothes, too, but Lewis was still wearing his sneakers. They'd slow him down, and he was slow enough already. But the three of them couldn't delay another second on the island. Kaya tightened and streamlined her outfit. Cracked her knuckles. Pointed at the roiling water. Then she lowered the weight into the water and slid off the edge. The heavy mass pulled her headfirst toward the warm, clear depths, and she gazed down at a city unlike any she'd ever seen.

9
GRAVITY AND GOLD

KAYA told herself to be patient. But could Lewis and Hanna swim any slower? Even with the stones pulling them down, she had to pause and wait for them to catch up every ten seconds. The Erasers were probably on the island already, questioning the triplets. The agents would follow them into the water soon. And they wouldn't swim at this plodding pace. Kaya needed to get her friends out of the open water and into somewhere safe.

She studied the scene below. The flooded underwater world was as alien to her as it was to her two friends. A submarine passed from one building to another, and she led Hanna and Lewis around a warped, twisting tower and down toward the city floor. Through the windows of the oddly shaped buildings, she spotted people working at desks and relaxing in their homes. A very large and very shirtless man stepped up to one window and stretched his arms out wide. She winced. For the first time, she wished she wasn't wearing goggles.

The rest of the city, however, was utterly beautiful. How strange it was, too—swimming down through this world from above felt like drifting through impossibly thick air. Here, people didn't crowd the streets the way they did in Ridge and other cities. Everyone was weightless in the water, and there was little gravity to drag them down, so they were spread out. She hung in the water, marveling at the city. But this wasn't some sightseeing trip.

There was work to do.

First, she had to figure out how to find her dad and the professor. If she and her friends had guessed correctly and they were in Evenor, where would they hide? The city wasn't nearly as big as Ridge, but it wouldn't be easy to search. The upper levels of the buildings were mostly offices and homes, from what she could tell, with shops and restaurants below. People were swimming in and out of holes in the rock walls of the cave, too. Their version of doors, maybe? Kaya was kicking past a popular sports shop called Nemo's Locker—a store that would have lured her inside on any other day—when Hanna grabbed her ankle. What did she want? They couldn't speak, not with the breathers covering their mouths and noses.

Hanna was holding up her hand, telling her to wait.

She and Lewis dropped their stones, rose slightly, and swam over to the Nemo's window. Lewis pointed through the glass. Then he swept his hands over his shirt and pants.

Seriously? They wanted new clothes?

The last thing she wanted to do was shop. The Erasers would be scouring these waters for them, and soon. Then again, if Kaya was going to help these two sneak through Evenor, different outfits might help. The warship was camouflaged; she needed to help the Sun People hide, too.

A mother and son swam out of a tunnel carrying a

watertight bag with the Nemo's logo. Kaya waved for her friends to follow her, but when she neared the opening, she realized the water was all rushing out. The currents ran in one direction; this was the exit. As for the entrance? Hanna was already swimming through it. Kaya spotted her legs disappearing into the tunnel, Lewis following behind her. She could have screamed.

They were supposed to follow her.

Kicking hard, she raced inside.

Squeezed between them.

Kaya was leading this misguided shopping trip. Not these two sunbrained visitors.

Light glowed through an opening. She sped ahead, grabbed a set of handrails, and pulled herself up out of the water and into a hallway. Kaya reached down and grabbed Lewis by the wrists, yanked him up until he could get both hands on the railing. Next she helped Hanna. When they were out of the water, she pulled off her breather. The two of them did the same. Lewis was stomping his sodden foot clothes, squeezing out the water.

"Quiet," she whispered. "You want clothes?"

"Clothes, equipment, swimming gear," Hanna said. "Whatever we can find. I'm not running around Atlantis in rags again. And this"—she pointed to her shirt—"is a little obvious."

Kaya studied Hanna's short dark hair, dark skin, and small eyes, and Lewis's brown hair and those spots he called freckles. His eyes, although slightly bigger than Hanna's, were still small compared to those of an Atlantean and set strangely far apart. Yes, they needed new clothes, but wearing their breathers around on dry land wouldn't be the worst idea, either. She'd known kids who did that when they were sick. A pair of wet/dry goggles also wouldn't hurt. Plenty of Atlanteans wore them everywhere, and the best models had lights around the edges that helped you see when you were walking through dark tunnels or swimming in the depths of a kelp forest, hunting. With the right gear, they might actually go unnoticed. But it wasn't going to be cheap, and Kaya was out of coins. She'd spent her savings helping the Sun People the last time. She eyed the waterproof pack around Hanna's waist. "What do you have to trade?" she asked.

Hanna removed a few small devices, each one with a tiny glass screen. "An antique iPod, a second-gen flip phone, a few other items."

"You brought all that?" Lewis asked.

Hanna shrugged. "Trading worked last time."

"Do you have anything useful, Lewis?" Kaya asked. He shrugged and looked away. "I guess we'll hope your stuff works, Hanna. Let's go."

Following the curving hallway, they passed advertisements for a popular hair gel, story stations, and a flavored drink. Kaya tensed when a man walked toward them, but he was so focused on his bag of spicy kelp chips that he didn't even look up. Lewis stopped in front of a poster for the worst musical group in the history of Atlantis. "Ha! Look! Narwhals are funny. Narwhals in a band? Funnier."

"Their music is torture," Kaya informed them.

In Nemo's Locker, racks of clothes were spread around the

room. The walls were lined with swimming gear: dozens of varieties of goggles, beautiful fins, the sleekest swimsuits. For a moment, Kaya forgot everything—her dad, the Sun People, the war—and gaped at all the gorgeous gear. The clerk behind the one checkout counter barely noticed them, and the only other employee, a girl around her age, was helping a customer. Otherwise, the store was empty. That was good. Kaya encouraged her friends to crouch. "You're too tall," she reminded them.

Lewis was already picking through the clothes. His sneakers made squishing sounds when he moved. The other customer, a small, round man, thanked the clerk and walked out. Once he left, Kaya asked Hanna for one of the gadgets to trade. Then she hurried over and turned an emergency bolt to lock the door. The glass clouded.

"Hey! We're open," the clerk said. "What are you doing?"

The other employee rushed over. "Oh my gosh, are you robbing us? That would be epic. We've never been robbed before. Have we, Mr. Gannos?"

"Last month," the clerk replied. "You were off that day. Sometimes I suspect it was you, but the thief was far too clever."

"Thank you," the girl replied.

"We're not robbing you," Kaya insisted. She crossed the small store and laid one of Hanna's little devices on the desk.

The clerk nodded approvingly. "This is . . . unusual."

"Valuable, too," Kaya replied.

"That's for me to decide," the clerk answered.

"Well, while you're deciding, we'd like a little privacy."

"We?" the girl asked.

Kaya's two friends, their clothes soaked, stepped into view.

"We're from the Rift," Lewis said.

The clerk stared in silence. The girl said nothing. Kaya had to give Lewis a little credit. The Rift was a region in the ridge that had been cut off from the rest of Atlantis centuries before. No one really knew what the people from the Rift looked like, or if they even were people, in the normal sense of the term. But the Rift angle had worked before the High Council had announced that the Sun People were real.

Now? The clerk guessed the truth instantly. He smiled and palmed Hanna's device. "Then the store is yours," he said.

The two Sun People shopped excitedly. They kept calling each other over to inspect one item or another. The girl steered Lewis to the men's section and discouraged him from sampling one of the foil packets in the display cases near the counter. He thought it was some kind of energy gel or a packet of cheese to keep in your pocket, but it was actually an ointment for wounds. Kaya kind of wished the girl had just let him taste it. His reaction probably would've been hilarious.

Every so often, Kaya reminded them to hurry. She stood at the door, listening for suspicious noises in the hall.

Finally, Hanna and Lewis piled their things on the counter. They'd already changed into new full-body suits. Hanna didn't look too bad, but Lewis had chosen the ugliest color Kaya had ever seen, a brownish-green hue that reminded her of fermented kelp. The girl had said something about the suit being on sale, but wasn't the idea to blend in? Kaya would've asked him to pick another one, but they'd wasted too much time already. Each of the Sun People had also grabbed two additional outfits made of the latest cooling, self-drying fabrics, all with hoods to hide their strange hair; top-of-the-line goggles; and waterproof vacuum backpacks to stow their new gear.

Kaya was actually getting a little jealous.

She wanted a pair of the goggles.

The clerk sorted through the piles slowly, checking the prices, then slipped the items into one of the two backpacks. He checked his tablet occasionally. Adding up the figures, Kaya guessed. Was that one gadget worth enough for all their gear? Kaya wasn't so sure.

A noise startled her.

Not in the hall, though.

Hanna apologized; she'd dropped a small box.

Relax, Kaya told herself. Everything was fine.

Meanwhile, the girl was leading Lewis toward a cloudy glass door.

"Whoa, whoa, whoa," the clerk said. "That's not for you."

"Why not? What's in there?" Hanna asked.

"Gravity suits," he replied. "Serious buyers only."

"We're serious," Hanna answered.

"We need to go," Kaya reminded them.

"Can we just look?" Hanna asked.

Kaya huffed. "Fine. Quickly!"

The clerk whistled a high-pitched, complex tune. The door slid open, and Kaya squeezed into the small room with her friends. The lights glowed a bright yellow, and the equipment inside was insanely cool. New gloves with stronger thrusters to give you better control and more boost as you moved through the air. Ankle straps so small you could hide them under the cuffs of your pants. All the gear looked light and thin. Normally, Kaya covered her gravity gear. Most people couldn't afford the equipment, so you were better off disguising it. But you could probably wear these suits all the time without people jealously calling you a spoiled floater or a rich brat.

Suddenly, she thought of Susan Silver. This was exactly the sort of equipment the woman wanted. And there was no way Kaya was letting that amoral urchin get her moisturized hands on one of these suits.

"I want one," Hanna declared.

"Two please," Lewis added.

"I don't know if those devices will be enough to cover them," Kaya started.

"How about we find out?" Hanna suggested.

The girl pulled two of the best models off the wall. She held one up to Hanna, checking the size, but it was slightly too small. The fit looked right for Lewis, though, so she gave him that one and passed Hanna another. Her boss appeared in the doorway. "Wait a second," he said. "I already told you. Serious buyers only."

"Then let's make a deal," Lewis suggested.

"A quick one?" Kaya pleaded. "We really need to keep moving."

After the clerk hurried back to his stool, Lewis placed his hand on the counter, reached down, and removed one soaked shoe, then the other. What was he doing? Foot water spilled out as he emptied each one on the floor. With great care, he placed them side by side in front of the clerk, arranging them as if they were sacred, holy relics from the early days of Atlantis. Thin puddles spread out from the soles.

Kaya was slightly embarrassed. No one in Atlantis wore the ridiculous foot coverings of the Sun People. Did Lewis really think this man would be interested?

The clerk glanced at the door, then at Lewis. "What are these?"

"These," Lewis explained, "are extremely rare Jordan 50s."

The girl turned one of the shoes toward her and inspected it. "You put them on your feet?" she asked.

"Yes," Lewis said, almost impatiently, "but that's not really the point."

"What is the point, then?"

"They're Jordans! When you put them on your feet, the whole world knows that you're above average. Special. You're, well . . ."

"Someone who wears Jordans," Hanna finished.

"Exactly!" Lewis replied.

"I remain uninterested," the clerk replied. "No more trades. This gravity gear is worth too much. I'll only accept gold."

Again, Kaya noticed the clerk glance at the door.

She followed his eyes.

A loud clunk pulled her attention back to the counter. Lewis had fished a stack of shining gold coins out of his pocket and set them down on the glass. What the . . . Kaya looked to Hanna, but she seemed equally stunned. The clerk deftly picked one off the top of the neat pile, turned it around in his fingers, then flicked it up into the air. He caught the coin before it fell, then placed it carefully back atop the pile and smiled. "That'll do!"

Hanna was glaring at Lewis now.

Kaya was completely confused. Where had he gotten all that gold? And why hadn't he offered any when Hanna was buying the clothes?

The door rattled.

"Who's that?" Kaya asked.

The clerk held up his hands. "I'm sorry. If I'd known you had this much gold—"

"You turned us in?" Hanna asked. "Unbelievable!"

Kaya glanced back at the coins. She'd ask Lewis about that later. Now she watched the door. "Is there another way out?"

"No," the girl said.

The door shook again.

Kaya wished that shark hadn't grabbed her blaster. But she'd figure something out. She rolled her shoulders. Breathed in deep. Clenched her fists. "Open the door," she said.

The girl disengaged the emergency lock and jumped out of the way as the glass slid into the wall. Kaya crouched, ready to face a horde of angry Erasers.

And then her breath promptly left her.

The Erasers weren't waiting in the hallway.

Hair soaked, breathing heavily, eyes huge, her friend Rian stood alone in the doorway, frantically glancing left and right. He scanned the clothing racks and display cases behind Kaya.

"You're shopping?" Rian asked. "Now?"

"No, we—"

He pointed to his earpiece. "The Erasers are on their way. We don't have much time."

"How many of them?" Kaya asked.

Rian paused before replying. "All of them."

10

DO NOT BREATHE

LEWIS forgot his Jordans. This was no minor tragedy. You didn't just leave a treasured pair of classic high-top sneakers in some random Atlantean store and keep running. You went back to get them! Yet no one seemed to understand this rule; they didn't even consider letting him turn back. Hanna reminded him that if he did reverse course, the Erasers might grab him. Freedom or high-tops? The decision was harder than he'd expected.

Hanna wasn't looking too happy with him, to be honest. She suspected, or knew, that he'd made a deal with Silver—that much was obvious. Hanna understood that Lewis didn't have gold just lying around. Those coins were probably worth as much as a hovercar, or even his family's entire house. Yet she didn't say anything. She was letting him keep his secret for now. But it wasn't like they had time to stop and talk, anyway.

Racing after Rian, they sprinted through the Atlantean mall, past gadget stores and clothing shops and through a food court. A man sucking green noodles from a steaming bowl glanced up at them. He paused midslurp, noodles dripping.

Three girls mauling their seaweed-stuffed wraps stared at him as if he had seven heads.

Maybe Lewis had picked the wrong color for his new Atlantean outfit. Silver and gray seemed to be more their style.

A little boy yanked his hand out of his mother's grip and pointed at Lewis, then Hanna.

"This way," Rian called to them.

A door in the wall was marked with bold red writing that Lewis couldn't decipher. Their new Atlantean guide pressed a square metal button beside the frame, then waved them through. Rian was barely taller than Michael, but bulkier, and probably older than Lewis, too. He had a slightly flattened nose, and his silver hair was cut short. His eyes were a grayish-blue color, his cheeks slightly red. His hands and feet were wide, and he kind of smelled like salt.

As Lewis slipped past him and through the doorway, Rian looked back the way they'd come. Lewis followed his gaze. There were no Erasers behind them . . . yet. But the girl from the store was there in the distance. She was across the food court, watching them. Or maybe him? Lewis thought they'd had a connection. At one point, while he was browsing, he'd made her laugh. Now she was following him. His heart leaped, danced, bowed. Sure, she was from Atlantis. Her eyes were weirdly big. The silver-white hair was a little strange, and she was kind of short. But what if she had a crush on him? And what if he liked her back?

Kaya yanked him by the sleeve.

Lewis leaned out for one more glance.

Two men and two women sprinted into the food court,

each of them wielding those sonic blasters that looked like flutes. The girl from the store pointed them down a random hallway. The noodle slurper glanced toward Lewis and his friends, as if he was considering redirecting the Erasers. Instead, he resumed slurping, too ravenous to get involved.

The agents rushed the wrong way.

"We're not safe yet," Rian whispered, yanking Lewis inside and closing the door behind them.

The hallway was dark, night-shadow black.

They ran, following Rian, and Lewis felt hopeful. Two of the triplets had tried to turn them over to the Erasers. That clerk in the store, too. But the girl had tried to help them. A few more friends like her, and they might actually evade the agents.

"How did you find us?" Kaya asked Rian, breathing hard.

Still running, Rian pointed to his earpiece. Lewis could barely see him in the darkness. "Naxos tuned me in to the Erasers' private channel. We've been swimming all over the city looking for you, and I happened to be nearby when that clerk sent in the tip. You're lucky I got there before the Erasers. There are dozens of them swarming around."

The hallway split. The group paused at the juncture. Hanna leaned over with her hands on her knees.

"You said 'all of them,'" Kaya noted.

"I was being dramatic, not literal," Rian confessed.

Lewis tried to think. Rian said he'd been with Naxos. And Naxos was the one who'd promised to take care of his father. "Was there anyone else . . ."

Lewis was too nervous to even finish his question, so

Hanna did it for him. She gripped Rian by the shoulders. "Did you see the professor?"

The Atlantean boy wriggled free of her grasp. "Yes, he's up and moving around. He asks a lot of questions."

Lewis was too relieved and excited to respond.

Hanna hugged him briefly, and hard.

He knew his father would survive.

He knew his dad wouldn't give up.

"He's annoying, right?" Hanna asked, smiling.

Rian nodded. "And huge. I've never seen anyone eat so much."

"That's fantastic!" Hanna exclaimed. "He'll be fine. If he's eating and barraging you with questions, he's back to his normal self. If his mind is healthy, his body will catch up eventually."

They heard footsteps in the distance.

"We need to keep moving," Kaya reminded them.

Right, and Lewis needed to see his dad. Talk to him. Look him in the eyes. "Where is he now?" he asked.

"That's where I'm taking you," Rian said. "You all have breathers, right?"

Hanna popped hers on, then clicked a button on the waistband of her new clothes. Her outfit and backpack suddenly became skintight. Lewis fumbled with his own controls. How had she figured hers out so quickly? Seeing him struggle, Hanna told him to hold still. She pulled his breather and his new goggles out of his pack, then clicked something on his belt. He felt like someone was pressing a high-powered vacuum to his chest. All of the air between his clothes and his skin was instantly sucked out. His backpack, with the gravity gear stuffed inside, shrank to a lump on his back, less like a bag than a very, very large wart. He slipped on the goggles. The lights around the lenses turned on automatically; he could see much farther down the dark hallway. Hanna squinted at him, silently reminding him that they still needed to talk about that stack of gold coins. She wasn't going to let that slide, but she wasn't going to bring it up in front of the Atlanteans, either.

"Let's go," Rian ordered.

They rushed ahead to a watery hole as wide as Lewis's outstretched arms. He glanced back the way they'd come. Was it weird that he wanted to see the girl from the store one more time? He'd really only had one crush before—but Ashley was in his science class, not a resident of Atlantis. If he didn't get a chance to talk to the girl from the store again, he wondered if he could write her letters. He could train a dolphin to deliver them and bring back her replies so Jet and Kwan would know he wasn't making the whole thing up.

The dolphin could be named Johnny.

Water splashed against his legs.

Rian was gone.

Hanna dropped through the hole next.

Lewis stared down into the blue water.

Yes, they were running from a band of dangerous Atlantean agents, but there was a slim chance a girl had a crush on him, and they were going to see his dad. Life wasn't so horrible. He smiled and pressed his breather to his face as Kaya shoved him down into the water. The current pulled him along feetfirst; he couldn't even see where he was going. The tunnel turned and swerved and spat him out into the slightly colder open water between buildings. He flipped upside down as if he'd just cannonballed into a pool. Hanna was hovering next to Rian, the two of them turning their hands back and forth to keep themselves upright.

The new suit was incredible—Lewis felt like a dolphin. The goggles were amazing, too. The scene was as clear as an aquarium.

Rian started swimming toward a towering building. He was unfairly fast. Was he showing off?

Lewis pulled and kicked after him, watched as Hanna followed Rian into a tunnel. Sucking air through his breather, he swam harder. A window below them spilled yellow light into the water, and he saw a little girl standing on a couch, leaning against the glass and playing with some kind of toy. The tunnel was just above her. Kaya slipped through next. Lewis jetted in after her. The current pulled him for five meters before his fingers felt dry air and he pulled himself up. Now they could rest for a second, he hoped. Maybe enjoy a quick snack?

Lewis pushed his goggles up onto his forehead and removed his breather. The girls were already hurrying away.

"Where are we?" Lewis asked.

Rian shrugged, then peeled off his breather. "I don't know. An office building, I think. We need to keep moving. What are you doing?"

Wasn't that obvious? This running-away-from-the-Erasers business was strenuous. He wasn't an Olympic swimmer. "I'm taking a second."

"Not yet," Rian replied. "Come on, follow me."

The Atlantean boy pushed through a door into a stairwell, then began hurrying down the steps two at a time. Kaya and Hanna were already exiting into another hallway. This time, Rian didn't wait or look back. On dry land, however, it wasn't that hard for Lewis to keep pace with him. Rian's feet turned out to the sides when he ran, like a duck. Lewis could easily beat him in a footrace.

Ahead of them, a door slid open. Two women stepped into the hall, then froze.

Confused? Frightened? Shocked?

A little of all three, Lewis decided. He bowed briefly as he passed them.

The group skipped the next waterhole and looped around the building until they came to another, larger exit. Kaya was plunging in when Lewis arrived; Hanna was already gone. Rian popped on his breather, crouched, and dove in after them. This time, Lewis made sure to go headfirst. He dropped to his knees, knifed through the hole, and pulled his arms down to his sides. The current was slower here, the space darker. When they popped out into the open water, though, his chest was aching.

The towers were different here on this side, and farther apart, too—it would be a long swim across. Streams of bubbles rose up from somewhere below them.

Rian and Kaya were swimming ahead.

Hanna was between the Atlanteans.

Lewis's chest felt tighter still.

What was wrong with him? Was this anxiety? His dad always talked about anxiety as a pressure in his chest, and

Lewis felt like a dinosaur was stepping on his sternum. A big one, too—not one of those little feathery lizard birds.

The water rushed past his lips and mouth.

He felt it against his skin.

His breather!

Lewis had forgotten to put it back on before diving into the hole. The device was in his hand; he was holding it like a baseball. He tried to clamp it back over his mouth and nose. The seal wouldn't take. He couldn't breathe. The goggles still worked, though, and Lewis could see his friends swimming all the way across to another building. A pool's length at least. He'd never make it that far. Lewis had no choice; he turned back toward the office building.

A man kicked into a tunnel below him.

Could Lewis reach it? His lungs were screaming for air.

He had to relax. As he swam down, he tried to remember the yoga words he'd learned when they did stretching and breathing exercises in school.

Namaste, he thought. Vinyasa. But his body was overruling his brain, as if dozens of muscle-bound, tank-top-wearing weight lifters had stormed into his tranquil yoga studio, shouting for the peaceful yoga master to hoist a barbell. One of the weight lifters in this unsettling vision had a boom box, too, and it blasted the head-smashing guitar solos of some heavy metal band. Lewis imagined the yogi ignoring it all and holding her pose as if she were alone in the universe. Lewis had to be like that yogi, but his lungs were begging him to suck in air that wasn't there. How long could he resist?

Twenty seconds?

Ten?

The tunnel was too far away. He didn't think he could make it.

Then he imagined the Erasers behind him, swimming closer and closer. Any second, one of them was going to clamp a hand around his ankle. So he swam faster. He clawed at the water with his hands, pushing against it with the insides of his outturned feet. Five strokes. Six. Every second that passed felt like a victory.

He was close to the tunnel entrance.

Seven strokes.

Eight.

Closer.

His head was aching now, too. The weight lifters were shouting, red-faced, flexing their huge muscles in anger. Yet the yogi remained peaceful. Vinyasa. Namaste. Cappuccino. That last one wasn't a yoga word, but it felt right, somehow, and Lewis sensed a faint current of water growing in strength, carrying him into the building. He reached out over his head, managed one final, powerful pull, and cruised headfirst through the opening. Lewis steeled himself for the last few precious seconds.

Do.

Not.

Breathe.

He dolphin-kicked gently, afraid that a more intense motion would force his body to revolt, and then, with a final desperate effort, Lewis launched himself up through the waterhole and onto the floor, drawing in a massive, beautiful breath of air.

And another.

And another.

He was alive.

Right?

Yes. He was lying on his back in the middle of a hallway in some random office tower in Evenor, but he was alive.

At any moment, one of the Erasers might burst up out of that water and grab him. He couldn't just run, though. What if Kaya, Hanna, or Rian came back for him? He had to wait—it was worth the risk.

Lewis breathed in and out, exhausted.

He pulled himself to a sitting position against the wall, watching the waterhole.

His friends did not appear.

Neither did the Erasers.

The air felt cold, and he started to shiver.

Slowly, with each breath, a little of his energy came back. The weight lifters, exhausted, trudged from the yoga studio, taking their boom box with them, allowing the yogi to stretch in peace and tranquility. Lewis pushed his goggles up onto his forehead.

The water was motionless.

The Erasers weren't coming.

Neither were his friends.

A terrible and vaguely familiar feeling closed its grip around him like a monstrous hand. Once, when he was younger and his parents were still together, he'd gotten sep-arated from them at an outdoor fair. He couldn't remember all the details, only that his mom and dad were arguing about something when a very large stuffed alien caught his interest. Lewis weaved through the crowd toward the glorious green creature before realizing that he had not told either of his parents where he was going. He'd been scared. Terrified, even. Someone brought him to a security guard, who then lifted him up onto the counter of a booth and yelled through his bullhorn, asking if any parents were missing a kid. There was music in the background, too, and Lewis, nervously, had started dancing. The dancing had relaxed him, and his moves drew an increasingly large and admiring crowd. At some point, there were cheers. Eventually, his mom and dad had burst out of the forest of people and grabbed him. A bearded man with red suspenders booed, wanting more dancing. Despite the success of his first public performance, the experience was scary, and he shivered whenever he recalled the moment he realized he'd lost his parents.

The moment he realized he was alone.

As Lewis imagined Hanna, Kaya, and Rian swimming or racing through Evenor, and his father recovering somewhere nearby, and his mom and Michael and Roberts up on the sur-face, he realized that feeling at the fair didn't quite compare.

This time, Lewis wasn't just lost.

He was lost in Atlantis.

11

THE SURVIVOR

KAYA wanted to scream. How had they lost him? The three of them had sprinted back and searched every floor of the office building. Lewis was gone. Hanna was nervously wringing her hands. Thinking, Kaya guessed. Rian kept glancing back over his shoulder and past her down the hall. This was all his fault. Kaya jabbed a finger in his direction. "You shouldn't have raced ahead like that," she said.

Rian heard her but didn't reply. He pushed his hand through his short hair and stared back at her. Kaya was immediately annoyed with herself. Why was she blaming him? This wasn't his doing. Kaya had agreed to let the two Sun People return to Atlantis with her. She was the one who'd decided not to drop them in the ocean near the shore. So she should have been looking out for them. Especially Lewis. Why hadn't she swum behind him?

She apologized to Rian.

He accepted silently.

"This isn't your fault either, Kaya," Hanna said. "We're *all* responsible. The important thing now is that we find him."

"Where did you leave the warship?" Rian asked. "Would he go back there?"

"Maybe," Hanna guessed. "But he's a pretty good swimmer. He should have been able to keep pace with me. My guess is that his breather broke, and if that happened . . ."

"There's no way he'd make it up to the ship," Rian said.

Again, Kaya blamed herself. She should have suggested buying new breathers at the store, not relying on borrowed gadgets.

Rian lowered his voice. "The longer we stay here looking for him, the greater the chance of bumping into the Erasers. We need to regroup. I say we go to your dad, Kaya."

Kaya swallowed. "He's close?"

"Very," Rian answered.

Hanna shook her head. "You two go, and I'll find Lewis."

"No," Rian replied.

The certainty in his voice surprised Kaya.

Annoyed, Hanna sneered. "I'll make my own decisions," she said.

Rian shrugged. "Look, I'm not suggesting we leave him here for good. But the vote is tomorrow, and if anyone has to be in Ridge City by then, it's you, Hanna."

Kaya eyed him. Why Hanna?

The Sun Person pointed her thumb at the center of her chest. "Me?"

"Yes," Rian said. "The warship is the first piece of evidence. Your dad said you need to be there, too, Kaya. They'll want to hear from one of our own people. But he explained that he really needs a Sun Person, and the professor, well . . ."

I gather he's a peaceful man. He told us some story about how he'd only been in one fight his entire life, when he was twelve years old, and he lost to a kid who had a broken arm."

Hanna chuckled. "He loves that story."

"Yes, but as your dad pointed out, Kaya, the professor is huge. He's intimidating. I'm guessing that seeing you, Hanna, will be far more convincing."

"Why?" Hanna pressed.

"You're too young to be a soldier," he explained. "Kaya's dad, Heron, thinks that if the High Council meets you or Lewis, they'll know the invasion story is a lie."

For a moment, the three of them were silent.

Rian was right.

Kaya knew it.

Hanna, too.

But she wasn't ready to give up looking for Lewis. "We can't just leave him out here."

"I agree," Rian said, nodding. "But before we continue our search, we should regroup. The others might have a better idea about how to find him. They helped me track you down, after all."

Hanna breathed in sharply through her nose, then exhaled. "Fine. Let's go."

Satisfied, Rian popped on his breather and slipped into a nearby waterhole without another word. Kaya hesitated. Was she ready for this? She hadn't seen her father since the battle outside the factory. Since he'd destroyed and then rebuilt her faith in him in a matter of hours. All her life, she'd thought he was just an engineer. Then she'd discovered he actually worked for the Erasers, the very people she was running from. The same nefarious group that had thrown her friends in prison. Yes, he'd eventually turned against them. He'd protected Kaya and the Sun People. But it hadn't been immediate. She'd had to risk her own life to sway him to their side.

What was she going to say to him?

What was he going to say to her?

What did he even think of her now?

Hanna elbowed her gently, then threw her arm around Kaya's shoulders and gave her a brief, affectionate squeeze. "Hey," she whispered, "it'll be fine. He's still your dad."

Was it that obvious? Kaya pressed the heels of her hands against the sides of her head. Then Hanna slapped on her breather, fastened her goggles in place, and slid into the water.

Right.

Onward.

Kaya followed Hanna through the short tunnel and into the open water. They kicked down the side of the building toward the city floor. The walls reminded Kaya of spiraling coral. She glanced in each window they passed, hoping they'd spot Lewis inside. She wouldn't have been surprised to see him eating a meal with some family, dousing his food in hot sauce. But there was no sign of him.

She wanted to believe he'd be fine. That he'd make friends and find people to help him. But what if the Erasers grabbed him? He couldn't dance or charm his way out of that.

She wanted to kick harder, swim faster. But she had to stay behind Hanna.

Slowly, they wove between the bases of the spiraling

buildings. Rian kept darting ahead impatiently, then stopping to wait. The water grew slightly cooler the deeper they went. They swam past stores and offices and a great assembly hall packed with people. The crowd in the auditorium rose to its feet as they kicked by, cheering wildly. Not for them, though. A woman onstage was shaking her fist, red-faced with energy.

Finally, Rian slowed at the base of a wide, jagged wall. He scanned the water behind them, then kicked through an opening in the rock. Kaya followed Hanna into the current, around a gradual bend, and into another, narrower tunnel. She thought they'd have farther to travel. Another few minutes, at least. That way she'd have more time to think of what to say. But when she pulled herself up out of the water and into an unfamiliar room, then slipped her goggles up onto her forehead, her father was staring back at her.

She wasn't ready.

She hadn't prepared herself.

Her dad wasn't smiling.

He didn't move toward her.

She spat out her breather.

Kaya didn't care what had happened.

She didn't care that he'd been an Eraser.

This was her dad, and she jumped to her feet, hurried across the room, and hugged him.

Someone applauded loudly. The claps hurt her ears. Rigid at first, her dad relaxed in her arms. He started whispering that he was sorry over and over. Kaya didn't know how long they stood like that, but when she finally pulled away, she remembered the professor. When she'd last seen him, they'd been worried he might not survive. Now, the enormous man was leaning on Hanna, one of his huge arms draped over her shoulders. The clapping had to have come from those giant hands. His face was pale and gray, more the pallor of an Atlantean than the color of a Sun Person. He gave Hanna a final squeeze and started slowly toward a nearby chair. A whalelike tail with two footholds—a monofin—leaned against his seat.

Naxos had probably gotten it for the Sun Person to use as a swimming aid. But the professor didn't look fit to walk, let alone kick.

Naxos shuffled toward Kaya shyly. He extended his hands; Kaya knocked them aside and hugged the inventor. Yes, he was partially to blame for this whole disaster. He was the one who'd warned the Erasers of a possible invasion in the first place. But he'd redeemed himself. He'd shown Kaya, Hanna, and Lewis the way out of Atlantis, and the professor wouldn't be alive without him.

So, yeah, he deserved a hug.

Not a long one, though.

Kaya backed away, noticed an odd drawing on the wall behind him—a map of some kind. She was about to ask about it when her father embraced her again. "I'm so relieved we found you," he whispered, "and so happy that you're safe."

His eyes were swimming with love.

"Actually, I think we found you," Hanna noted.

"Ha! That's my faithful assistant," the professor laughed.

"Assistant? More like partner," Hanna said. She moved to his chair and crouched on the floor beside him, then nodded toward the monofin. "Trying to be a merman, Professor?"

He chuckled. "A gift from Naxos. Too snug for my oversize feet. But it might fit you," he added, watching the waterhole.

Kaya felt a chill. The man was expecting his son to pop through that water. "Where's Lewis?" he finally asked.

Not one of them was strong enough to answer at first. Hanna and Rian were both looking to Kaya. Why her?

"Ah, I assume you left him with the warship? I hope you made him promise not to touch anything. He's not very good at keeping his promises, but it would decrease the chance of disaster, at least. Was he the one who deciphered my message? No, no. Don't tell me. Of course he was! I've had so much time to think down here these last few days, lying in bed, doing nothing. I have a wonderful idea for a screenplay. I'm working on a cookbook, too, focused on Atlantean delicacies. Strictly sea vegetables. A possible best seller, I suspect. Alas, I've been thinking about my parenting as well, and I see how I might have fallen short in a few critical areas over the years. I'd so like to apologize to Lewis, too, but I'm glad he's back in the ship, for his own safety." He stopped. His brow furrowed. "What is it, Kaya?" He turned to his research partner. "Hanna? What's wrong?"

Kaya, Hanna, and Rian looked at each other, silently arguing over who should tell him the truth. The professor squinted, his thick eyebrows scrunching closer together. Carefully, he stood. "Hanna, where is my son?"

"Professor," Hanna started, "I'm sorry, but . . ."

"But what?"

"We lost him," Rian said.

Nice, Kaya thought. Way to be subtle.

"Where did you lose him?"

"Here in Evenor," Rian added. "Don't worry, he's close."

The professor dropped heavily into the chair.

Kaya started explaining. Hanna and Rian tried, too, and Kaya's father attempted to reassure him. Naxos lobbed in a few words as well. They were all trying to convince him that Lewis would be okay. But the professor remained quiet, and soon they stopped making suggestions. They waited, watching him. Kaya hadn't thought it was possible to feel worse about losing Lewis, yet she'd sunk to an entirely new level. "This is all my fault," she said. "I'm so sorry."

Kaya's dad crouched on the floor beside the huge Sun Person. Her father, who supposedly hated people from the surface, was comforting the professor. He had his hand on the man's shoulder. For a while, the professor didn't move. Then he drew in a great deep breath and stood. He seemed even taller. Larger in every way. And determined. Kaya could see that he was done with whatever injuries he'd suffered during his escape from the underwater prison. He no longer had any patience for his ailments.

"This is not your fault, Kaya," he said. "Naxos, Heron, and I will scour this city together, combing through every hidden corner like a school nurse searching for head lice, until we find my son."

No one responded. Head lice? Kaya didn't understand.

Rian held up his hand. "We can't miss the vote."

"The boy's right," Naxos added.

153

"What are you thinking, Richard?" Kaya's father asked.

"I did not say we are *all* going to search for my son," the professor said. He motioned to Naxos and Kaya's dad. "Can one of the drillships make the trip in time?"

"Easily," her dad said.

"Drillship?" Hanna asked. "What drillship?"

"Not one, but several," Naxos replied, jumping into the conversation eagerly. "A fascinating and fortuitous find! I've been exploring over the past few days, and I found a dozen brand-new, highly advanced drillships, complete with gravity drives, stationed in abandoned shafts around the perimeter of the city."

Rian leaned toward Hanna and whispered, "We use drill-ships to carve out new tunnels."

"Yeah," she said, "I figured."

"I didn't know they had gravity drives," Kaya added.

"I'd heard rumors that some of my colleagues—excuse me, *former* colleagues—in the Erasers had developed a new model of drillship," Naxos continued, "but the project was as secretive as our warship effort."

"Why would the Erasers build drillships?" Rian asked.

Kaya had the same question. It annoyed her that he'd asked first.

Naxos brightened. "I'm not sure, but look at this," he said, pointing to the drawing on the wall. "Here we have the surface of Evenor's waters. This," he added, pointing toward the ceiling, "is north. These markings here, here, and here"—he noted a few of the circles spread along the border of the water—"signify the locations of the drillships I found. Notice anything?"

Kaya stepped closer, tilted her head. Did they form a circle?

"They're evenly spaced," Hanna noted. "Why's that?"

Thrilled, Naxos held his arms out wide. "I don't know! But I do love a mystery. A construction project, perhaps? New tunnels connecting to different cities?"

No, Kaya thought. The Erasers weren't in the construction business. She turned to her father. "Dad? You don't know anything about them?"

He shrugged. "I'm at a loss."

Naxos was still smiling. His ignorance excited him. Kaya found not knowing to be infuriating. She preferred solved mysteries.

"The spacing aside," her father added, "the drillships are marvelous machines, and they will serve our purpose perfectly."

The professor coughed. "Might I interrupt your technology debate to return to more important matters?"

Right. Naxos apologized. Kaya did the same. "Sorry, Professor, you were saying?"

"Well," he continued, "as I was explaining, the three of us will search this city for Lewis and you three"—the professor pointed to Kaya, Rian, and Hanna—"will continue on to Ridge City in the warship. I expect that we will join you there soon with my son in one of these wondrous Atlantean drillships."

"And if you don't get there in time?" Kaya asked. "What are we supposed to do then?"

The professor nodded to her father. With a slight but

proud smile, he eyed Kaya. Although he addressed all three of them, in her heart, she knew he was talking just to her. "You three have proven yourselves to be highly capable," he replied. "If by chance we do not make it to Ridge City in time, then you'll have to stop this war yourselves."

12

LOST IN ATLANTIS

LEWIS sprinted through an empty hallway. His stomach was growling angrily. All those wonderful snacks were stashed away in the warship. His toes were cold. His feet felt naked without his Jordans. Oh, and he was lost.

This was the worst trip to Atlantis ever.

He popped on his breather, slipped his goggles over his eyes, dropped into the nearest waterhole, and followed the current out into the open. He tried to swim like Kaya with his arms above his head, dolphin-kicking. Lewis did not think about how he was alone. He didn't think about his dad. And he definitely didn't think about what would happen if the Erasers found him and he ended up in one of those underwater jail cells. Would he grow old inside? Would he get those long, yellow, curved toenails that old men have? Would he start to smell all weird? His fear of this foul, ugly-nailed future made him swim harder and faster.

The water was slightly chillier near the bottom. Wide windows surrounded the base of one building, casting out green and yellow light. He kicked across to them, then hung in the cooler water, sweeping his hands back and forth. Hundreds of people inside were seated shoulder to shoulder. At the back of the space, a woman stood on a stage. She was holding her arms out wide, dramatically pacing back and forth. Kaya had mentioned that storytellers were pretty popular in Atlantis. The lady they'd met the last time they were here, Elida, was awesome. Maybe the woman onstage was telling a story? Lewis needed something to take his mind off his current situation. A story would be nice. He could sneak inside, listen, relax, maybe find a snack.

Then he could concoct a plan to find his friends and his dad.

Another swimmer darted into a tunnel above the window to his right, and Lewis followed the figure inside. He popped out into a hallway and descended a set of stairs.

Outside the auditorium, a row of vending machines called to him, begging him to try Atlantean snacks. The pictures were brightly colored, red and orange and green, with glittering letters. He couldn't read the weird Atlantean script, but each machine also had pictures of the food and drink inside. One machine was entirely dedicated to different kinds of kelp chips. A few appeared to be spicy, based on the red-and-orange labels. He'd tried the hot sauce in Atlantis during his last visit, and that had been delicious. The chips looked delectable, but he was thirsty, too. He checked the neighboring machine. Juice boxes! They probably tasted like seaweed, but he loved, loved, loved juice boxes.

He unsealed one of his pockets and started to search for coins.

Then, for the second time that day, he kicked himself.

He didn't have Atlantean coins.

Lewis didn't even have any gold left—he'd used it all to pay for the suits.

Actually, he had negative money, since he still owed his little brother twenty bucks. Once he got the suit to Susan Silver, though, he wouldn't have to worry about that ever again. He could buy all the juice boxes he wanted whenever he wanted, and they'd have actual juice inside, not brewed or blended seaweed. He could buy snacks that were coated in gold! Eating a precious metal might not be healthy, but it would be worth the indigestion.

Until he returned to the surface and brought the suit to Silver, though, he was penniless.

Frustrated, he kicked one of the machines with his bare foot. Inside, a motor turned.

A leathery fish bar fell into the dispenser. At least it was something. He grabbed the bar, straightened his wig, adjusted the goggles on his forehead, and snuck into the auditorium. The Atlanteans inside were packed onto long stone benches. The floor sloped down, so he sat at the back, against the glass, and stretched out his exhausted legs. He wriggled his pale, itching toes and bit into the bar. A little chewy, but not totally gross.

The woman onstage wasn't merely a storyteller. She was a whirling tornado of energy and excitement. He was late to this story, but it didn't take him long to catch her drift.

She was talking about Sun People.

He sat up straighter.

"They did not come to fight!" she yelled. "They did not

come to steal our precious technology, as certain members of the High Council would have you believe! They came here in peace! My mentor, the great storyteller Elida, met these noble heroes from the surface." A few people in the crowd gasped. "One of them was built like a mountain, but he had the friendly manners and warmth of a playful seal. This is the professor, a great and noble teacher, famed among the People of the Sun for his theories of Atlantis.

"His brilliant partner is a young woman, hardly older than a girl, but no mere child in terms of her intelligence, bravery, and uncanny beauty."

Lewis bit his lip. He could hardly breathe. Now the storyteller was getting to the best part—the part about him.

"There was a boy, too, and when these three first arrived, we didn't welcome them. No! Our war-crazed leaders immediately mistook their visit for an attack and began to chase them through the tunnels and waterways . . ."

She kept talking. Lewis stopped listening.

There was a boy, too.

That was all she had to say about him? What about his intelligence? His cunning? She hadn't even mentioned his charm! He'd been brave, too. Lewis felt like a popped balloon, soaring one second, plummeting to the ground the next. Despite this narrative betrayal, though, he forced himself to listen again, and the story was actually pretty gripping. When she detailed their escape from the underwater prison, how his dad had braved the icy, poisoned water to free them, the audience gasped. A woman in the back row wiped tears from her eyes. People stood and cheered when the storyteller told of how they'd defeated the Erasers.

The Atlanteans didn't despise the Sun People.

The audience was giving them a standing ovation.

These people didn't want to go to war with the surface.

This was all a tsunami-size misunderstanding.

Another thing she'd said troubled him, though. The storyteller had sworn to the crowd that the Sun People had come in peace, that they hadn't snuck into Atlantis to steal its precious technology. That had been true the first time. Absolutely. But now? Lewis had a gravity suit in his bag. The technology wasn't stolen. He'd paid for the gear, and if he gave it to Susan Silver as promised, he'd be able to use hundred-dollar bills as toilet paper. His mom, his dad, Michael, Roberts—he'd help them all. But then Silver would copy the Atlantean technology and pass it off as her own invention.

What this storyteller had told the audience would turn out to be false.

If Lewis was really honest with himself, if he put himself into an imaginary headlock and twisted his arm behind his back, he might admit that what he was doing was theft.

Or maybe not?

He hadn't thought this hard since his last math test a month earlier, right before the end of the school year. Was he failing here, too? His brain was bursting. His head itched; he pulled off the wig and scratched his scalp vigorously, as if he could dig all these annoying questions right out of his mind.

The storyteller went silent.

Lewis looked up.

The woman onstage was staring at him.

Her eyes were like spotlights showing everyone where to focus.

Others followed her gaze. A few at first, then more. Soon, hundreds of Atlanteans were eyeing Lewis. The attention changed something in him, activating some unknown program in his brain. He didn't run. He didn't speak. But deep in his mind, he did begin to hear a faint beat.

Lewis stood, ditching the wig on the ground. The beat grew louder, a sort of *boom, boom, cha-cha-cha*.

Yes, the music was playing only in his head, and yet it felt so real.

A giant audience was watching him.

He wasn't quite ready. He hadn't practiced nearly enough. There were nuances left to master. Yet one fact was unavoidable.

The raptor's time had come.

He pulled his elbows in tight to his ribs and held up his forearms, letting his hands dangle limply. His head was pitched forward but steady. He lifted one knee, then the other, then quickened his pace to keep up with the *cha-cha-cha*. The crowd was mesmerized. They'd never seen a Sun Person before, let alone one doing a newly invented dance based on a long-extinct predatory dinosaur. There was no applause. There were no cheers. He was simply too wondrous; the crowd was in shock. And yet, at the peak of his brilliance, he noticed a group bursting onto the stage.

Three very imposing, very angry-looking figures.

Two were Atlantean men he didn't recognize.

The third, the leader among them, had the short blond hair and firm jaw of his third-grade teacher, Mrs. Finkleman. The last time he'd seen this Atlantean, they'd been in the warship factory. Lewis was happy to see that she'd survived, even if she was one of his mortal enemies. But she didn't look thrilled to see him. Her eyes narrowed. Lewis stared back with equal intensity—if this was a stare fight, he'd make sure it was a tie. These Atlanteans were Erasers—he was certain of that—but this wasn't the same group that had tracked them through the mall.

Lewis shot the leader one last ferocious look, then turned his attention to the audience. He bowed, as it would have been wrong to deny his adoring crowd this simple gesture of thanks, and then he lifted his fist and shouted, "FOR ATLANTIS!"

The crowd erupted into cheers.

"Stop the Erasers!" someone shouted.

"Block their way!"

"Don't let them get away with this!"

The crowd swarmed around the agents, holding them back. The Atlanteans were trying to help him escape, and he seized the opportunity, dashing out the door. On the stairs, he pulled his goggles down over his eyes, then opened his breather and pressed it over his mouth and nose. He found a waterhole with the current flowing out and dove through without thinking. Out in the open water of the city, he swam around the corners of several buildings, then through a narrow space between two curving structures crowded with windows.

Where was he supposed to go now?

He decided to return to the one safe place he knew. Esmerelda.

Lewis turned and coasted up the side of a triangular tower, staying close to the wall. At the very top of the building, he grabbed on to a railing with one hand and studied the scene below. Thankfully, no one had followed him. He released his grip, floated up to the surface, and popped his head out slowly, like a cautious and—he thought—slightly handsome frog. A few small islands floated nearby. There had to be hundreds of them spread across the water. How was he going to find Esmerelda? He ducked down and noticed that the islands were connected by a web of long lines. He held one, pulling himself forward, then recognized a tower in the water below. They'd swum past that building when they'd first arrived. That meant the island of the triplets—and Esmerelda—wasn't far away.

A sudden and completely unexpected emotional volcano erupted within him. His face felt suddenly hot. Deep behind his eyes, tears formed. He clenched his teeth, squeezed his eyes shut. Could you cry underwater, or while wearing goggles? Normally, when Lewis was about to cry, he imagined a crew of microscopic gnomes blocking his tear ducts on command, preventing unexpected emotional outpourings. Typically, the trick worked. But where were his trusted gnomes now? Off at some rambunctious garden party, undoubtedly.

Lewis made no effort to stop the tears. He swam onward, using the web of lines that stretched between the islands to yank himself along. The ropes were slimy and strung with seaweed, but he moved faster this way, hand over hand, and before long, he was crawling up onto the shore near Esmerelda.

He found a hiding spot between several large boxes packed with seaweed and salted fish. Earlier, they'd seen Rass fishing; he probably preserved and sold his catch. The crates stank, but his seat was soft and surprisingly comfortable. A little too damp, though—Lewis felt like he was resting on a pile of ramen noodles.

He told himself he could wait a little while. His friends might still turn up. Maybe even his dad.

But what if they didn't? What if the Erasers had grabbed them?

If his father and his friends were thrown back in prison, no one would be able to convince the High Council that there had been no invasion. Atlantis would vote to attack the surface, and the president would surely strike back. Other countries would probably jump into the fight, too.

The whole thing would be a colossal, devastating mess.

An entirely unnecessary war.

Unless he stopped it.

What if Lewis had to save the world by himself? Typically, you needed superpowers or really large muscles to do stuff like that. All he had was a letter from the president, a harmonica, some Atlantean gear, and a quiver full of half-finished comic dance routines.

Lewis stood up. Had he grown? Maybe. He felt taller. His arms looked scrawny; he was bummed he didn't have bigger biceps. Maybe pecs, too. But his Atlantean outfit was heroic. The greenish-brown color wasn't gross; it was distinct. Special. Even the wart-like pack on his back felt right, almost like it was his own wart. He decided to call it Wally.

Lewis and Wally were going to save the world.

Inspired, he started composing a quick little song:

He didn't have muscles and he wasn't that tall,
but Lewis was the hero who saved us all.
He was brave and daring and a little bit bold.
His dances were amazing and his toes were cold . . .

The song needed work, and a beat, but this wasn't the time for wordsmithing. You weren't supposed to sit around writing lyrics while saving the world. Superheroes didn't procrastinate, and he needed to get the ship to Ridge City as soon as possible.

Inside the hut, he heard arguing. One by one, the triplets burst out of the house. Lewis leaned out of his hiding spot. Seaweed clumps were flying, and Rass stumbled backward with what looked like a spiny urchin stuck to his forehead.

A plan began to form in Lewis's mind.

There was no reason to trust them. In fact, there was evidence that he should do exactly the opposite. The triplets had already duped him once. But Lewis preferred to trust people. He'd kept his faith in his dad after all those times he'd cancelled their visits and trips to the mountains. He'd trusted Kaya and Hanna, too, and that had mostly worked out. Lewis had even given James Bond another chance after the sleepover incident, and the pug had never doused his sheets again.

What if Rass and Fenitia redeemed themselves?

What if they helped him save the world?

Fenitia spotted Lewis first. "They're back!" she exclaimed. A sodden fish cake smacked against the side of her face. "That got in my ear, Argon!"

The food fight stopped. The triplets hurried over.

"What are you doing here?" Rass asked him.

Argon looked at Lewis kindly. "Are the others okay?"

"I'm not sure," Lewis admitted. He eyed the three siblings, then glanced back in the direction of Esmerelda. The warship was still invisible, but he could see the light flickering strangely near the ground. The Atlanteans were watching him, waiting. He turned back to Argon. "Do you know how to drive?"

13

NO MOOD TO WAIT

KAYA walked back and forth over the squishy ground. She wanted to kick something. Esmerelda was gone. This was definitely not part of her plan, and now Rian was asking if she was sure they'd left it here. Seriously? Of course she was certain! You didn't forget where you'd left a stolen warship.

Meanwhile, Hanna was wondering aloud who had taken Esmerelda. Was it the Erasers? The triplets? That didn't matter to Kaya. Not right now. The real question was what to do next. Her dad, Naxos, and the professor were searching the city for Lewis.

"On to the new plan," she said.

"What's the new plan?" Hanna asked.

That was a good question. Kaya hadn't gotten that far yet.

Walking to the island's edge, Rian turned and motioned to Hanna. "We still have you, Hanna," he said. "And you, too, Kaya."

"And?" Kaya responded.

"And if we can get you two to Ridge City in time, the High Council might listen to you."

He had a point. If the government leaders met Hanna, they might change their minds about the Sun People. Kaya hoped Rian was right and that she could appeal to them, too. Maybe they'd listen to her because she was an Atlantean. Not only that, but the daughter of one of their former colleagues. One little problem remained, though. "How do we get there?"

"What if we took one of those drillships?" Hanna suggested.

Sure. That might work. But they didn't have all day to search for the right caves. Kaya thought of that crude sketch in the hideaway. "We need that map Naxos drew on the wall."

"I'm not swimming back there," Rian said. "The city is swarming with agents."

The three of them couldn't return together. Hanna was too slow. Faster than Lewis, certainly, but not quick enough.

"No one has to swim back," Hanna said. "I have the map."

The drawing had been sketched on a rock wall. "I don't understand," Kaya replied. "What do you mean?"

Hanna tapped the side of her head. She shrugged. "My brain's a little weird. Maps, diagrams, formulas, equations . . . I only need to see them once. Which way is north?"

Confidently, Rian pointed to the right of the triplets' hut. He was off by at least ninety degrees. Kaya laughed, grabbed his still-pointing forearm, and swung it to the left. He shrugged, not bothering to argue. Hanna turned northward, closed her eyes briefly, then nodded to the right. "If I'm remembering the map correctly, and have my bearings right, then the nearest one should be somewhere around there."

The dry outer walls above Evenor gradually sloped downward to the waterline. The section Hanna indicated wasn't very well lit, but it looked like a ledge ran along the side, above the lake. There were a few openings scattered about as well. Kaya squinted. They'd have to get closer to be certain. "Let's go," she said.

"I'll lead," Rian added.

At the island's edge, Rian slid through a gap in a long row of waist-high flowering shrubs and into the water. Hanna followed, and Kaya checked behind them, studying the neighboring islands and the mist overhead, hoping to see an odd glimmer or wrinkle of light. Something to suggest that maybe Esmerelda was still nearby. That the ship had simply been moved, not stolen.

Instead, she noticed three figures climbing up onto one of the brightly colored garden islands in the distance. Removing their breathers, they pushed their goggles up onto their foreheads and surveyed the scene. One of them started to turn in Kaya's direction. Her hair was short and blond, and Kaya recognized her from the factory.

Finkleman! That's what Lewis had called her, anyway.

Before the Eraser noticed her, Kaya dropped down, ducking behind the row of shrubs.

This was bad. If Finkleman had been sent all the way to Evenor, then they were in serious trouble. Maybe Rian's statement about all the Erasers looking for them was more accurate than he realized. Kaya eased out of her hiding spot, crawling on the soft ground and peering around the side of the shrub.

The two men with Finkleman both carried sonic pistols.

With her back to Kaya, Finkleman pointed to a tour boat in the distance.

Her partners quickly slipped on their breathers and goggles and dove into the water, barely making a splash. Then Finkleman turned slowly in Kaya's direction. Kaya drew back immediately. She counted to ten before edging forward to look again. When she did, Finkleman was gone.

They were safe for now.

But what about Lewis?

How would he ever survive with so many agents scouring Evenor?

What if Finkleman and the Erasers had already grabbed him?

That, Kaya reminded herself, wasn't her responsibility. Her dad and Naxos would find Lewis. They'd rescue him if need be. Her job was to get Hanna and herself out of Evenor.

Immediately.

Kaya slid into the water alongside her friends. Quietly, she told them what she'd seen, and Rian suggested they hurry. The three of them pressed on their breathers, pulled their goggles over their eyes, and slipped below the surface. The light trickling through the water was weak, but Kaya kept Hanna in sight and glanced back often to make sure they weren't being followed.

Rian reached the outer wall first. At the water's edge, Kaya slid her goggles up onto her forehead and waited with Hanna. The water around them was as smooth as glass, which meant no one was sneaking up from below.

Up on the ledge, Rian hurried to their left, peered into a

large tunnel, then waved for them to join him. Hanna climbed out. When Kaya stood, her hands were shaking. Was she scared? Nervous? Either way, it was annoying.

Rope was strung back and forth across the opening of the cave. Piles of rubble spilled out onto the ledge. Collapsed tunnels like this were the kinds of places every kid in Atlantis was taught to avoid from an early age. If a tunnel had collapsed once, it might do so again, and you didn't want to be inside when it did. Rian stood just inside the entrance, Hanna right beside him. Was he waiting for instructions?

"Get inside," Kaya said.

As Kaya stepped in between the ropes, Hanna pointed back behind her, into the distance. "What's going on over there?" she asked.

Across the cave, the air was thick with mist, so it was hard to see, but it looked like half a dozen cruisers were speeding toward the western wall of the cave. Kaya squinted. Something was happening—some kind of emergency. And it was right near the tunnel through which they'd entered the city. She thought she saw a few unusual watercraft floating on the surface, too. But the mist and the distance made it impossible to be certain.

Plus, they had the Erasers to worry about. Finkleman was way too close.

Kaya led them forward into the cave.

The built-in lights on Hanna's new goggles illuminated the otherwise-dark interior. She looked around and let out a long, breathy, "Whoaaaaaa."

A narrow, cylindrical metal ship rested on the ground in

front of them. Five exhaust pipes extended from the back, each one large enough that Kaya's arms would barely reach around them. Deep channels extended along the length of the vehicle. The front was a single ridged cone inlaid with sparkling clear stones. Rian marveled quietly, but Hanna couldn't contain herself. She was actually bouncing with excitement.

She stroked one of the exhaust pipes lovingly. "Whoa, whoa, whoa! Don't tell me this is the drillship. And are these diamonds on the front? Makes sense, I guess—hardest stuff on Earth. But seriously, are you kidding me? This thing's straight out of a comic book!"

Rian added, "It is pretty amazing."

Hanna started inspecting the back, the sides, studying every square inch. "I figured you'd have to have some ridiculous technology to carve out all these tunnels. For a little while, I was thinking it was done with laser ablation, you know? But that would be too slow. Old-fashioned grinding and Newtonian physics works best, right?"

What was she talking about? Kaya glanced at Rian. He shrugged. He was clueless, too. Hanna was speaking another language now: the language of science and engineering. Not one that Kaya's translator could make sense of easily.

"Right," Kaya replied. "Exactly."

Rian glanced at her sideways, smiling at her fake certainty. He knew her well enough to know that she had no idea what Hanna was talking about.

"This is so old-school," Hanna continued. She spun to face them. "So I bet the diamond drill grinds the rock in front while these"—she pointed to a bunch of strange rods with handlike extensions—"push back against the walls. That way, the drillship keeps moving forward, right? And all the rock that's pulverized gets kicked to the back thanks to these." She ran her hand along one of the channels in the side of the ship. "Right? Don't you think?"

"Sure," Rian said.

This was all very interesting. Kaya was glad Hanna was so impressed. Really. But they were in a rush. "I don't care how it works," she said. "I care about whether it's going to get us to Ridge City in time."

"Then let's get inside and check it out," Rian replied.

"Wait," Hanna said.

What now? Kaya stifled her frustration. Hanna was staring blankly at the back of the ship. "What's wrong?" Kaya asked.

"We need to name it first."

"Name what?" Rian asked.

"The ship," Hanna answered. "Lewis would name it, right?"

A wave of guilt washed through Kaya. She'd been thinking so much about the meeting, her dad, herself. She'd almost forgotten they'd lost their friend.

Her dad would find Lewis. She truly believed that. But naming the ship would be a kind of tribute to him. A reminder that he was still with them. In spirit, at least.

"Dave," Hanna decided. She crossed her arms over her chest. Her head bobbed slightly. "We'll call it Dave."

Wide-eyed, thoroughly confused, Rian stared back at Kaya. "Can we get inside . . . Dave?"

Kaya looked back over her shoulder. She couldn't see out to the lake. But Lewis and her father were down in that water somewhere. Kaya wished she'd had the time to tell her dad everything, all about the surface and the dinners and that weird Susan Silver woman and her Sunshine Corporation. Kaya had so many other questions, too. She was desperate to know more about the Erasers, her mother, why her father had lied to her about . . . well, almost everything. Or everything that really mattered. A part of her was still furious with him. Sorry for him, too. And mad at herself for the way she'd treated him at times. But her dad was on the right side of this fight now.

The side Kaya knew her mom would be on, too.

In a weird way, she felt closer to him than ever.

At the door to the drillship, Rian was holding out a metal rod the size of his index finger. The device emitted a range of notes, varied in pitch, speed, and frequency. Kaya pressed her hands to her ears. The chaotic mix of sounds was painful. What in the world was he doing?

The door slid open.

Oh. Right. The little gadget was a lock whisperer. The best models could open any door in Atlantis, and Rian had been asking for one for his birthday for the last five years at least. His family was definitely odd, but she didn't think his parents would actually give him a gadget used by burglars and thieves. "Where'd you get that?" Kaya asked.

"From the same person who sent me here," Rian replied. "Long story, but she had me spy on the High Council first, then gave my parents a free vacation and pretended she was my babysitter—yeah, I know, it's weird—and asked me to sneak up to Evenor with a transmitter for your dad so he could contact you." Rian paused for a breath—he'd blurted everything out in a rush. Then he pointed to his goggles and held up his breather. "She gave me this gear. Not a bad deal."

That was one way to look at it—but she'd made him risk his life, too. "What did this woman look like?" Kaya asked.

"Short hair. Blond. Kind of fierce."

His description matched Finkleman—that was odd. "Well, if you meet her again," Kaya said, "we'll have to thank her."

A light breeze flowed into the tunnel. A passing cruiser, maybe. The thought of the Erasers out there searching for them made Kaya increasingly impatient. Thankfully, Hanna was already in the ship, slipping into the pilot's seat. Rian leaned over the instrument panel. "I'll drive," Hanna said.

"You know how?" Rian asked.

"I'll figure it out."

He huffed and focused on the panel.

The door closed behind Kaya.

With one hand on a small dial, Hanna smiled at Rian. "See? I've got it."

While they studied the controls, Kaya inspected the rest of the interior. This was going to be a long, long trip. The cabin was cramped, with only two seats. There was no viewing glass in front of them, either, since the massive drill was in the way. There were a few tool kits—they'd keep Hanna occupied for hours. A deflated raft was rolled up in a corner for emergencies. Kaya found a medical kit, a few boxes of kelp bars, and a faucet linked to a water supply. She tested the water. Slightly metallic, but drinkable. A tall metal door revealed some kind of fold-down toilet. That was good. Not very private, but good.

Overall, Dave wouldn't be a terrible ride. Luxurious? No. Definitely not. But they'd survive. She repositioned the raft and sat on the floor with her back against the makeshift cushion. Rian could have the seat next to Hanna. To start with, anyway.

The drillship was vibrating—a high-frequency pulse that Kaya felt in her spine. A humming sound came from the front.

"Hanna, wait," Rian said. He was annoyed; Kaya could hear it. "Let me read through this stuff for a few more minutes."

But Hanna was in no mood to wait.

The whole inside of the ship rumbled, and Kaya heard a deep crunch as it secured itself to the walls of the tunnel, then an earsplitting roar as the vehicle began drilling through the rock.

"How do we know where we're going?" Hanna asked.

Rian lifted his hand off the control pad. "The ship is packed with sonic sensors. There's a clear tunnel up ahead." He closed his eyes, pointed slightly to their right. "Over that way," he added. "If we can get into that passageway, we can shut down the drill and drift."

"We need to get to Ridge without being noticed," Kaya reminded him. "This ship is going to attract way too much attention cruising through a standard tunnel."

Excited, Rian nodded. "I don't think we need to worry about that."

"What?" Kaya asked. "Why not?"

Hanna interrupted them. "Can I start driving now?"

"Not yet," Kaya answered. "Rian, what are you talking about?"

He held his hand over the control pad. "The ship's computer is loaded with maps. Not just any maps, though. They have all kinds of unmarked tunnels on them. Here, let me show you. I'll bring up Ridge." After a few seconds, he called her over and leaned out of her way. Kaya placed her palm on the pad. "Do you feel that?" he asked. "That's a tunnel running right underneath Government Square in the center of the city! I'm telling you, that's not on any normal map."

"So what?" Hanna asked.

"So I think we'll be able to find our way to Ridge City without anyone spotting us."

"Dave," Hanna corrected him.

"What?"

"Without anyone spotting Dave."

The two of them glared at each other. Not angrily, though. They were competing. Kaya needed them to work together. They needed roles. Kaya looked at Rian, then Hanna. "You're the navigator," she said to Rian. "Hanna's driving." Rian began to protest, but Kaya cut him off. "Nobody finds hidden routes like you do, Rian. If you don't tell us where we're going, we're lost."

She waited. Had it worked? She wasn't lying.

Finally, Rian nodded. "You have to listen to me, Hanna."

"If I listen, I can drive?"

"Yes."

That was all Hanna needed to hear. Her smile widened as she placed her hands on the pads in front of her seat. Slowly, she eased them forward. The grinding, whining roar of the drill intensified, and Dave drove into the rock.

14

HIS UNUSUAL ARMY

THANKFULLY, Lewis wasn't alone anymore. The triplets weren't the worst companions, either. Fenitia was steering their invisible warship through a tunnel with light traffic. The brothers were arguing, and Lewis was stretched out on one of the bench seats. He was proud of himself. He'd opened Esmerelda's door on the first whistle. Or maybe the eleventh. How many attempts he'd needed wasn't the point. He'd done it, demonstrating his superior musical ear, and now they were on their way to saving the world. Once he'd shown the triplets the invisible vehicle, weaving together the rest of his plan was easy. He hadn't even thought about it all that much.

The warship had to be in Ridge by tomorrow.

There was no sign of Hanna, Kaya, or Rian.

He didn't have a clue how to find his dad.

He didn't know how to steer anything bigger than a bicycle.

And he really, really didn't like being alone.

Inviting the triplets along was the obvious choice. Naturally, the three of them had been surprised when Lewis had asked for their help. Fenitia had confessed that Argon had swayed her opinion, and that she'd come to feel terrible about having cheated Lewis and his friends. Rass had grumbled and growled in agreement. Lewis wasn't sure he actually wanted to help, but apparently the Erasers hadn't given the triplets the promised reward for turning in the Sun People, so he was out for revenge.

The one unfortunate development? Rass and Argon had insisted on bringing a few crates of fish to sell in Ridge City— five, to be exact—and the warship was bursting with an unholy stench. The upside? If the Erasers took back Esmerelda, the agents would have to scrub the inside for days to clean out the stink. The other bonus? Lewis had been reunited with his backpack. That meant snacks. Glorious, delicious, soul-soothing snacks. He offered Argon some beef jerky. The triplet said it smelled like home. He happily gnawed off one end as Lewis paused between bites of a delightfully normal granola bar.

"How long will it take to get to Ridge?" Lewis asked.

"We have to go through Cleito first," Fenitia explained. "It seems your ship is low on power reserves, so we'll have to travel slowly. We should be able to make it by late morning, though."

"She drove a tour submarine for decades," Argon said. Quietly, he added, "The company fired her, though. It's no wonder, either. She's one of the worst drivers in Evenor."

"I heard that!" Fenitia protested. "Those last four accidents were not my fault."

The last *four*? Lewis didn't want to ask how many had come before that.

"Neither of us can drive, though," Rass added, "so she's our best option."

A lone ferry floated on the waterway below them. Esmerelda was still in stealth mode; the driver and passengers didn't notice them drifting overhead. Fenitia started explaining that Cleito, their next destination, was named after the wife of the sea-god Poseidon. Or one of his wives, anyway. Lewis remembered learning something about Poseidon's brother, Zeus, dating a swan. Or maybe he became a swan? The Greek gods were weird.

One of the triplets switched on the soundscape and tuned to a news station. A man and a woman were debating what they called "the surface question," which seemed to be whether Atlantis should invade. Argon pointed the remains of his beef jerky at Lewis. "Is there room for us Atlanteans up there?"

This was a difficult question. Was there enough space for millions more people? Not in his town, or even his part of the country. Europe, Japan, China, Africa—he'd heard they were all pretty crowded, too. Siberia or Antarctica might work, though. There were steam rooms in Siberia. And that red soup Roberts made once. What was it? Oh, right—borscht! He loved that word. As for the South Pole, sure, it was cold, but the place had lots of water, and there were penguins. The Atlanteans would probably love penguins. Everyone did. Lewis could talk to the president about renaming the place Atlantarctica or something, unless that would confuse people from Atlanta.

He described it for the Atlanteans, leaving out the part about the cold. "Can you swim there?" Rass asked.

Maybe? Lewis wasn't sure. But they didn't need to know that. "Totally."

"I like it," Argon declared. "If there's a whole world up there, Lewis, we Atlanteans ought to try to be a part of it, don't you think?"

Lewis yawned unexpectedly. He didn't mean to be rude.

Fenitia smiled back at him in an awkward but sort of motherly way. "Maybe you need some sleep?" she asked.

Him? No! Never. He was a hero now. Heroes didn't nap. They trained. He leaped to his feet and attempted a few push-ups. This time, he made it to five. Then, with Argon's help, he tested out the gravity suit, in case he needed to use it. He bounced and drifted off the walls and ceiling in the back of the ship. The thrusters in the gloves were supercool. Argon said they were a new feature, and they made it easy to change direction. After cruising around the cabin for a while, Lewis tried push-ups again with the suit on and managed to crank out fifty. Sure, they were much easier when you were weightless, but still, he was getting stronger! His arms looked no bigger, but he felt more muscular. Mentally, he was ripped.

All the training was exhausting, though.

A few more yawns escaped him.

He lay on the floor to rest briefly. Ideas started ricocheting around in his head like restless, frantic houseflies. He thought of the Erasers and Hanna and Kaya and his father and mother and Roberts and Michael and Susan Silver and Johnny the mail-carrying dolphin.

After an eternity, they arrived in Cleito, which reminded him of pictures he'd seen of ancient desert cities. Lewis was eager to sneak out and explore, maybe test the gravity suit outside, gather a few details to share with his father when they were reunited. A breath of non-fishy air would have been nice, too. But the triplets thought that going out in the open would be too risky for him, so they left Cleito quickly through an enormous tunnel heading south. Fenitia encouraged them all to sit down, and the warship maintained its slow and steady pace. The trip, she said, would take all night and into the morning. Saturday morning, he realized. Normally, he might have a soccer game or play pickup with his friends.

Instead, he'd be sneaking into an Atlantean city.

A perfectly normal weekend.

Lewis's brain wouldn't let him sleep, so he decided to make use of the remaining hours and begin plotting his memoir, a semi-fictional but mostly true story of his adventures in Atlantis. The book would be a graphic novel, obviously. In the story, he would change his name to Troy, and he would be a lacrosse player whose hair flowed like ocean waves. There would be monsters in the memoir, too, and he would lull them into a trance with the soothing sounds of his harmonica. As he imagined his masterwork, his yawns intensified, and when they finally arrived in Ridge City, he'd been in a deep, dreamless sleep for hours.

Esmerelda slowed and shook slightly, jostling him.

Lewis rubbed his eyes. Fenitia was still in the driver's seat. Her brothers stood beside her. After a quick stretch, Lewis joined them at the control panel.

"We made it," Fenitia said.

The city was a wonder and so different from Evenor. The multicolored buildings gleamed and shined. Some looked like crystal churches. Intricately carved and sculpted balconies stood out from the sheer rock walls, and waterways threaded through the alleys, curving and flowing in all directions. The streets were crowded with people. Antigravity cruisers drifted through the air. Esmerelda veered around one of the dozens of enormous steel columns stretching from the floor to the ceiling of the cave. The ship drifted slowly upward.

"It's beautiful," Argon said.

Rass gazed out at the city silently.

A few of the crystal-and-glass buildings were familiar to Lewis from his last trip to Ridge City. He thought they might be near Kaya's neighborhood. Argon threw his arm around Lewis's shoulders. The smell was horrendous, but the gesture was welcome. "Thank you for trusting us, Lewis," he said. "I never thought I'd see Ridge City for myself."

"I never thought we'd leave Evenor!" Fenitia declared. "Lewis, while you were sleeping, we did receive a message—"

He jumped. "Who was it?"

"Didn't give a name. An Atlantean, though. Asked if we had the visitor."

His shoulders sagged. He'd been hoping it had been his father. Maybe it had been Kaya's dad or Naxos. "And what did you tell him?"

Fenitia pointed ahead and to the right. "I told him yes. He said to bring you and the ship to Capitol Tower. According to my maps, it's over that way."

"We've been listening to the soundscape," Argon added, "and according to the news, the High Council is meeting in Capitol Tower as we speak."

Lewis's heart started beating faster. Yes, it could have been Kaya's dad or Naxos. But what if the message had been from the Erasers? What if this was a trick?

Lewis had to take that chance. He would deliver the warship to the High Council. Sure, the triplets were helping, but they were more like assistants. Lewis couldn't depend on Hanna and Kaya now. This was his mission and his alone. Forget Susan Silver and her money. Lewis was going to save the world.

He felt sick.

An excited Argon patted him on the back. Lewis gulped and gritted his teeth.

Then Argon threw his arm around his brother's shoulders. "We did it, Rass!"

The Atlantean said nothing. Esmerelda turned slightly. Argon backhanded Rass in the shoulder. The greasy-haired, snaggle-toothed triplet didn't look the slightest bit excited. His thin, gray lips quivered, and he was working very hard not to look Argon or Lewis in the eye. He glanced back behind them. Slowly, Lewis turned, too, fearing the worst.

Three cruisers were drifting behind them, all in a row.

Three black cruisers with darkened windows.

The Erasers had found them.

"Seriously? You turned me in *again*?"

"What? No!" Argon protested.

Fenitia was equally outraged. "We'd never—"

She glanced back at Rass, then went quiet.

"I'm sorry," Rass said. "They offered quite a reward."

"We should have left you in Evenor!" Argon declared. "How do they even know we're here? The ship is invisible."

Rass tapped his ear. "I've kind of been telling them."

Furious, his brother reached into one of the crates, pulled out a codfish the size of Lewis's thigh, and began slapping Rass in the head with the silvery swimmer. Rass cowered, holding up his arms to block the blows. Shiny fish scales and flecks of salt stuck to his hands and forearms and the side of his face. One of the cod's eyes popped out and became tangled in his hair.

Meanwhile, Fenitia was frantically searching through the controls. "Should I fire at them, Lewis? This ship's loaded with sonic blasters."

She was asking *him*? Yes, of course she was asking him! He hurried to the control panel. "How far are we from Capitol Tower?" he asked.

"That's it right there," Fenitia said, pointing to one of the strangest buildings Lewis had ever seen. More sculpture than structure, it looked like a cross between a giant piece of seaweed and a skyscraper. He actually blinked twice to make sure he wasn't imagining things.

Behind them, the cruisers were pulling closer. And sure, Esmerelda was a highly advanced warship, but its pilot was no soldier. There was no way they were going to beat those cruisers in a blaster war. Lewis grabbed the Velcroed touchscreen device off the dashboard and scrolled through the controls. Thankfully, Dr. Lin had made this part super simple. There were two large buttons near the bottom of the screen labeled VISIBLE and INVISIBLE. He tapped on the former.

Now there would be no hiding Esmerelda.

Now all of Ridge City would see them returning the warship.

"Don't blast them," Lewis said. "But try to get us closer to the tower."

Fenitia answered, "I'll do my best."

Esmerelda swooped down toward the tops of the buildings. In a rush, Lewis laid out his gravity gear. He buckled on the chest plate, slipped his hands into the fingerless gloves, then strapped on the ankle pieces. The fish fight had stopped—Rass was picking scales off his forearms and face. Argon helped Lewis tighten the suit, and it fit perfectly. He slipped his goggles over his eyes. Wally was snug against his back, and he patted the harmonica in his pocket. He thought of everyone who was depending on him. He felt as if his friends, his parents, his little brother, and even the president were all watching him from far away, cheering him on. He felt taller. Stronger, too. And ever so slightly more handsome. He wished the girl at the mall could see him now.

Lewis was ready to save the world.

"We're getting close," Fenitia said.

Argon pointed back at the cruisers. "They're getting closer!"

"Take us higher," Lewis said, "above the tower." He said it firmly, too, as if it was an order. He was feeling more heroic by the moment, and he glanced down at his biceps again. Were they slightly larger? Yes. Definitely.

Esmerelda veered toward the roof of the enormous cave. Through the back, he watched the cruisers. One vehicle accelerated, pulling up alongside them. Lewis tightened his weird new clothes. He patted his harmonica and the letter from the president for good luck.

"Open the door," he called out to Fenitia.

His stomach felt sick again, awash in bilious waves of bravery.

Argon nodded solemnly. "You can do it, Lewis."

This bit of encouragement was all he needed.

Lewis stepped toward the edge, holding the door frame.

Capitol Tower loomed below the ship.

The streets and waterways of Ridge City were far beneath him.

Suddenly, Esmerelda swerved. Several crates of fish slid across the floor. One slammed into Lewis from behind, throwing him forward. The box crashed against the doorway, bursting open. Hundreds of glimmering cod and countless strands of seaweed spilled into the air around him, and Lewis and his unusual army rained down on Capitol Tower.

$\approx$ 15 $\approx$

WORTH PROTECTING

KAYA woke in a panic. How had she slept? And why had Rian and Hanna let her? This was no time to relax! She had to plot. Plan. Think. Yet she'd been so exhausted that she hadn't been able to do any of that clearly. Even now, her mind was in a fog. She sat up, her back against the deflated raft. Her arms and legs were heavy. She didn't feel like she was waking up from a nap so much as returning from another planet. After a moment, she realized Dave was silent. The drillship wasn't moving.

"Where are we?" Kaya asked.

"A tunnel outside Ridge City," Rian answered. "We're almost home."

Ridge City? Already? "I know I napped, but—"

"That wasn't a nap," Hanna said. "That was hibernation. You slept for ten hours. We must have punched through three or four piles of rubble and stone with the drill, and each time we were full-on shaking!"

Grabbing the armrests on his seat, Rian reenacted it for her. "It was wild," he agreed. "And you didn't move at all."

"I actually checked your pulse a few times," Hanna added, "to make sure you weren't in a coma or something."

Okay. That was embarrassing. Kaya took Hanna's outstretched hand and climbed to her feet; the girl was thin but strong. For a Sun Person, anyway. The depth of Kaya's nap shouldn't have surprised her. She had never slept well on the surface. Their world was too bright. Even at night, the moon cast that whitish-gray light all over everything. Her head ached just thinking about it. Ten hours, though? And straight through those rumbles? That was serious. But good.

She felt refreshed.

Ready.

And absolutely ravenous. Rian sensed that. He tossed her a kelp bar.

"Thanks," she said. "Did you hear from my dad or Naxos?"

"No," Rian replied, "but they'd know the Erasers would be listening."

"He trusts you, Kaya," Hanna added.

Hanna didn't need to add that, but Kaya didn't mind hearing it, either.

"How much time do we have?" Kaya asked.

"We don't know," Hanna said.

"It's still morning," Rian explained, "so we got here ahead of schedule, but . . ." He stopped himself, then turned up a dial on the control panel. "Here, listen."

The familiar voice of a reporter came through the speakers:

"*. . . Glandor Thrall, reporting live from Government Square. Due to unexpected events, the much-anticipated vote has been* *moved to this morning. As we speak, the High Council is meeting in Capitol Tower, debating if Atlantis should proceed with our counterinvasion—"*

Rian turned down the sound.

"We need to go," Kaya mumbled, her mouth still stuffed with food. She finished the bar and licked her fingers. Rian was smiling at her. "What?"

"You always make fun of me for doing that," he said. "Did they even feed you on the surface? Was anything good?"

Hanna was listening, and Kaya didn't want to seem ungrateful. "Chocolate," she said to Rian. "You'd like chocolate." She nodded to Hanna. "The trip was okay?"

"She's an awesome driver," Rian responded.

"And your friend here is a pretty stellar navigator," Hanna added.

Outside, the tunnel walls were rough but well lighted. Water trickled down the rock. Kaya leaned out through the open door, ran her finger along the smooth, wet stone, and glanced up and down the tunnel. Ahead of them, the passageway was sealed off—this was some kind of construction site. A temporary wall had been built with a door in the center. Kaya heard movement on the other side, the hum of cruisers drifting past in either direction. "This is one of those hidden tunnels?" she asked Rian.

He nodded and pointed at the control panel. "There are so many of them. It's amazing. I thought I knew all the hidden routes in Ridge, but these passageways are everywhere."

"Where exactly are we now?" Kaya asked. Rian explained

that they were on the northern edge of the city. "Can you get us closer to Government Square?"

"Not without getting noticed," he said. "There are other underground routes, but we'd have to travel an open tunnel to reach them, and I don't think Dave is going to slip by without someone alerting the Erasers. We'd be surrounded in minutes."

"What if we leave the ship and drift?" Hanna suggested. "I have that new gravity suit, and Rian brought yours, Kaya."

Would that work? Maybe. They could take turns carrying the third person along. Kaya had tried a tandem drift with Rian once before, though, and it had drained her suit's power. Would they make it all the way to Government Square? Not to mention that the whole idea was to cross the city without the Erasers noticing them. Drifting across Ridge with one of them dangling wasn't exactly subtle.

Rian grabbed his pack, reached inside, and pulled out a tightly rolled bundle. He tossed it to her underhand. "I should have given this back to you earlier, Kaya. You two go."

"No," Kaya replied, "we're not splitting up."

"Yes, we are," he said. "There's only enough gear for two of us. You're the one who has been to the surface. Your mom and dad, everything you've seen and done . . . you're the one who needs to talk to them, Kaya. You're the one who needs to stop this vote."

She started to protest. But Rian was right, and the mention of her parents filled her with unexpected strength. The last tendrils of sleep pulled back. Her father had faith in her. Her mom had died trying to find a way to bring Atlantis and the surface world together. She'd died on a quest for peace. And now Kaya had to complete the work her mother had started. So what if she was young? This was her job to finish.

"Okay," she said at last. "We'll go."

Rian said nothing at first, but he was definitely looking at her in a funny way. She wiped her mouth with the back of her hand—nothing there. Subtly, she ran her tongue over her teeth, feeling for stray seaweed bits. Rian's eyes were larger than she remembered, and they matched his hair, though they were slightly bluer. He pulled some kind of necklace over his head. A green crystal hung from the chain, and Rian reached out and hung it around her neck. Then he looked at the floor and added, "It's for good luck."

Kaya didn't know what to say to Rian, or how to say it—and she didn't know he was into crystals, either. But she needed luck. They were only an arm's length apart, yet it could have been a hundred miles. She felt a hand pressing against her back. Hanna was pushing her forward, and she and Rian quickly hugged. Awkwardly at first, then even more awkwardly. If there were such a thing as an awkwardometer, it would have measured an eleven out of ten.

Maybe a twenty.

Then Hanna rescued her, pulling on the back of Kaya's shirt. She was laughing, which was annoying, and Rian's face was red.

"What are you going to do?" Hanna asked Rian.

He coughed, tightened his expression, wrinkled his fore-head in concentration. The awkwardometer was still at nine, easy. "Create a distraction, maybe, so no one notices you two?" he suggested. "I'll figure it out."

Hanna was already gearing up. She had her ankle straps all wrong, though, so Rian fixed them for her. Then she reached into her bag and removed the shirt she'd been wearing at the start of this adventure. She held it by the shoulders, gazed wistfully at the illustration on the front, and then suddenly tore it along one of the seams with two powerful tugs. This left her with a single long piece of fabric, which she wrapped around the bottom half of her face, below her nose. The disguise wasn't perfect, but combined with the hood and the goggles, it would at least increase their chances of sneaking across the city unnoticed.

"By the way, Mr. Navigator," Hanna said, turning to Rian, "where are we going?"

Hurriedly, Rian checked the maps stored in the ship's memory. "Straight through that door, then turn right, toward the city center. Follow that tunnel, and you should pop out into the fifth quarter in a few minutes. From there, it should be smooth drifting."

"And you?"

"Me? I'll meet you there eventually."

Kaya squinted at him. "Promise me you're not going to do anything crazy?"

"I promise nothing," he replied with a smirk.

The three of them jumped out of Dave and made their way to the front of the ship. Kaya was about to give Hanna a quick lesson on how to operate the suit when the girl from the surface crouched on the stone floor of the tunnel like some human-size spider. Hanna pushed off with her hands and feet, launching herself up and forward. Kaya tried to warn her to slow down, but Hanna crashed into the flimsy door. Kaya rushed over to her, worried she was injured, but Hanna was elated. "I just flew!"

"I know, but listen—"

"I mean, I flew!"

"Drifted," Rian called out.

"What's the difference?" Hanna called back.

Kaya wasn't sure, and she was eager to move on. "Never mind," she said. "Good luck, Rian!" she yelled, and then she pushed through the door and into the much-larger tunnel. Cruisers zipped past in both directions, racing to and from the city. "Ready, Hanna? Follow me."

Kaya pushed off and stayed close to the wall, a safe distance from the speeding vehicles. As the tunnel turned, she heard a grinding noise. Behind them, the spinning tip of the drillship was powering right through the wall and into the tunnel. Cruisers swerved left and right, up and down, barely avoiding a massive crash, and Rian steered Dave straight into the chaos.

Perfect, she thought. Nice and subtle.

Hanna grabbed her arm, yanking her forward, and the two of them cruised low, below the drifting vehicles. Hanna had worn her goggles, which was smart, since they were moving fast and the air was dustier than expected. Kaya spat some rock dirt off her lips. A tiny bug flew into her eye, so she pulled on her goggles as well.

The tunnel did lead to the fifth quarter, as Rian had said,

and Kaya felt a wave of relief roll through her as they soared out of the passageway and into open space. She dialed up her drive and coasted higher, above the waterways and ferries, the crowded streets and towers. Hanna followed. Part of Kaya wanted to reach back and hold Hanna's hand, to guide her, but her friend wasn't one to be led. Hanna cruised ahead as they approached a cluster of the powerful metal columns that helped support the cave ceilings. There was something joyful in the way Hanna drifted, looping and winding between those beams. Something playful that reminded Kaya of how utterly fantastic her world really was—and how Atlantis needed to be protected.

Yet the sunstruck surface was so beautiful, too. The stars at night. The moonlight. Even the trees—the way their leaves danced in the breeze. The people she'd met were wonderful. Or most of them, anyway. Lewis's mother was strong and caring at once. His little brother was hilarious. She respected Roberts, too, even if he and Kaya had often balanced on the edge of an argument. She shivered at the thought of Susan Silver, though.

No, the Sun People weren't all perfect.

But neither were the Atlanteans.

The lights in the cave walls overhead were like the stars in their night sky, only brighter. The crystal and glass embedded in the city's buildings sparkled.

She needed to protect Atlantis. Absolutely. But she didn't want the Sun People to be harmed.

Kaya had to bring the two worlds together.

And soon.

At the edge of Government Square, the streets and water-ways were more crowded than she'd ever seen them. All of Ridge City seemed to be packing into the area in anticipation of the vote. She reached a hand to her earpiece and tuned into the soundscape, moved through the channels. Nearly every single station was talking about the Sun People, the approaching vote, the threat of invasion.

Kaya pointed to a break in the crowd ahead, and she and Hanna cruised to the ground. Hanna landed deftly on her feet, and they hurried ahead. "What are we doing?" Hanna asked.

"We'll walk the last few blocks," Kaya explained. "I'm afraid the Erasers will stop us if we make a scene."

"You mean like that?" Hanna asked, pointing toward Capitol Tower.

High above the city, a swarm of drifting figures was chasing a lone individual through the air. She couldn't be sure, but Kaya was pretty certain she recognized the suit. No one else ever wore that putrid shade of brownish green. Arms tucked against his sides, Lewis was speeding toward Capitol Tower like a human torpedo.

16

HOW TO SAVE A WORLD

SAVING the world was so much harder than Lewis had expected! And so dramatic. You couldn't just press a button and call it a victory. Nope, you had to perform seriously brave acts, so now he was plummeting straight for the fifteenth floor. The wind ripped through his hair. Fortunately, the sickness in his stomach had been replaced by a warm, pleasant feeling. He was having . . . *fun*. Did this mean he was actually courageous? He still wasn't certain, and that probably wasn't a good sign. But this wasn't his main concern.

The Erasers were right behind him.

During the fall from Esmerelda, he'd grabbed one of the fish—he wasn't sure why. Lewis held on to the cod, reached down with his free hand to the dial at his waist, waited until he was about the length of a basketball court away from the top of the tower, and then turned on his drive.

He'd been hoping the change would be gentle. But when the suit switched on, his whole body, inside and out, felt like it had been given a massive, violent shake.

Immediately, he stopped and hovered in the air.

A half dozen Erasers were speeding toward him.

He braced himself. Five of them zoomed past and swerved around him. One reached out and clipped his outstretched arm, sending Lewis spinning like a top. But he was still free—not one of them grabbed him successfully. The top of Capitol Tower was close. He cranked up the thrusters in his gloves. He flew faster and faster, up and onto a wide balcony that wrapped around the top floor. Lewis shut down the suit and landed—a little too hard. Pain shot up through the heels of his bare feet. But it was definitely nice to be standing on solid ground again.

Lewis peered into the building through a tall window. A dozen or so people were sitting around a huge table. They were old, and they all wore robes. That meant that he'd found either the big important war meeting or the waiting room for a spa. Half the people had their backs turned in his direction, and he couldn't see the whole room, but he managed to pick out Demos, the devious old dude with the long, pointed chin. The leader of the Erasers, Demos was the one who had locked Lewis, his dad, and Hanna in that underwater prison. He'd lied to them, too, and ordered his agents to blast them out of the water after Lewis had made a deal with him.

Directly behind Demos stood Lewis's other Atlantean nemesis, Weed Chin. The Eraser had what looked like a small patch of seaweed growing on his face. Somehow, like Finkleman, he'd survived the battle outside the factory. Weirdly, this was a relief. Lewis wasn't exactly happy to see the heartless brute right there in the room, but he was glad Weed Chin was alive. They were enemies, but that didn't mean Lewis wanted him crushed in the deep sea.

At first, none of them noticed Lewis. They were all staring toward the left side of the room. An image was projected on one of the walls. It looked like a digital presentation, complete with bullet points and a bar chart. Lewis had made a few of these for school, and his mom was always making them for work. But who was doing a slideshow in Atlantis?

The view changed. A map of what looked like the Caribbean appeared. Or maybe it was Australia. Lewis needed to pay better attention in geography. One of the robed people stood and slammed her hand down on the table. Demos rose to his feet and started pointing at her.

There was a noise behind him—agents landing on the balcony.

Lewis turned. Five Erasers were heading toward him.

Several more were drifting down to join them.

He was still holding the fish. He raised it menacingly.

None of the agents appeared too frightened by the cod.

Lewis spun around and knocked on a tall glass door between the windows. Someone must have whistled; the door slid open.

Immediately, Demos pointed a long, crooked finger at Lewis. "That's one of the invaders!" he shouted.

Lewis glanced behind him. The swarm of Erasers was steps away.

"Grab him!" Demos yelled.

This was not part of Lewis's plan. In truth, he didn't really have a plan. Generally, he'd been hoping the robed people would invite him inside and listen to him, maybe offer him some snacks while he told his side of the story. He did not want to be grabbed. Or thrown back into prison.

Weed Chin raised a menacing flute in Lewis's direction.

The agents on the balcony were right behind him.

Panicked, Lewis tossed the fish at Weed Chin.

The creature flipped head over tail as it soared through the air.

The confused Eraser dropped his weapon and caught the cod with both hands. Forget stench or even flight—if Lewis had a superpower, it would be confusion, and this time, he'd struck with all his might. Perplexed, Weed Chin stared at the fish. No one moved, and Lewis dashed into the room, switched on his gravity drive, and pushed off the floor. His momentum carried him forward. Someone called his name. The voice was familiar, too. But there was no time to look: Lewis pounced on the table and soared right up over the gleaming bald head of Demos. He eyed a doorway in front of him, planted his foot on the back of an awestruck Eraser, pushed off hard, then grabbed both sides of the door frame and pulled himself through.

He crashed into the opposite wall of the hallway.

His left foot tingled and turned numb. A shot from a deadly flute, he guessed.

The hall was lined with doors. Drifting fast, he pushed through one to his right and floated up a stairwell. He heard footsteps behind him. Crashing. People shouting, too.

The stairs stopped one flight up.

He slid open another door and pushed out onto the roof of Capitol Tower.

Switching off the drive, he ran, limping on his numb foot, to the edge of the roof. The air was thick and hot. A dense cloud hovered just below the ceiling of the enormous cave. He might be able to drift up there and hide in the mist. But then what?

His attempt to join the meeting had failed terribly. But he'd done one thing right, at least—Esmerelda was here in the city. Maybe he could use the ship to stop the vote.

Unfortunately, the ship was nowhere to be seen.

Behind him, the Erasers burst through the doorway.

At the head of the pack, Weed Chin aimed his flute.

Lewis leaped backward off the roof.

His stomach did cartwheels.

The ground raced toward him. He flipped, dropping headfirst.

The muddled mass of Atlanteans packed into the square below was getting closer and closer with every fraction of a second. The windows were flying past. Lewis switched on the gravity drive again, ready for another stomach-clenching stop.

But he kept falling.

Faster and faster.

The ground was close.

Too close.

He could see the faces of the people on the street. They stared up at him, wide-eyed with horror. After everything he'd been through, he was going to end up as a pancake on an

Atlantean sidewalk. And he didn't even like pancakes! Sure, he tolerated them occasionally if they had chocolate chips, but he was more of a waffle kid.

Frantically, he turned the dial on his drive back and forth. Then he smashed the thing with his fist so hard it was like punching himself in the gut. The world stopped moving. A few meters off the ground, he swerved, and then he was soaring again, cruising over the heads of the Atlanteans.

Behind him, the Erasers were dropping from Capitol Tower. There was still no sign of Esmerelda and the triplets anywhere.

Lewis had to hide. Aiming for the far side of the square, hoping to disappear down an alley or crowded street, he swooped toward the ground. Someone was calling his name. Not the voice from the meeting, though. This time it was two people.

A wonderfully familiar pair—Kaya and Hanna.

"Drop!" Hanna yelled, pointing above him. "They're coming!"

He powered down the drive, and Hanna reached up, grabbed him by the wrist. The crowd pressed in all around them as the three of them hunched down, everyone moving toward Capitol Tower. His foot still tingled as if it were asleep.

"You made it!" Lewis said.

"Keep moving," Kaya urged him.

They pushed him through the crowd, crouching low. He limped along as fast as he could.

Hanna looked at him and winced. "Why do you smell like fish?"

What about his injury? Did neither of them notice his limp? Apparently not. "Did you find my dad?"

"Yes. Long story, little time," Kaya said, glancing back over her shoulder. "We need to find a way inside Capitol Tower."

"And soon," Hanna added.

They kept walking, but Lewis stopped. "Where is he? Where's my dad?"

Hanna swung around and grabbed him by both shoulders. She leaned in so close that their foreheads were almost touching. Her breath was warm and smelled strange, almost like onions, which didn't make any sense at all, since he hadn't seen any root vegetables in Atlantis. "Don't worry," she said. "He's good. He was up and moving around and talking way, way too much."

Lewis couldn't help smiling. "Is he in Evenor?"

Looking back over her shoulder, Kaya pointed to a trio of Erasers drifting over the crowd. Other agents were on the ground, shoving through the crowd, ripping off people's headgear to see if they were Sun People in disguise. She grabbed Lewis's arm above the elbow and pulled him forward. This time, he didn't resist, and the three of them started moving again. "We don't know where he is right now," Kaya answered. "We left him in Evenor to look for you."

That was unfortunate, but at least he was okay.

Lewis caught Hanna eyeing his gravity gear. Was she wondering again about where he'd gotten the gold? Did she suspect him of making a deal with Silver? He needed a chance to explain the whole thing to her without Kaya around. But this wasn't the time.

"Look!" someone shouted.

Another Atlantean cried, "They're attacking!"

Near Capitol Tower, Esmerelda was flying in ever-shrinking circles. The electronic skin was malfunctioning. Light played across the surface, flashing and glimmering. The ship drifted downward gradually before crashing to the ground in front of the government building, skidding and screeching to a halt—Lewis could hear the glass grinding against the stone.

Kaya stopped. "Who is driving the ship, Lewis?" she asked.

"Lewis?" Hanna pressed.

He would've appreciated some time to explain this decision, too. They really weren't going to like his answer. "I don't know how to drive," he reminded them, "and I didn't have any other options."

"Who is piloting the warship?" Hanna demanded, her voice stern.

"The triplets," he admitted. "Rass turned me in again, but Argon is still on our side. Fenitia's a pretty good driver. She used to pilot a tour submarine in Evenor. Apparently, she does have a tendency to get in accidents, though."

Neither of his friends replied. He counted that as a victory.

The three of them weaved through the Atlanteans at a near sprint. Jolts of pain shot up through Lewis's foot, but it was getting slightly better. If only he'd been wearing his Jordans. They might have protected him.

A big-eared man bumped into him, then stared in wonder as he looked Lewis in the face.

Lewis glanced back over his shoulder. Two Erasers were

still hovering above the crowd. Others were drifting over to the crashed warship or pushing through the people on the ground. The Atlanteans all around them were shouting and yelling. Lewis heard mutterings about Sun People, the High Council, invasions, war.

They ran faster. Up ahead, a shallow waterway crossed in front of Capitol Tower like a castle moat. The crowd pressed right up to the water's edge but no farther. On the other side, in front of the building, a half dozen guards holding sonic blasters stood watching. These folks actually wore uniforms. Yellow ones, with little patches on the sleeves. Several more of the guards surrounded the crashed warship. Esmerelda's doors were still closed—the triplets were probably too frightened to step outside. Either that or they were deep into another fish-slap fight.

Gathering his breath, Lewis pointed to the uniformed guards. "Who are they?"

"Government security," Kaya explained.

"Not Erasers?"

"Not Erasers."

Someone tugged at Wally, and Lewis swung around to face a woman with very short, very straight white hair. She was looking past, not at him. Her lips were thin, her eyes even larger than those of the standard Atlantean. The jowls below her jaw quivered when she spoke. "Out of my way," she said. "I'm a reporter, and the announcement is due any moment."

Bowing his head, Lewis apologized, then looked back across the waterway at the front of Capitol Tower. Two of the guards in yellow moved to stand on either side of a raised podium in front of the building. "What announcement?" he asked.

"They moved the vote forward," the reporter explained. She pushed ahead until she was right at the edge of the moat. "New developments, apparently." She nodded to the podium, where a pack of ten Atlanteans now gathered after hurrying over from the crash site, holding what looked like microphones. "All of Atlantis will be listening," she continued, "and I'm supposed to be up there with the other reporters, so if you don't mind—"

The woman turned silent as Hanna reached back and grabbed Lewis by the wrist.

The Atlantean's already-large eyes turned impossibly wide as she studied Hanna. Then she looked Lewis over as if she were seeing him for the first time. He wished he still had the wig. Awkwardly, he smiled. The woman jerked back.

Then Hanna totally stole his spotlight. She had been using the hood of her suit to cover her head and an old concert T-shirt to mask part of her face, and now she pulled them both off, and removed her goggles, too. She stood up to her full height. With her dark skin, long limbs, and short dark hair, his friend looked nothing like an Atlantean, and she towered over the reporter. Her stance was regal, powerful—the posture of someone you'd bow before—and Lewis found it really annoying. He stood on his toes, trying to close the gap.

When the reporter tried to speak, she stumbled on her words. "You're . . . I didn't . . . you don't . . ."

Hanna smiled. "We're done with secrets, right? This is

me. I'm not covering myself up or hiding what I look like anymore. If our worlds are going to mix, Atlantis is going to have to get used to the human variety show." She pointed toward the surface. "Up there, we come in all different colors, sizes, and shapes."

What in the name of Atlantis was Hanna talking about? "Not *all* shapes," Lewis said, correcting his friend. "No one's triangular, for example. Or no humans, anyway. Aliens? Maybe. We haven't found any smart ones, though. Not yet. But if we did, and if they were shaped like triangles, they'd probably have to live on a planet with lots of moving sidewalks and elevators, because it would be really hard to walk or climb stairs if you were that shape."

He'd lost her—the woman was studying Hanna again, and Kaya, too. "You're the daughter of Heron!" the woman said. "Your friends here don't look like invaders. They look like . . . children."

"That's because we are kids," Lewis replied.

"I'm more of a young adult," Hanna insisted.

"And we're explorers, not invaders. I am pretty brave, though," Lewis added. He leaned in. "I literally just learned that, like, five minutes ago. There were signs, you know? But now it's official. You can all me Steelheart if you want."

The reporter shook her head, puzzled. "I don't understand. The Sun People came here to steal our technology in preparation for war. That's an invasion."

"No," Kaya said. "This is all a misunderstanding."

"A big, stinking, hairy mess," Lewis added.

"Hairy?" the reporter replied.

"Never mind that," Hanna said. She pointed up at the tower. "This is all wrong. We're kids. His father, the other supposed invader, is no soldier, either. He's a scientist."

"And they didn't steal our technology," Kaya noted.

Lewis pointed back toward Esmerelda. "The warship is right there."

"Exactly! We returned it," Hanna noted. Then she glared at Lewis. "We are not stealing anything. Right, Lewis?"

He paused. The suit felt suddenly heavy. Tight, too. Hanna's stare was like some kind of emotional laser, a powerful beam that filled him with sickening guilt. "Right," he muttered.

"That's the stolen warship?" the reporter asked. "Are you certain?"

"Yes," Kaya said. "We're certain."

"And you're the girl, Kaya! Daughter of Heron, the traitor—"

"My father is *not* a traitor," Kaya snapped, her voice strong. "He's a hero."

The reporter started patting her chest, searching frantically for something. From the folds of her coat, she pulled out what looked like a microphone and what Lewis guessed was some kind of handheld transmitter. She tapped the top, then spoke in a dramatic tone. "This is Glandor Thrall, reporting live from Government Square, where I've just met two of the supposed invaders. Their names are . . ." Her eyebrows rose expectantly as she held the microphone out in front of Hanna. Deftly, Lewis moved it toward him, and the woman whispered, "All of Atlantis is listening, young man. Say your name."

He'd always liked the name Steve. Antonio was a good one, too, and he was planning to call himself Troy in his memoir. This would be a perfect time to switch. But no—his father might be listening. Lewis wanted to make him proud.

He cleared his throat. He didn't want his voice to crack.

Then the ground shook. Alarmed, Hanna and Kaya both stared down.

"What is that?" Hanna asked. "An earthquake?"

"I hope not," Kaya answered. She turned to Thrall, then grabbed Lewis by the wrist. "You can do your interview later. We need to go."

A footbridge stretched over the moat toward the entrance of Capitol Tower, but a group of guards stood at the near end, blocking people from crossing.

"I don't think we're going that way," Hanna noted.

Kaya jumped into the moat. "Follow me," she called back.

Hanna nudged him, and Lewis leaped into the chest-deep water. Thrall stayed right behind them, narrating their movements, reporting live. He'd missed his chance to introduce himself to Atlantis, yes, but this livestream wasn't so bad. Lewis felt like he was a star athlete with his very own play-by-play announcer.

The ground shook again.

The water in the moat pulsed.

He really, really hoped it wasn't an earthquake.

Someone shouted, "It's the Sun People!"

Thrall continued the play-by-play, detailing their movements for her listeners.

The ground was vibrating now, and Lewis watched as two Erasers squeezed through the throng and leaned over the moat. Both aimed their sonic blasters. A third Eraser—a burly woman with a wide, crooked jaw—pointed what looked like a miniature trumpet directly at him.

"STOP!" the woman roared.

Lewis held up his hands.

Hanna was at his side now, but Kaya had already climbed out of the water and up onto the other side.

Thrall kept rolling with her play-by-play.

"Let them go!" someone shouted.

The lead Eraser extended both her arms, holding back the other agents. Realizing, Lewis guessed, that blasting them in front of all those people wouldn't be very popular. Once again, the crowd was on his side.

"They aren't invaders! Leave them alone!" another Atlantean yelled.

"They're just kids!" someone else shouted.

Suddenly, the ground began to buckle. Several people stumbled into the moat. The burly Eraser lost her balance and splashed backward into the water.

Hanna pointed at a spot ahead of them in the moat, near the footbridge.

Something was glimmering in the water. A narrow metallic cone was breaking through the bottom of the moat, sparkling and spinning, growing larger as it rose higher and higher.

Hanna leaned back slightly. "Dave?"

Dave? Who was Dave? Lewis was confused, but Hanna looked fully stunned. And Kaya? She was smiling.

The spinning tip of the strange cone popped up out of the water, and behind it was . . . some kind of vehicle. The current rushed toward it faster and faster. The vehicle had cracked through the moat, and now the water level was dropping fast. Already, it was down below Lewis's waist. "What is that thing?" he asked.

"A drillship," Hanna answered.

Sure. Was that supposed to be obvious? "Who's driving?" Lewis asked.

With a smile, Kaya replied, "Rian."

"The kid from Evenor? What's he doing here?"

"Providing us with a needed diversion," Kaya said. She reached down to help them. "Let's use it."

Lewis grabbed her hand, and she yanked him up out of the moat with ease. Behind him, the drillship fully breached the floor of the moat, launched forward, then crashed down again, soaking everyone nearby.

A half dozen Atlanteans jumped into the water and formed a wall blocking the Erasers from Lewis and his friends. A thick-necked agent tried to drift over them, but someone leaped up, grabbed the Eraser by the ankle, and yanked him down.

The door of the ship slid open. Rian sprang out. He darted up onto the opposite bank of the moat and called across to them, "What are you waiting for? Go!"

Two of the yellow-uniformed guards dashed across the footbridge, heading straight for Rian. Lewis would have to thank Rian and this Dave dude at some point.

"Rian!" Kaya yelled. "Watch out!"

Her friend crouched and disappeared into the crowd as the girls raced ahead. Lewis followed Kaya and Hanna toward the entrance to Capitol Tower.

The crowd was still watching him. Hanna, too. But mostly Lewis. The Atlanteans were more interested in the Sun People than Rian and his drillship.

As Thrall continued her breathless narration, Lewis turned to his fans. He pumped his fist high in the air. "FOR ATLANTIS!" he yelled.

The Atlanteans roared their approval.

"You're ridiculous," Hanna called back to him.

But she smiled briefly, too—for the first time since they'd been reunited.

The first smile since he'd paid for the suits with Silver's money.

Hopefully, she wouldn't stay mad at him forever.

Two security guards stood on either side of the podium. Others lined up around the entrance to Capitol Tower or clustered around the warship. Esmerelda was twenty or thirty paces away, its door still closed. The triplets, Lewis guessed, were hiding inside.

A yellow-uniformed guard raised her sonic rifle as Kaya approached. "Stay where you are," she warned.

Kaya stopped. Hanna and Lewis stood on either side of

her. "We need to get inside," Kaya said. "We need to talk to the High Council."

Before the guard could reply, the tall doors swung open slowly. Two more Atlanteans in yellow uniforms emerged from the building. Behind them walked a man with a thick brown beard, an embarrassing ponytail, and one of the ugliest Hawaiian shirts Lewis had ever seen.

Hanna was speechless. Kaya gasped. Lewis? He was just plain confused.

What was Reinhold doing in Atlantis?

17
CONSPIRACIES AND LIES

THE scientist smiled awkwardly at Lewis. Reinhold scratched at his beard. His plump fingers were free of cheese puff dust, but scattered with green flecks. There were traces of green and orange in his mustache, too—spicy kelp chips, Lewis guessed. Of course *he'd* gotten to try them, while Lewis himself had been denied the pleasure. More importantly, what was his father's best friend doing in Capitol Tower? How had he made it to Atlantis in the first place?

Reinhold moved toward them as if he were looking for a hug or a high-five. Hanna held out her hand like a traffic cop. The scientist stopped. He looked guilty. Of what, though?

Another group was walking out through the glass doors, and for a second, Lewis hoped it was his mother and Roberts, that they'd come all this way to rescue him. Maybe the president had loaned the three of them a submarine and painted it with polka dots, as he'd imagined. But they would've said something when he'd drifted through the conference room.

His mom wasn't in Atlantis. Neither was Roberts.

Triumphantly, Susan Silver strode out of the building.

"Oh no," Hanna groaned.

"Not her," Kaya added.

"Children!" Silver exclaimed, spreading her arms wide, "so glad you could join us!" Lewis stared at Silver, then back at Reinhold. "This time I do know what you're thinking, young man," she said. "Dr. Reinhold Bae here works for me."

"Have you been working for her this whole time?" Hanna asked.

The scientist shrugged. "A little consulting on the side, feeding her vital information, keeping her updated on your father's findings. She realized that if Atlantis really had figured out how to control ocean waves without so much as shifting the seafloor, they must have fabulous technology. Of course, we didn't know *how* amazing until you returned and told us during those wonderful dinners about everything you'd seen."

Lewis felt like he'd been dropkicked in the stomach.

"They trusted you," Kaya said. "His family trusted you."

Right! And they'd fed him, too, and Reinhold had been a terrible and gluttonous guest. Most nights, the scientist had served himself first. He had always grabbed the best pieces of chicken, the broccoli that was roasted perfectly. Lewis was left with the charred bits.

"How could you?" Lewis asked. "You said you were watching out for my dad!"

The broccoli-hogging chicken thief waved off Lewis's

outrage. "Your dad is a genius, Lewis, but he's completely impractical. He could have made a deal with Sunshine Corporation himself if he'd had the foresight."

Quietly, Lewis replied, "You said you were his friend."

"I am his friend!"

"Yeah, right," Hanna snapped. She pointed her finger at Reinhold's chest, as if she were going to poke him in the sternum. "Why go behind our backs? Why lie to the professor?"

"Oh, about fifty million reasons."

"Give me one," Lewis said.

"What?"

Hanna lowered her voice to a whisper. "He doesn't really have fifty million reasons. He means fifty million dollars."

Oh. Right. Lewis felt supernaturally stupid.

Hanna pointed to Silver. "How did you find us?"

"The electronic skin has embedded tracking devices. That part was simple. But the journey? So boring! Thankfully we were able to make up some time via helicopter, and my submarines are surprisingly fast. Now we're all here! That Evenor place was fascinating."

"Delicious snacks here in Atlantis, too," Reinhold added. He held up his fingers and wiggled them. "Spicy kelp chips! Who knew?"

Not Lewis—he still hadn't been given a chance to try them, and it didn't seem like the right time to ask Reinhold if he had extras.

Hanna spun around to face Kaya. "The cave! When we spotted all those cruisers across the cave above Evenor, that had to be them arriving."

Kaya glared at Silver. "I'm surprised the Erasers didn't lock you in prison," she said.

The billionaire waved her hands in the air dismissively. "At first, I thought they'd present a problem. My plan was to grab as much technology as we could find, then hurry back home and leave this little attacking-the-surface problem to you, but they met us immediately upon arrival. A lesser person would have seen this as a failure, but I recognized an opportunity! I instructed them to take me to their leader, and they complied."

"She's very convincing," Reinhold noted. He motioned to the podium. "They'll be down to announce the details of our agreement any minute now. The High Council loved my slideshow. They were mesmerized."

"You did a slideshow in Atlantis?" Hanna asked.

"One of my best," he said. "Until you almost ruined it, Lewis, with your little chase across the table and up the stairs."

Before Lewis could answer, Silver made a small, excited sound. She clapped, then pointed to his new gravity gear. "Is that my suit?"

No. Not now. He'd momentarily forgotten about the deal.

"What's she talking about?" Kaya asked. She was blasting eye lasers at him. She glanced at the suit, then Silver, and a terrible sensation grew in Lewis's gut. This wasn't the taste of bravery, though. He felt weak, almost dizzy with guilt. How was he going to explain himself?

Maybe there was no point in trying.

Maybe he was just as despicable as Reinhold.

Sure, his dad's supposed friend was a traitor and a liar, as self-centered in his work as he was at the dinner table. But was

Lewis really any better? He'd paid for the suit, but it didn't belong to him. And it didn't belong to Susan Silver, either, even if he'd used her money.

The gravity gear belonged to Atlantis.

Lewis wanted to rip it all off and smash it to pieces.

His friends were watching him, waiting for him to explain.

He stammered, "Y-you don't understand. I wasn't—"

The billionaire reached forward and grabbed his wrist, inspecting one of the gloves. Her hands were cold and weirdly smooth. "We had our doubts about whether you'd come through," she began, "so Reinhold and I followed the three of you here to procure the technology ourselves. Yet you delivered, Lewis. How impressive!"

Kaya was watching him. "You really made a deal with her?" Kaya asked quietly.

"Yes, he did," Silver answered for him.

"That's not yours to trade," Kaya said. "That belongs to Atlantis."

Lewis backed away. This wasn't fair! He hadn't given the woman anything yet. "I was thinking about doing it, but now . . ."

"But now what?" Kaya asked.

"Now I—"

"Don't listen to the little rat," Silver replied. "I have his letter right here."

The billionaire reached into her pocket and began unfolding a familiar piece of paper—his note to his mom. Lewis had scribbled out everything he could in that short letter. He'd crammed it with apologies. He'd packed it with pleas for forgiveness. And he'd explained in very clear words that he was going back to Atlantis not only to rescue his dad but to make them all wonderfully, fantastically rich.

As Silver read his note aloud, pausing at times to laugh at his "pedestrian" word choice and "utterly robotic" voice, Lewis felt like the layers of rock and miles of ocean above his head were falling directly on top of him. What would Kaya and Hanna think of him now? What would his dad say when he found out? And his mom—the fact that the letter was here in Silver's manicured hands meant that his mother hadn't even seen it. His mother and Roberts and Michael were probably terrified they'd lost him again or furious that he'd lied to them just to sneak off on another adventure. The presence of that letter meant he'd broken his mother's heart . . . again. And based on the way Kaya and Hanna were glaring at him, Lewis was pretty sure he'd lost a pair of friends, too.

He didn't want to save the world anymore.

He just wanted to go home.

Silver chuckled.

She shrugged, crumpled the paper, and tossed it to him. The balled-up note hit him in the chest. "Keep it," she said.

Everything Lewis had been thinking and feeling started gathering somewhere deep within him. His face shook. But if he cried, Silver would win. Well, she'd pretty much won already, but his tears would make it a devastating victory. She would probably laugh even harder. He clenched his teeth and held back the emotion on his own, with no help from the gnomes. You could never depend on imaginary friends when you really needed them. Lewis found his own strength instead.

He'd make this right.

Somehow, he'd make it right.

Silver rolled her eyes dramatically. "Are you about to *cry*?"

Surprisingly, Hanna jumped to his defense. "Leave him alone."

The billionaire shook her head. "Why are we fighting? We should be celebrating! We're about to change the world. We'll go far beyond gravity suits." She pointed to her ear and tapped her throat. "These translators you mentioned, for instance. They gave us each a set. Amazing! Atlantis has completely mastered natural language processing. Companies have spent billions trying to solve that problem!" She whirled around, looking out at the city. "There's so much here," she added, her tone turning dreamy. "I've been negotiating with the leader of the High Council, a charming gentleman named Demos, on a deal to license the rights to all Atlantean technology. When their attack is finished, I might be the world's first trillionaire! Me! Can you imagine that?"

"What do you mean, when their attack is finished?" Kaya asked.

Reinhold bit his lip.

"Have they voted?" Hanna pressed.

Silver exhaled heavily. "Well, that's the thing. Demos had made up his mind. The others on the council simply couldn't see his reasoning, so he had to take control. You should all thank me—he had a much larger war in mind, but I convinced him to take a more focused, precise approach. A splendid little war rather than some messy global confrontation." Her eyes widened, and she smiled. "Ah, here he is now."

The guards outside the building parted, clearing the way. The crowd gradually stopped cheering and chanting and started murmuring, questioning, wondering. Thrall had crawled up out of the waterway, and she was still speaking into her microphone, a solemn look on her face. The Erasers were still watching them, too, and Lewis noticed the two yellow-uniformed guards leading Rian over the footbridge. Lewis started toward Hanna, then stopped himself. Did she even want to be near him?

He didn't dare stand next to Kaya, either.

A dozen armed agents marched slowly through the doors. Weed Chin walked beside Demos, who had changed into a different robe—a silvery one embroidered with gold patterns around the collar and cuffs. His bald head gleamed, and his already-pointy chin looked even longer. His small mouth formed a barely noticeable smile, and he wore a thick, color-ful belt with a blaster holstered at his right hip. Reinhold and Silver began clapping. Weed Chin and the Erasers ordered the yellow-uniformed guards out of the way; Demos whispered something to Weed Chin, who pointed his weapon at them. The other Erasers copied him. The security guards quickly set their sonic blasters on the ground and backed away.

Reinhold nudged Lewis. "That's Demos," he said, his voice cheery. "Such a great guy. Really forward-thinking."

"We already know him," Hanna replied. "A little too well."

Demos glanced at Esmerelda and nodded. The warship's glass was clouded, so they couldn't see inside, but the vehicle was surrounded by Erasers. One of them whistled. Lewis recognized the familiar notes.

The door slid open.

A pale arm extended out, holding a fish by its tail.

Weed Chin fired his blaster. The cod dropped to the ground. Rass stepped into view, smiling awkwardly, and his siblings followed. "I'm on your side," Rass insisted. He pointed his thumb at Fenitia and Argon. "These two are despicable."

The Erasers herded the triplets toward Lewis, Hanna, and the others.

The crowd fell silent as Demos stepped up to the podium. The only voices were the murmurs of Thrall and the other reporters detailing the events for listeners all over Atlantis. A large black cruiser floated out of a garage at the base of the building. Lewis felt his heart beating faster. He didn't understand what was happening.

Demos looked out over the massive crowd, then spread his arms wide and began to speak. "Citizens of Atlantis," he announced. His voice boomed off the walls behind him, blasting out of speakers set all around Government Square. Thrall and the other reporters held out their microphones. "I will be brief," Demos continued. "This is a sad and solemn day. I have discovered that your trusted representatives on the High Council of Atlantis are traitors. They attempted to give away our precious technology to foreign invaders, endangering our world. But I stopped them. The conspiracy is real, and so is the invasion." He motioned to Esmerelda. "We have four of the invaders here among us now."

As Demos pointed toward their group, someone pushed Lewis from behind. An Eraser growled at him, shoving him and his friends toward Demos.

"Don't let the appearance of the two younger ones fool you, my fellow Atlanteans," Demos said, pointing directly at Lewis and Hanna. "They are uniquely skilled and highly trained warriors. They stole one of our most advanced warships and attempted to give it to their accomplices on the surface. Fortunately"—he nodded at Esmerelda again—"I retrieved the vehicle."

That wasn't even slightly true! Lewis started to protest, but one of the Erasers pressed a sonic pistol against his ribs. Lewis pretended to zip his lips. The Atlantean didn't understand. Did they not have zippers in Atlantis? "I'll be quiet," he whispered.

"Why's he calling us invaders, too, Susan?" Reinhold asked. He nodded at Lewis. "*You're* the invader."

"These other two," Demos continued, nodding at Silver and Reinhold, "tried to make a secret deal with my fellow High Council members to give Atlantean technology to the Sun People. Again, though, I stopped them." He let his shoulders rise and fall. "You're welcome, Atlantis."

Kaya shouted, "You're lying!" The reporter, Thrall, spun toward her.

"Must be a new wrinkle in the plan," Silver guessed quietly. "I doubt he'd actually turn on me, of all people."

"My dear citizens," Demos continued, "rest assured that our technology is secure and that these invaders will be locked away for a very, very long time."

Lewis stiffened. Was he really going back to that prison? And would Kaya and Hanna even want to be in a cell with him now?

The crowd reacted with a mix of cheers and boos. There were shouts about the Sun People and the threat of war. The reporters started hollering questions. Demos smiled, clearly enjoying the attention. He pointed to Thrall first. She adjusted her microphone. "Question from the *Atlantean Times*, sir?"

"Ah, one of my favorite soundscape programs. What is it, then?"

"If the High Council was packed with traitors," Thrall began, "who will govern in their place?"

Demos coughed, then adjusted his posture. He stood straighter, stronger. "I will."

"Until?"

"Until the future of Atlantis is secure, naturally."

Another voice boomed above the rest. "Warren Lando of the *New Atlantean*."

"Another wonderful program. I love that little tune you play at the start of each segment. Yes?"

"What was the outcome of the vote for war?"

Now Demos turned solemn and cold. He clasped his hands below his long chin. "An important question. Sadly, our fears have turned out to be all too real. The Sun People not only exist, as you see—they are more violent than we even imagined." He paused, letting his voice resound through the cave. "But we will not be intimidated!" he shouted. Scattered cheers followed.

Lewis was stunned. Were the Atlanteans actually buying this story? The part about him being a highly trained warrior was cool, but it was a lie. He wasn't Steelheart. If he were given a warrior name, it would be Faintor because of his tendency to pass out before a fight.

Demos raised his fist. "Atlantis is the greatest civilization the world has ever seen, and if the Sun People want war, we will give them war and take the surface for ourselves!"

18
ALL OF ATLANTIS

KAYA studied the madness exploding around her. This was an absolute disaster. Ridge City was in chaos. Half the crowd was shouting for war. The rest was yelling for peace. She tried to get Rian's attention, but he was busy escaping from a pair of Erasers. As she watched, he dropped to the ground and grabbed one of the men by the backs of his knees. He pulled both the man's legs forward, toppling him, then squirmed free and planted his foot right in the middle of his back. He darted between two reporters as the other guard struggled to grab him.

Someone grabbed Kaya's arm from behind—an Eraser. She spun free and backed away as Demos ordered his agents to hurry Kaya and the four Sun People inside. But Kaya wasn't going anywhere. She scanned the faces in the crowd. Stood up on her toes, trying to see into the distance. Lewis kept looking at her with those pleading, searching eyes.

What did he want her to say? That she forgave him?

She couldn't be bothered.

Not now.

Kaya had bigger problems to solve, and no small part of

her was hoping help would arrive. Hanna stood close to Lewis, protectively. Maybe Hanna would think of something. But where were her dad and Naxos? Even Rian had slipped away, out of sight.

Kaya touched the green crystal hanging from her neck. Any kind of luck would be welcome.

The reporters were all trying to slip inside Capitol Tower, but the Erasers formed a barrier, keeping them back. They shouted in frustration. Thrall's face reddened. "More secrets," she growled. "The last thing Atlantis needs is more secrets."

The woman was absolutely right, Kaya decided.

They needed to be open and honest.

With Atlantis, yes.

But also with the world above.

Kaya thought about what Thrall had said earlier, when she was trying to interview Lewis. What was it again? Right—that all of Atlantis would be listening.

She had an idea, a desperate plot that just might work.

The Erasers pushed Kaya and the Sun People toward the entrance to the tower. One of them practically ripped Kaya's backpack off and searched its contents. Another pushed her from the side. This was her chance. She pretended to stumble.

Grasped Thrall by the elbow.

Pulled her close.

"What are you—"

"Are you broadcasting live?" Kaya asked, her voice low but firm.

"Why?" Thrall whispered back.

Kaya nodded to the upper floors, then to the reporters being ushered away. "You're not getting in there," Kaya said, "but it looks like I am."

The woman needed no more explanation.

Hurriedly, Thrall adjusted a few dials and pressed her microphone and transmitter into Kaya's hands. Then, acting the part of the aggrieved Atlantean, Thrall pushed her away. "Get off me, you traitor!"

The one Lewis called Weed Chin stepped between them. "Leave her alone," the Eraser growled at Kaya. He nodded to the reporter. "By the way," he added quietly, "if you need an inside source on the daily life of a daring agent, I could—"

Weed Chin jerked back as Demos called to him. "Get them upstairs. Now. And have a few agents bring a pair of cruisers to the top floor. After we collect our friends on the High Council, we are going to embark on a little journey."

One Eraser tossed Kaya's pack to her, and another shoved her forward. She managed to keep her balance and hide the microphone and transmitter in her bag. Once inside the Tower, the four Sun People, Demos, and a half dozen of his agents rode the elevator to the top floor in silence. Lewis was still looking at her. He kept adjusting the chest harness of his gravity suit, as if it were making him uncomfortable now. She hoped he felt guilty. He couldn't just sell Atlantean technology, and especially not to an amoral shark like Susan Silver.

On the top floor, the self-proclaimed ruler of Atlantis strode out of the elevator and down the hall to a room overlooking the great city. The other eleven members of the High

Council of Atlantis sat around a long table. Not one of them rose. Not one of them spoke. And they all had odd steel collars around their necks.

A group of Erasers stood behind them, sonic weapons ready.

A younger, bearded councilor who reminded Kaya of her father wriggled in his seat. His jaw seemed to be locked, as if his teeth were cemented together. Kaya held her pack at her waist and stayed close to Lewis, using him as a shield, ignoring all his hopeful, pleading glances.

Carefully, Kaya edged the microphone out between her thumb and forefinger. The transmitter vibrated slightly; she hoped that meant it was active. If it was, then Atlantis was listening.

"What are we doing here?" Kaya asked.

"What happened to them?" Hanna added, nodding to the other councilors.

"Right, yes," Demos answered cheerily. "They were calling me all kinds of despicable names. The collars lock their jaws and mute their voices. Wonderful invention."

"I could use those at board meetings," Silver mused.

A white-haired woman glowered at their captor. Her eyes bulged. Kaya recognized her. The woman was one of the leaders of the High Council. Yet Demos laughed at her; his face was glowing with confidence. "Let me guess, Alexandra— you're thinking I'm not going to get away with this. Well, I already have. All of Atlantis thinks you're a traitor."

"I don't understand," Kaya said. "Did the High Council vote against the war?"

"Let her talk," Hanna pleaded.

"You really shouldn't mute a powerful woman," Silver added.

The woman, Alexandra, squirmed in her seat. She moved her chin in small circles, as if trying to break free of the steel collar. Finally, Demos sighed. "Oh, very well, let her speak," he said, "but only her."

An agent leaned in close to her collar and whistled.

"Of course we voted against the war!" Alexandra replied. "Now I can see for certain that our vote was the right one." She nodded at Lewis and Hanna. "These two clearly aren't soldiers, and whoever crashed that warship is obviously no fighter pilot."

"Exactly," Hanna said.

"This invasion was all a great lie from the start! When the reports came from Evenor about this one here"—she pointed to Lewis—"dancing in front of all those people . . . well, then we were certain."

The room was quiet for a second.

Even Lewis was silent.

Kaya thought she saw the hint of a smile on his face.

"This is a disaster, Demos!" Alexandra continued. "If you go ahead with this war, your son will have died in vain."

What was she talking about? Kaya turned to Demos. "Your son?"

"This is not about him," Demos growled, ignoring her.

"Of course it is!" Alexandra replied, her voice calm. "What happened to your son, and Kaya's mother, was a terrible tragedy."

The mention of her mother made Kaya feel instantly cold. A familiar pit formed in her stomach.

"No," Demos snapped. "It was an act of war, and our response was weak. They strike first, and we send harmless waves at their coasts? That's not a show of strength."

"I wouldn't call them harmless," Silver interrupted. "Many people died. The entire world economy changed. Corporations that weren't run by peerless thought leaders like myself were completely broken and—"

"Quiet!" Demos snapped. "Unless you'd like to feel the sting of a sonic blaster?"

The shark sneered and pressed her lips closed.

Kaya remained focused on Alexandra. "You mentioned my mother. You're talking about the mission."

"Your mother and Demos's son were both part of a failed diplomatic trip to the surface," the woman explained, her voice heavy with sadness. "I still regret letting them go—"

Demos slammed his hand on the table. "You regret it? You didn't lose your son!"

Alexandra closed her eyes and breathed in deeply. "As I was saying, Kaya, they were two of a dozen crewmembers who were chosen. Demos's son was a brilliant scientist specializing in the health of the oceans. Given their passion for the truth and your mother's curiosity about what the surface was really like, they were two of our best candidates. Then, tragically—"

"The Sun People killed them!" Demos cut in. "A clear and simple act of war!"

A dramatic cough to Kaya's left pulled their attention away from the two leaders. Reinhold took a hesitant step forward.

"If I may?" he asked. No one protested. He continued, "The deaths were more of a communication error than an act of war. Lewis, your father was right. That mysterious explosion off New York years ago? That was an Atlantean ship—the vessel you're talking about now, I presume. The navy tried to communicate with it but received no reply. No submarine we've ever built could even approach that speed, so the navy assumed it was a torpedo headed for the city. They had no choice but to destroy it before it struck land." He looked at Kaya, then Demos. "I'm sorry."

"We're all sorry," Silver added.

The woman sounded completely insincere, and this whole explanation was maddening. "My mom died because of a *communication* problem?" Kaya asked.

Silver shrugged. "World wars have started over even smaller misunderstandings, sweetheart," she said. "It's clear that both worlds are too blame, as your waves have cost us many, many lives, but I'm willing to look past these squabbles and move forward with our plans."

Demos didn't even acknowledge her. "Yes, Alexandra, I lost my son." He faced Kaya. "You, child, lost your mother. There is no excuse for what the Sun People did, and it's proof that they can't be trusted!"

Kaya swallowed. This was more than she was ready to hear. Or process. She adjusted the microphone, breathed through the pain and confusion.

"But you can trust me," Silver said to Demos.

"And me," Reinhold added. "You're going to love the islands we suggested."

"What islands?" Hanna asked. "What's happening in the islands?"

"We suggested a few spots to invade," Silver explained. Her voice became strangely sweet. "We still have a deal, right?"

Demos shook his head. "Do you really think I need you two?" he asked. "I'm now the ruler of Atlantis, the most technologically advanced civilization in human history. I don't need help from any Sun People. The two of you have served your purpose. As for you, Alexandra . . ." He nodded to Weed Chin, then pointed to the balcony, where a cruiser was gliding into place alongside the railing. "We'll put the Sun People back in their little submarines and send them home. Take the others to the Stone Barrens."

Alexandra slumped. "Demos, you wouldn't—"

"Of course I would! You've lorded over the High Council for more than a decade, Alexandra. Your time is up." He looked at each of the muted councilors in turn. "As for the rest of you, I gave you an opportunity to side with me, but you missed your chance. Don't worry, though—I'll call ahead and ensure that our finest prison cells are ready for you."

This was a perfect opportunity. Kaya had to bury her emotions . . . again. She had to keep him talking. "But these are elected members of the High Council," Kaya protested. "You can't just dump them in prison. They were chosen by the people of Atlantis."

"The people don't know what they want!" Demos snapped. "The High Council is finished. Don't you see? My Erasers don't need to operate in secret anymore. This is the new age of Atlantis, the one in which we will finally show the world our power. I can't have the members of our defunct government interfering. So, yes. Prison. For all of them."

"And our deal?" Silver asked.

"There is no deal!" Demos roared. "You've already told me what I needed to know. These islands you've described sound perfect for the new Atlantis, and for that advice, I thank you and grant you your freedom. But if you won't be quiet, I'll take back that gift and throw you in prison with the rest of them!"

Reinhold winced. Silver turned silent, and a change came over her. Not a look of shock, exactly, or even disappointment. Something deeper and more profound—a kind of darkness. She reached into her shoulder bag, removed a rectangular device, and began tapping on the surface.

Never mind Silver, though. Kaya had Demos to think about. She probably should have been frightened. He was planning to throw them all back in prison. The details of her mother's death weighed heavily on her, too, and she struggled to stifle the pain.

But Demos was talking.

Her scheme was working.

She wondered if her dad was out there somewhere, listening. Or her grandmother and Rian. That weak, pleading look was gone from Lewis's face. Hanna was staring at her, too, and there was urgency in both their eyes.

Encouragement.

Faith.

She had to keep pressing Demos. "What do you mean when you say we're going to show the world our power?"

Kaya asked. "Your warship factory was destroyed. How are we going to war with the surface? And why do you even want a war?"

Demos exhaled. He ran one of his fingers along the golden collar of his robe. "Many of our warships survived that incident, and we have additional factories throughout Atlantis, along with a wide range of gravity weapons that would cripple the primitive cities of the Sun People with ease. Atlantis could crush the surface, child. Now, you ask why? I don't want war. But it's necessary. Atlantis is in danger. The changes in the sea, the rate of collapse in our cities, our dwindling food supplies and growing population . . . I would say we have a few decades, a century at most."

"Until what?" Hanna asked.

"Until we cannot safely feed or house millions of Atlanteans," Demos responded. "The Sun People won't simply make room for us up there on their already-crowded surface."

"There's always Atlantarctica," Lewis mumbled. "It has penguins."

Kaya wanted to kick him.

Demos stopped. "What?"

"Ignore him," Hanna replied. "Go on."

Kaya adjusted the microphone in her hand. She was trying to think of what to say next, how to push him to detail more of his plan, when Reinhold interrupted.

"That was the focus of my presentation, Kaya," Reinhold explained. "The deal was that in exchange for the rights to sell your technology, we'd find you Atlanteans a nice place to invade and settle down. Ireland might work, but it's a little too damp and gray in the winter, so some place warm was our top choice. A tropical island would be a seamless fit, really."

Silver went on tapping at her device.

"You can't just *give* them an island," Hanna protested.

"No," Demos explained, "we plan to take these territories by force."

"That's the war you want?" Alexandra asked.

"A simple little war," Demos said with a shrug. "More of a targeted invasion."

"A classic land grab," Reinhold added.

"How do you know the citizens of Atlantis will support this?" Kaya asked. She thought of another line—one that was pure bait. "Atlanteans aren't fools."

Demos rolled his eyes. "Wrong! The people of Atlantis will stand behind my war because they are easily led. I have them all convinced that these children are dangerous invaders and that we are only acting out of self-defense."

The other members of the High Council were squirming in their seats. Their faces were twisted with anger and frustration. One of them tried to stand. An Eraser shoved him back down.

Demos had swallowed the bait. Kaya's ploy was working better than expected.

Lewis held up his hand, palm out. Don't ruin it now, Kaya thought.

Demos snarled at him. "What?"

"Well," Lewis said with a shrug, "you're pretty much in charge of Atlantis now, and you haven't even picked a title for yourself." He motioned to the muted High Council members.

"Since they're out of your way and this is your show, I feel like president isn't grand enough. Has Atlantis ever had an emperor before?"

Demos pulled at his long chin. "Not for a thousand years," he murmured.

The old fool was actually pondering the idea. Kaya had to stifle a smile.

"You could be Demos the First," Hanna said.

"You're going to need a throne, though," Lewis added, "and a staff with those pointy things at the end."

"A trident?" Hanna said.

"Exactly!" Lewis replied. "The emperor of Atlantis definitely needs a trident." He pointed to Demos's robe. "And while I like the fancy trim, you should probably get more colorful outfits, too."

Amazingly, the man was considering Lewis's advice. Demos faced Alexandra, as if he were waiting for her approval. He stood slightly taller, with his shoulders pressed back. "What do you think, old friend?" he asked. "Does Demos the First suit me?"

"The people aren't going to believe you," Alexandra snapped. "They've seen the supposedly stolen ship."

Casually, Demos waved a hand in the air. "A mild complication. I have additional plans."

One of the other Erasers whispered something to Weed Chin. The green-chinned agent scanned the room, and Kaya avoided his gaze, staying focused on Demos. She moved slightly closer to Lewis, hiding the microphone as Hanna asked, "What additional plans?"

"Our drillships have dug tunnels all around Evenor," Demos said. "The caverns are inlaid with explosives. One command from me, and that backwater city will collapse completely under water and stone."

"You're lying," Alexandra said.

"Why would you destroy Evenor?" Lewis asked.

"Fear is a great motivator," Demos replied. "Once the people learn that another one of their cities has collapsed, they'll support my plan to colonize the surface. It's all for their own good."

Another High Council member started to stand in protest, only to sit again as two agents raised their blasters. But Demos wasn't lying, Kaya realized. She and Rian and Hanna had seen one of those tunnels for themselves. Plus, Naxos had said he'd found the advanced drillships all around Evenor. Still, how could Demos think about destroying an entire city? And such a beautiful one, too, crowded with Atlanteans!

"Those drillships were supposed to be used for good," Alexandra exclaimed. She motioned to the silenced Council members. "We approved the funding because we thought they would be used for construction. We thought they'd be used to make Atlantis safer."

Demos sneered. "Yes, well, this isn't the first time I've misled you fools."

"You wouldn't destroy Evenor," Kaya said. "Not if you really cared about Atlantis."

His frustration was obvious as he replied. "Don't you understand? I'm doing all this for Atlantis. We need to begin moving to the surface. This will help convince the people. And all we'll lose is one little city! Don't misunderstand me—it will be a difficult decision. But true leaders make difficult choices."

Without looking up, Silver added, "That much I agree with."

"When the city is destroyed," Demos explained, "I can blame the Sun People for it."

"There are many ways to honor the memory of your son, Demos," Alexandra said, her voice laced with panic. "A violent invasion is not one of them."

"This is not about my son anymore, Alexandra," he replied. "Don't you see? I'm talking about a new age of Atlantis. No more hiding beneath the sea. No more sending waves to scare the Sun People away. No more worrying about our future as a civilization."

A small, hesitant cough came from Lewis. He'd been so quiet, and now his voice was flat, almost sad. "But . . . how could you? There are people in Evenor."

Demos raised his long chin. "All great acts require sacrifice," he pronounced.

The Eraser next to Weed Chin removed his earpiece and gave it to the lead agent, whose expression changed dramatically. He tugged at the clump of green hair on his jaw, then pulled at Demos's robe. "Sir?"

Demos ignored his trusted agent.

"We should have barred you from the council years ago," Alexandra said. "I should've known you were trouble when you started your little group of enforcers. Your so-called Erasers."

"Yes, you should have! But you didn't. And now you're

sitting there, about to go to prison for the rest of your life, and I am Demos the First, supreme ruler of Atlantis."

"And part of the Caribbean," Reinhold added.

"The people of Atlantis aren't brainless fish, Demos," Alexandra cut in. "They'll never fall for your treachery."

Urgently, Weed Chin tried again to interrupt. "Sir? I think you—"

"Quiet!" Demos yelled. The self-appointed emperor swept his arm wide in the direction of the city below. "They'll never fall for my treachery, Alexandra? They already have! Don't you see? Our fellow Atlanteans *are* brainless fish. They're mindless urchins, all of them! They will do what I say, because the High Council is finished. I am the ruler of Atlantis now, and as my first official act—"

"Sir!" Weed Chin shouted.

"What?" Demos snapped.

Weed Chin gulped visibly. "Sir, everyone's listening."

"I know that," he said. "That's why we muted them. So they wouldn't interrupt me. And I will mute you, too, if you continue."

"No, I mean, everyone." His lieutenant pointed out at the city. "This entire conversation, everything you've just said, is being broadcast all over Atlantis."

His eyes bright with urgency, Demos looked at each of them in turn, searching for the one who'd tricked him. Kaya tried really hard not to smile. When his stare landed on her, though, she could see that he knew. His glare became venomous. His whole body tensed. His jaw quivered. She could almost feel Weed Chin eyeing her, too. And maybe she shouldn't have taunted Demos. Maybe she should have kept quiet. But as Kaya remembered everything he'd done to her and her family and friends, how he'd put all of Atlantis in danger because of his own twisted version of reality, she wanted him to know who had outsmarted him. Who'd beaten him.

She held up the microphone and transmitter.

"You're finished, Emperor."

19

A VERY LARGE SUM

LEWIS wanted to raise his fists and cheer, maybe climb on top of the stone table and toss confetti up at the ceiling and watch it snow down on the hairless head of the emperor. No one else was celebrating, though, and it would take a really long time to make that much confetti, so he stayed quiet. Not to mention that Demos didn't exactly look beaten. One of his Erasers tore the microphone and transmitter from Kaya's grip and hurled them to the floor, then picked up one of the chairs and crushed the devices.

The transmitter cracked and splintered.

Demos laughed.

Was this funny to him? They'd just tricked him into revealing his deceitful plan. All of Atlantis now knew the truth. The emperor was ruined—Lewis had kind of been hoping he'd cry.

A shining black transport was hovering outside. The windows were tinted, and the cabin was enclosed. The glass door to the balcony slid open, and one of the agents grabbed a stool from the meeting room and set it against the railing to form a step up into the ship. The Erasers began prodding the silenced High Council members toward the transport.

"I don't get it," Lewis said, speaking to no one in particular. "We won. Didn't we?"

Demos smirked. He motioned to the crushed microphone and transmitter on the floor. "Oh, you mean that?" He shrugged. "A mere annoyance. You've made my life more difficult, yes, and I suppose you've saved Evenor, Kaya—I can't destroy the city now. But as far as I can see"—he nodded toward his agents, who were shoving the others into the transport—"I'm still emperor."

One of the agents tried to pull Kaya forward. She wrestled free of his grip. "I'm not going with you," she insisted.

At the railing, Demos laughed coldly. "You are mistaken, child. You are going to prison, and you will stay there for the rest of your miserable life. Don't worry, though. You won't be alone. When we find your traitor father, I'll make sure he joins you."

"You're the traitor," Kaya snapped back at him. Two of the Erasers grabbed her by the elbows. Again, Kaya shook free. "I can walk by myself."

Lewis didn't try fighting. He stood between two of the agents. He felt weak. Powerless. Defeated. He glanced at Hanna—her eyes were darting around.

Hopefully, Lewis thought, she was concocting a plan.

As she stepped into the transport, Kaya addressed Hanna. "Goodbye," she said, "and thank you . . . for everything."

Then Kaya looked at Lewis directly.

The gravity suit felt suddenly heavy on him.

He looked down at the gloves, the chest harness.

The suit, his secret agreement with Silver—it was all a terrible mistake.

Words didn't mean anything now, but he had to say something. "I'm sorry, Kaya. I'm so sorry."

Kaya nodded and backed into the ship.

Demos and Weed Chin followed.

The door slid closed, and the ship drifted away.

She was gone. After all they'd been through, she was gone.

A second transport drifted up to the railing.

The remaining agents pushed the Sun People toward the vehicle. Hanna's mouth was twisted in concentration, as if she were working through a difficult math problem. Reinhold was nervously tugging at his beard. He looked even more frightened than Lewis himself. But Silver? She was busy. During the meeting, she'd pulled some kind of old-fashioned smartphone-type device out of her bag, and she was thumb-typing furiously. Was it some kind of digital journal? Or was she composing an irate poem as an outlet for her anger?

Lewis tried to sneak a glance at the screen. Silver shielded her device.

Meanwhile, Hanna watched the Erasers with intensity. She was plotting, Lewis realized. And he hoped she'd come up with a plan fast. Demos had said that his agents would take them back to their submarines, but Lewis wasn't ready to leave Atlantis. He couldn't go. Not yet, anyway. Not with Kaya headed for prison. And definitely not without his dad.

"Move," one of the Erasers growled.

Lewis felt the nose of a sonic pistol press into his back. His foot still tingled slightly, but the pain was gone.

Reinhold stepped up into the transport.

Still typing, Silver followed. She dropped into a seat across from the door, completely focused on her device.

Hanna leaned closer to Lewis. "Do you still have that sweatshirt?"

"Wally does." A quizzical look flashed over her face. Right—they hadn't been introduced yet. "My backpack," he explained, pointing over his shoulder. "Why?"

"We might have to fight our way out of this one, Lewis."

That was her plan? Lewis truly did feel horrible about Silver and everything. He wanted to prove that he was on Hanna's side. The right side. But a fistfight against some muscly and highly trained Atlanteans? That probably wasn't going to work out in their favor. He wasn't a coward or anything. He was a world-saver, capable of cranking through at least four push-ups, even more when he was weightless. But he was also a realist, and the truth was that he was an absolutely terrible fighter.

He appealed to Hanna's mathematical mind. "We're outnumbered," he noted.

She looked around. "What? No we're not. Four Atlanteans, four of us."

"I'm more of a negative two, so it's really four against two," Lewis explained. Then he nodded to Silver and Reinhold. "Plus, do you really think they'll help us? If they sit out, that would make it four against zero, or negative one, maybe, which is—"

"Quiet," one of the agents barked.

"My bad," Lewis replied. "Sorry."

The sonic pistol pressed into his back again. Lewis had one foot up on the stool when the driver of the transport hurried to the door. She had short blond hair, a slim frame, and the intensity of his impatient, demanding third-grade teacher.

This day was only getting worse.

He narrowed his eyes. "Finkleman."

She addressed the other agents. "Leave these Sun People to me. Demos wants you to stay here."

The agents glanced at each other. "Are you sure?" one of them asked.

"Message him yourself if you'd like," Finkleman replied. "But I wouldn't bother him today, if I were you. He's got bigger things to worry about than some fish-brained agents doubting orders from their superior."

That was more than enough. "All yours, then," the agent answered.

Lewis was still wearing the gravity suit. If he was quick, he could dash down the railing until he was clear of the ship and jump. That was a much better plan than fighting Finkleman.

"Don't even think about jumping," Hanna warned.

"So what do we do?" he whispered.

Hanna was watching the blond agent curiously. "Actually," she said, "I think we get inside the ship."

This seemed like a terrible idea, but Lewis trusted Hanna.

And trusting her had saved them before.

He stepped up on the railing and into the cruiser. Hanna

followed. Finkleman had moved back to the pilot's seat; the door closed behind them, and the vehicle drifted away.

The two of them sat close together, across from Reinhold and Silver, out of Finkleman's view. Lewis pulled Wally off his back and pulled out the strange sweatshirt. Quietly focused, Hanna started scrolling through the small digital touchpad.

Opposite them, Silver tapped her screen. She sighed. "There. All done."

"What's done?" Lewis asked.

"I sent out a series of messages, tweets, and other digital missives informing the world that Atlantis plans to invade and take over a coastal nation."

Was she serious? Lewis studied her smooth, unwrinkled face. Her expression was as blank and emotionless as a clean tissue.

Pulling on the sweatshirt, Hanna laughed. "That's impossible. I already used that bluff on the Atlanteans the last time we were here, and I know for a fact that there's no way you're getting reception in Atlantis. Especially not with some old-school smartphone."

Silver chuckled. "Ah, the ignorance of youth! You might be precocious, Hanna, but you have no idea what real money can buy. I fund and purchase the impossible daily." She held up the gadget. "This is not 'old-school,' as you say. This prototype is probably the most advanced communication device on the planet. It could stream movies on Mars! A few phone calls and messages from Atlantis? Not a problem at all."

After a pause, Hanna replied, "Seriously?"

"So it's like a superphone," Lewis said.

The billionaire paused, considering his suggestion. "Yes, I actually like that," Silver replied. "Legally, that wasn't your idea, though. I thought of it first. Right, Reinhold?"

"Of course, Susan. I heard you say it first."

Hanna interrupted them. "Wait. You seriously sent out those messages?"

"She's very serious," Reinhold replied.

There was a trace of fear in Hanna's tone as she replied. "But . . . why would you do that? We don't know for certain that they'll attack. We could still stop Demos. But if everyone on the surface thinks an invasion is imminent . . ."

"Then the surface will strike first," Silver answered. "Maybe not our own country, but one of the threatened ones? Absolutely. That's why I wasn't specific about the Atlanteans' plans. Most island territories barely have armies at all. So in my messages, I warned that they might invade France, Southeast Asia, the Indian Peninsula, or a coastal African nation. Surely one of them will attack to defend itself, and Demos's perfectly planned little war will become an absolute catastrophe. That's what he gets for lying to me. No one lies to me," she added, her voice calming. "I lie to them."

"You are a madwoman," Hanna concluded. She started to lunge for the phone, but Silver quickly pulled a sonic pistol out of her bag.

"Back in your seat," she ordered. "I borrowed this from your friend Kaya. Thankfully, Demos's goons did a terrible job of searching through my things. I'd be more than happy to see how these sonic weapons work."

Grimacing, Hanna leaned back.

The billionaire wrung her hands, a tight smile on her face. She edged forward in her seat. "I'm not a madwoman," she said. "I'm a competitor who despises losing, and I'm thrilled to see that this will all work out just fine in the end. Lewis, why don't you give that to Reinhold so he can start taking notes for my team."

"Give what to Reinhold?" Lewis asked.

Silver pointed the pistol at him now. "The suit, you imbecile. Remember our deal? Give me the suit."

At this point, Hanna was only half paying attention, busy with the sweatshirt. She'd pulled it on over her gravity gear, then activated something that tightened and stiffened the material. Lewis was pretty sure she was still listening at least a little, though, which meant he could finally show her that he wasn't on Silver's side anymore.

He took a deep and somewhat heroic breath.

He tried not to think of the money.

"No," he said at last.

He caught Hanna smiling. That slight grin was even better than his standing ovation in Evenor.

"You're having second thoughts?" Silver asked. "That's natural. I'll tell you what—give me a moment." She stared down at her bulky phone, typed, then waited. A ring tone sounded, and a man answered. "Marvel? This is Susan."

A crackly voice came through. "Yes, Susan?"

Hanna stopped fiddling with her sweatshirt. "You're talking to the surface?" Now she sounded more amazed than skeptical.

"Do you really think I'd venture all the way down here

without a signal? Marvel," she continued, "how long would it take you to wire fifty million dollars into the bank account of our friend Lewis's mother?"

Marvel paused. "A few minutes at most."

"Great. Don't do it yet—"

"You can if you want," Lewis cut in.

"No, wait for my word, Marvel," Silver replied. "All you have to do is give me that suit, Lewis, and the money is yours."

"Hold on back there," Finkleman called to them. "We've got to catch them before they get too far."

"Catch who?" Reinhold asked.

"Lewis?" Silver said. She was leaning forward. Her breath was minty. "I'll give you five seconds to agree."

Five *seconds*?

He wanted to decline. He knew he had to say no.

But that was some serious cash.

If he handed over the suit, his mom would be rich.

He'd be loaded, too. He'd ask for an allowance of a million dollars a year.

But he'd also be a liar and a cheat, and he'd lose two of his good friends.

Two of the best—and strangest—friends anyone could hope for.

Was that worth fifty million dollars?

He wanted to say no, but that was a very large number.

"Lewis, you can't," Hanna said, suddenly doubtful.

He exhaled. For emphasis, he pointed at Silver. "No," he said. "A big, giant, hairy no."

The billionaire was genuinely shocked. "What?"

"I don't want your money," Lewis said. After the words left his mouth, he realized they weren't quite true. "Well, actually, I do want your money. A lot."

His thoughts started drifting again, sailing toward his dream house. Every chair would be a massage chair. Every hallway would have a soccer goal— even the small ones. The goalies would be gnomes, and they'd always be there, ready to defend against him. There would be gnomes in the garden, too, and they'd sing songs about his bravery. Yes, it would be wonderful, but his friendships were still worth more than all that.

"I'm not going to cheat Kaya. Or Atlantis. I'm going to become a billionaire the old-fashioned way, by discovering gold in the mountains or marrying someone who turns out to be superrich. I'm not going to do it by lying and cheating." He patted his chest, tightened the straps on the gravity gear. "This suit is staying in Atlantis, where it belongs."

"Mine, too," Hanna added.

Silver shivered. Lewis thought she looked as if she'd eaten something unpleasant. An old lemon, maybe. "This feeling is so odd!" she said. "I don't like it. Is this rejection? It's terrible. You're not going to make me use this weapon, are you, Lewis? If Reinhold has to pull that suit off your unconscious little body, so be it."

Silver lifted the blaster.

At the controls, Finkleman yelled, "Get ready! We're right below the transport."

Momentarily distracted, Silver lowered the weapon. "Why

in the name of Steve Jobs would you pursue them?" she asked. "You're supposed to be taking me back to my submarine."

Finkleman climbed out of her seat. "Don't worry, I programmed the transport to take you back to Evenor," she said to Silver. Then, to Lewis and Hanna, she added, "Are you ready?"

"For what?" Lewis asked.

"We're going on a rescue mission."

"Since when are you on our side, Finkleman?"

"I've been on your side since the factory," she said. "I helped your friend Kaya's father escape, and I've been secretly working with him ever since."

Hanna snapped her fingers. "You helped Rian, too! He mentioned a blond woman with short hair."

"That kid is impressive," she noted. "Odd parents, though."

"But you were chasing me in Evenor," Lewis said.

"No," she explained, "I was preventing my former colleagues from catching you, Lewis. You wouldn't have gotten far from that auditorium if I hadn't steered them the wrong way and insisted that I'd seen you entering another building."

Was that really true? Lewis wasn't sure. His raptor dance had turned the crowd in his favor. The citizens of Evenor would've helped him—he was pretty much a celebrity there. But this was no time to argue. The important thing was that she was on their side. "Then we agree to disagree," Lewis replied. "Either way, this is fantastic. I didn't know you had it in you, Finkleman!"

"Why do you keep calling me that?"

The real answer might confuse her, Lewis decided, so he

devised another explanation. "Because it means 'brave and noble warrior' in my language."

"Oh, that works," she said. "As for switching sides, I'm trying to do the right thing. After what happened in the factory, I realized Demos was wrong."

"We saw you in Evenor, too," Hanna noted. "Or Kaya did, anyway."

"That's right. I kept the other agents occupied until you'd slipped away," Finkleman replied. "They nearly had you when you went looking for the drillship."

"Well, I'm glad you're with us now," Hanna replied. "We need all the help we can get."

Silver stomped her foot. "Hello? I'm threatening you!"

"Right," Lewis replied. "You were saying?"

The billionaire pointed the sonic pistol at him again. "The suit, Lewis. Give it to me now."

The last word was barely out of her mouth when Hanna leaped forward and lashed out at the weapon, knocking it out of Silver's moisturized hand. The blaster spun and slid along the floor, stopping at Finkleman's feet.

Hanna held out a hand to Silver. "How about you give us the phone instead?"

"Superphone," Lewis noted.

Silver clutched the device to her chest. "Absolutely not."

Hanna did not move her hand. "Give me the phone *and* remove the password protection so I'm not locked out, or my friend Finkleman here will program this transport to take you back to Capitol Tower. Then you can find your own way to the surface."

"Susan," Reinhold urged her, "please."

The billionaire's face briefly transformed into an angry, venomous scowl. She started to give Hanna the phone.

"The password," Lewis reminded her.

Silver finally did as she was told. Hanna tested a few screens, then pocketed the device with satisfaction as the door to the transport opened.

They pulled up alongside the other vehicle.

Hanna pressed a hand to Lewis's shoulder. "Hey," she said, her voice quiet, "you did the right thing. I'm impressed."

Proudly, he smiled. "I'm impressive."

Hanna called to Finkleman, who held the confiscated blaster in one hand and her own in the other. "What now?" Hanna asked.

"Now we get in there and help Kaya," Finkleman replied.

The door to the other transport slid open, and Weed Chin and four other agents stood facing them, each brandishing a deadly trumpet. Behind them, the councilors were bound to their seats. Kaya was sandwiched between two of the robed prisoners.

For a second, Lewis froze.

The agents raised their weapons.

At the sight of Finkleman, though, they paused. Weed Chin even lowered his sonic pistol.

Finkleman turned to Hanna and Lewis. "Ready?" she asked.

No! Lewis definitely wasn't ready. He'd need a few seconds, maybe even a year or two. Then he'd be taller, at least, and hopefully stronger, too.

But Finkleman wasn't going to wait.

She backed up several steps, then launched herself across the gap. Without a word to Lewis, Hanna followed, and the two of them plowed into the wall of agents, leaving him alone with his father's former friend and the bitter billionaire.

Hands in prayer position, Silver said, "One more chance, Lewis. Please?"

This time he answered with certainty. "No."

Silver shrugged. "Fine. But your friends aren't here to protect you now. Reinhold, please rip the suit off that little weasel before he leaves this ship."

The scientist glanced back and forth between Lewis and his boss. "But Susan, he's only a boy, and I—"

"How about another ten million dollars?" she suggested.

"Deal," he answered. "How do you want to do this, Lewis?"

Lewis backed against the wall opposite the open door. Reinhold approached, his scowl menacing. Their ship was still even with the other transport, but the distance between them was growing. The scene inside the other ship wasn't exactly inviting, either. A brawl had erupted—Hanna, Finkleman, and the Erasers were tangled in a violent scrum. Still, Lewis had to help them, and that meant he had to get past Reinhold.

The scientist's eyes were wild, his beard ragged and lightly dusted with tiny flecks of spicy kale chips. He held up his fists, then lunged for Lewis.

Immediately, Lewis switched on his suit, pressed the thrusters in his gloves.

The scientist was about as fast as an overfed house cat.

Reinhold's attempted tackle missed his midsection. The

scientist grabbed at Lewis's shins. Lewis powered up the thrusters, planted his bare foot on the bald spot at the back of Reinhold's head, and pushed off. He flipped forward, head over heels, as Reinhold crashed into the opposite wall. Now near the ceiling, Lewis steadied himself against the upper part of the door frame. He looked back. Silver was sneering up at him. A stunned Reinhold was shaking his head. Lewis grabbed the door frame with both hands, drifted back so his arms were extended, then pulled down as hard as he could, launching himself out of the transport and into the air.

Hanna and Finkleman had leaped the gap easily.

But the gap had been smaller then.

Now the other transport was moving too fast, and gravity suits weren't built for speed, not even with the thrusters. Lewis aimed for the front end of the still-open doorway, but he nearly missed the door entirely as the vehicle sped forward. At the last second, he managed to grip the frame. A hand grabbed his wrist and yanked him inside. Finkleman, her face red and newly swollen below one eye, practically tossed him toward the rear of the ship. Lewis tripped and tumbled into the robed legs of one of the councilors.

The transport was larger than Esmerelda, but the layout was similar, with long rows of bench seats on either side. Lewis couldn't see into the cockpit—the door to the front was closed. In the main cabin, the councilors were still immobilized and silenced. But the space between the seats was like a wrestling ring on a space station. The agents, Hanna, and Finkleman all wore gravity suits, so the fight moved between the floor, the ceiling, and the walls. Finkleman was grappling with two of the agents at once. On the floor near the still-open door, Weed Chin pointed his weapon at Hanna, but she slapped it out of his grasp and drove the heel of her hand into his chest. The green-chinned agent gasped for breath. Lewis was stunned. Where had Hanna learned that move? Another agent, upside down with his feet on the ceiling, pointed his weapon at her, but Hanna spun and snatched his flute, then grabbed another agent's wrist, twisted, and left him crumpled in pain.

Struggling to his feet, Weed Chin raised his fists.

Hanna spun and struck him in the sternum again, knocking him back.

Then she kicked each of the fallen weapons across the ship, out of reach of the agents. Finkleman had somehow pinned two of the Erasers at once, but Weed Chin and his men were back on their feet on either side of Hanna.

Now it was his turn, Lewis decided.

He threw himself bravely into the scrum. Fist clenched, he pounded Weed Chin in the shoulder. A bolt of pain fired through his wrist, and the punch was pointless.

Weed Chin laughed, then tossed Lewis easily to the ground, swatting him away.

Lewis felt as harmless as a housefly. Was he even that effective, though? At least houseflies were annoying. He was more like an ant. And yet the brief distraction had helped Hanna. Energized, she whirled and struck and battered them with her fists.

The agents staggered away from his friend. One of them backed into Finkleman, who was caught in a scrap of her own. She grabbed the Eraser by the shoulders, dropped onto her back, planted her feet on the man's chest, and kicked him out the door.

For a second, no one moved. Lewis stared at her in surprise, mouth open slightly. Even the real Mrs. Finkleman would never be that brutal.

"So, that happened," Lewis said.

"He has a suit," Finkleman reminded him. "He'll be fine."

Another agent charged at her, and after a brief grapple, Finkleman tossed him out the door as well.

Hanna adapted to the new plan with enthusiasm. She fought two Erasers at once, backing them toward the opening. Then she forced one out into the air as Finkleman threw the other. Lewis scanned the cabin. Only two Erasers remained, including Weed Chin.

The pair stood shoulder to shoulder at the rear of the cabin, away from the door.

The only remaining sonic blaster lay at the feet of one of the councilors. The robed woman kicked it toward him. Lewis picked it up and aimed at the Erasers. But he hated the feel of it in his hands—he didn't want to point a weapon at anyone, not even an Eraser. Thankfully, Finkleman took it from him and turned it around. "You were holding it backward," she whispered. "You would've blasted yourself."

Finkleman and Hanna faced the Erasers across the space, with Lewis beside them.

Strapped to their seats, the silenced councilors were watching eagerly.

Kaya's jaw was clenched. Her eyes were bloodshot with anger and frustration.

Finkleman ordered the two remaining Erasers to kneel. Weed Chin complied, but his partner, the burly woman from outside Capitol Tower, pulled what Lewis had to admit was a pretty sweet fake-out. She started to go down on one knee, then sprang forward. Lewis flinched, thinking she was going to attack, or maybe grab him and take him hostage. Instead, she slammed her hand against her waist, activating her suit's gravity drive, and leaped toward the ceiling. Finkleman was slow to react, and the agent kicked the weapon out of her hand and out the still-open door.

The agent's offensive was over as quickly as it had started, however; Hanna grabbed the woman by the ankle, pulled her down, and hurled her out into the air. Then she glared at Weed Chin. "Don't even think about trying that," Hanna warned.

The fight was over. Right? Yes! And they'd actually won. Lewis had never won a fight before. Did this one count? He thought so. Even if his role had been more of a secondary one, he still deserved some credit. He'd been a distraction, but a strategically important one. He might even include this scene in *The Epic Adventures of Troy Gates*. But he had to admit that the real hero—of this fight, at least—was Hanna.

Finkleman agreed. "Where did you learn to fight like that?"

Still staring at Weed Chin, Hanna waved off the compliment. "The shirt knows how to fight, not me," she explained. "That victory was well timed, too. The battery life on this thing is terrible. I don't think I could've thrown another punch."

"Wait," Finkleman said, looking up, "where's Demos?"

"He must have bailed before we got here," Hanna guessed.

Behind him, Lewis heard Kaya struggling against her restraints. She was red-faced from the collar keeping her speechless, too. He leaned in awkwardly close, copied the whistle he'd heard back in the conference room, and actually got it right on the second try. Or maybe the third. What mattered was that Kaya's hands were free and the weird collar around her throat shut down. Instantly, she jumped up and shoved Lewis behind her. "He's in there!" she shouted.

"Who?" Lewis asked.

"Demos!"

The door slid open.

The self-appointed emperor leaned through, aiming a sonic blaster.

One of the still-silenced councilors leaped from her seat and, with her hands still bound, lowered her shoulder and slammed into Kaya and Lewis. A weird buzzing sensation pulsed through Lewis's arms and back.

The robed councilor's whole body shook.

Yet Kaya and Lewis were fine; the blast wasn't nearly as bad as the shot to Lewis's foot.

The woman had sacrificed herself for them. She groaned.

Demos glanced back over his shoulder and out through the windshield. He tapped a control pad, then moved his sonic pistol between Lewis, Hanna, and Finkleman. "Out of my ship, now!" he roared.

Without waiting, he fired again. Anticipating the shot, Finkleman dove out of the way, and the blast hit Weed Chin. Demos glanced back at the windshield. Lewis realized he was trying to fend off a mutiny and drive the transport at the same time—an all-but-impossible task.

As the emperor turned back toward them, Lewis spotted a glimmering, whale-shaped hull emerging from the mist above them. Esmerelda! The invisible skin was still malfunctioning, so Lewis could clearly see that his friend Fenitia wasn't driving. The copilot was very familiar, though. With his thick shoulders and long silver hair, Naxos was easy to recognize. Plus, he was one of the first people they'd met in Atlantis, and his presence explained how the ship was moving again. Naxos had designed the vehicle himself; he must have found a way to fix or recharge it after Fenitia's crash landing.

The pilot was no stranger, either. Kaya's father had long hair and, even at a distance, bore a strange resemblance to a wizard. The last time Lewis had seen Heron, he'd been sending them to their doom inside the warship factory. Now he was leaning over the dashboard intently. He was clearly on a rescue mission, and although Lewis didn't know exactly what Kaya's dad was planning, he figured he might as well try to help.

One more time, Demos aimed his weapon.

While he wasn't particularly strong or brilliant, Lewis did have a talent for distraction. In a flash, he slipped the harmonica out of his pocket and lifted the instrument to his lips.

Behind him, he heard Hanna mutter, "Oh no."

He didn't have time to explain, and from where she was standing, his friend wouldn't be able to see Esmerelda. But the warship was steering ever closer.

The transport must have been running on autopilot—the emperor wasn't even bothering to look back out the windshield now. "You fool!" Demos shouted. "You really think I'll fall for one of your tricks again?"

"This isn't a trick," Lewis said. "One breath of air through this devastating mouth organ, and everyone on this ship will cry out in pain."

This wasn't really a lie. He was still in training; his tunes were deplorable.

Demos paused momentarily, but the story didn't sway him.

That didn't matter, though, because the brief delay was enough.

Neither the tyrant nor his sidekick had noticed the unusual ship cruising toward them, and they were completely unprepared when Esmerelda rammed the side of their transport.

The emperor stumbled and fell, losing his grip on the sonic pistol.

The weapon clattered to the floor.

Hanna kicked it to Kaya.

Their ship swerved and dove.

Lewis grabbed onto a railing near the ceiling.

The transport veered down and to the right. Apparently, the nudge from Esmerelda had switched them out of autopilot.

A pair of towers loomed in their path.

"Can someone steer?" Lewis pleaded.

Finkleman dashed for the controls. She straightened their course, narrowly squeezing between the towers. "Who just slammed into us?" she asked.

"Was it Rian?" Kaya wondered.

"I think it was your dad, Kaya," Lewis said.

Swelling with pride, Kaya stomped toward Demos, and he

scuttled away from her like a terrified crab, cowering beside Weed Chin in the back of the transport. She trained her weapon on them and watched through the still-open door as Esmerelda swooped up from below and pulled alongside them. Kaya smiled as her father turned his head to peer inside and started shaking his fist triumphantly. Did they whoop in Atlantis? Lewis wasn't sure, but it definitely looked like Heron was whooping and hollering. Naxos, meanwhile, stepped away from the dashboard and appeared to celebrate. Was he dancing? Yes, and his moves reminded Lewis of his own.

"Turn the ship around," Kaya called to Finkleman. "We're going back to Government Square."

As Finkleman steered, Lewis freed the rest of the High Council members one at a time with the power of his precise and perfectly tuned whistles. Had anyone ever whistled so heroically in the history of the world? He doubted it, and he decided that if *The Epic Adventures of Troy Gates* was ever adapted into an audiobook, he'd have to do the whistling himself, even if he wasn't the narrator.

This definitely felt like a time for celebration, but the others remained serious, especially the councilors. Once she was able to speak again, Alexandra demanded the sonic weapon. Kaya handed it to her without question, and she and her colleagues all started shouting at Demos. Alexandra ordered the former emperor and Weed Chin into seats, then bound them both in place.

The pair protested. Weed Chin claimed he'd just been following orders. Demos ranted about how they were all fools and how the surface would destroy them and everything Atlantis held dear. He didn't go on for too long, though. Another councilor joyfully slapped collars around their necks, muting them both.

The glass hull of the warship was glitching again. Lewis tried to see into Esmerelda's cabin, but the flickering light made it impossible.

"I don't think he's in there," Hanna said.

She'd read his mind again. But if Naxos and Heron had made it here all the way from Evenor, then his dad might be in Ridge City, too—even if he wasn't right there in the warship.

"What happened to the other Sun People?" Alexandra asked. "What of Silver and her colleague?"

"They're gone," Hanna explained. "Finkleman programmed the transport to take them back to their submarine."

"Finkleman?"

"That's me," the driver yelled back. "It means 'brave and noble warrior' in their language."

Kaya squinted at Lewis. "True story," he lied.

One of the councilors noted that Finkleman had earned herself a promotion or even a reward, as she'd demonstrated her loyalty to Atlantis by turning against Demos. Alexandra agreed, wondering aloud whether she might be the right person to lead a new, revamped group of Erasers—one that was focused on the needs of the people, not the wishes of one man. Lewis smiled. He was proud of Finkleman. She'd turned out okay, for a heartless villain. He was tempted to give her an affectionate pat on the back, but she was probably still in soldier mode. There was a chance she'd grab his hand

and sprain his wrist. Maybe he'd make her a thank-you card instead. Johnny could deliver it for him.

"I suppose it's good that the other Sun People are gone," Alexandra mused. "The two of them were intolerable. I'm glad we're finished with them."

"Well, that's the thing," Hanna said over her shoulder. She reached into her backpack and held out the superphone. "Silver sent a bunch of messages to the surface. She told people about Demos and his plans, trying to make them think Atlantis is ready to attack. If that's the case, they could be getting ready to defend themselves."

"Or even strike first," one of the councilors intoned.

Alexandra eyed the device, the kids, and then her fellow councilors. They clustered together in the middle of the cabin, discussing what to do next. Finally, one of the women announced, "We'll return to the tower at once."

One of the men groaned. "Another meeting? Now?"

"It's our job, Solon."

Demos and Weed Chin squirmed uncomfortably in their seats.

"What are you going to do with them?" Lewis asked.

"Oh, I believe Demos's beloved prison is a perfect place for them to spend some time reflecting on their decisions," Alexandra said. "Would the council care to vote?"

"Let's do it right now," one of the other members replied.

"All in favor?" Alexandra asked.

The councilors shouted their approval.

"I think that settles it, Emperor," Alexandra said. "You and your friends will endanger Atlantis no longer."

20

A Fragile Peace

NOW could Lewis cheer? Maybe just pump his fist once or twice? This definitely felt a little more like a victory. Yet the mood in the transport was still so serious. Everyone was deathly quiet as they cruised back to Government Square. Lewis almost felt like he was at a funeral. A real one, too. Not the kind he and Michael held for cracked pencils, broken action figures, and ravaged rotisserie chickens.

The thought of his little brother carried him out of the ship and back to the surface and his mom and Roberts. Back home. He had Silver's superphone, so he could actually tell them he was okay. But he wasn't ready to talk. Not yet. Not while he was surrounded by all these Atlanteans. He wasn't sure what he'd do if he heard his mom's voice. She deserved to know he was alive, though, so he entered her number, typed out a message as fast as his fingers would allow, and pressed send. Then he realized his mom might think the note was from Susan Silver, since he was using her phone. So he added, "That was me." A few seconds later, he finished with a third message: "Lewis."

Alexandra instructed Finkleman to land at the base of Capitol Tower. The crowd had not cleared the area. People were bunched around Rian's drillship, which was still stuck in the moat. They'd pushed across the footbridge, too, and clustered near the entrance to the building, where half a dozen armed agents formed a wall in front of the door. As Finkleman landed their vehicle, the crowd below cleared out of their way. Her glass hull still flickering, Esmerelda settled onto the ground nearby.

Lewis felt a nervous chill as he realized Kaya was standing beside him. She was ready to dash over to her dad, he guessed. But they still hadn't really talked about the suit or his deal with Silver. His first attempt to say something had failed. He gulped. "Kaya, I'm sorry."

At first she didn't reply or even react. She just stared at him with those large blue-gray eyes. She stayed silent for what felt like an eternity, and he was about to apologize again, as many times as he could, when she answered quietly, "It's okay."

He breathed out. "I didn't give it to her, you know."

"I know."

"How did you know?" he asked.

She pointed to the suit. He'd forgotten he was still wearing the gear. "Oh, right."

Laughing now, Kaya jumped to the ground, and Hanna slipped past him and followed her. The air was steamy; Lewis mopped a film of sweat off his forehead with the back of his hand. Atlanteans crowded the space between their transport and the warship. Lewis spotted Thrall interviewing Rass, using a new microphone, and he was happy for the traitor. Sure, Rass had turned Lewis in twice, but the guy had lived a difficult life—even he deserved a moment of fame.

Next, Rian darted out of a cluster of onlookers. A man and a woman wearing flower-patterned swimsuits and crystal necklaces trailed after him, staying close. Their hair was tightly braided and decorated with colorful beads. They looked like they'd been on an island vacation, and Rian must have noticed Lewis squinting at them curiously. "You did it!" Rian exclaimed. Then he nodded to either side. "These are my parents," he explained. "They just got back from a trip."

His mom grabbed Rian's shoulder with one hand, clutching her necklace with the other. "We hurried home when we heard about the Sun People," she said. She looked from her son to Lewis and Hanna and back. "I don't understand. You're friends with them, Rian? What's going on here?"

"You still haven't explained what you were doing in that drillship, either," his dad added.

Rian ignored his parents' questions. Kaya was heading for Esmerelda, and he rushed over and blocked her way. After a pause, he hugged her briefly, then let go and backtracked, his cheeks red. Lewis hurried forward for a better view and noticed that Kaya was blushing, too. And while Lewis was no world-leading expert on relationships, he did detect the stirrings of a crush.

"You're okay," Rian said, his voice soft.

"I'm fine," Kaya answered. She motioned to the drillship. "You promised you wouldn't do anything crazy."

The Atlantean boy laughed. "I made no such promise. And hey, it helped, right?"

"Definitely," Hanna replied. "Nice work."

The crowd was closing in around them when Kaya's father

squeezed his way through. Heron didn't pause when he spotted Kaya. He ran straight up to his daughter and embraced her, and Lewis was momentarily jealous until he heard a great, booming yell. His pulse quickened. His chest tightened with excitement. He stood up on his toes, his bare heels off the ground, and spotted a mountain of a man shoving his way through the Atlanteans. The enormous head covered with wild, thick hair was unmistakable. A pair of thick-fingered hands as big as catcher's mitts came into view, moving several Atlanteans aside, and suddenly Lewis's father was there before him in all his bright-eyed glory. He wasn't merely alive. His face was radiant with energy and happiness, and his voice was so powerful it sounded like it was blasting through a megaphone.

"My son the explorer!" he yelled. "Three cheers for Lewis!"

The first cheer rang out, then the second. Lewis thought—or hoped—that the cheers would multiply, prompting people to organize a brief but joyous parade. He didn't even care what they threw. Money would be great. But even dried seaweed would be fine.

The third cheer never happened, but he didn't care. Now his dad was limping toward him, leaning on Naxos. His father was using the Atlantean engineer as a crutch, and the poor inventor was sweating from the strain. Lewis rushed over to help. Naxos breathed a sigh of relief as Lewis took over. His dad leaned against him, wrapping his arms around his back, and Lewis pressed his face against his ribs, right below his armpit.

His father was alive.

He hadn't bathed, and the stench was significant, the heat from his armpits uncomfortably intense, but he was alive. Lewis had found his father at last. The emotion of the moment overwhelmed him; he didn't have time to summon the gnomes to close the gates holding back his tears. They rushed down his face.

The tears, not the gnomes.

Lewis wiped his eyes with his self-drying sleeves.

"You made it, son."

"So did you!"

"Nice outfit. Where'd you get that?"

Lewis paused. "It's a long story."

"Tell me later." His dad stepped back, studied him, and dropped his hands heavily onto Lewis's shoulders. "I'm surprised your mother let you return."

"Well, that's kind of a tricky story, too . . ."

"Hey," Rian said, grabbing Kaya by the elbow. He pointed to Finkleman. "That's the spy I was telling you about!"

"Yes, I know," Kaya replied. "Her help was essential."

The former Eraser shrugged. "They don't call me Finkleman for nothing."

Lewis noticed his father staring at her in confusion.

Pointing at the councilors, Hanna asked, "Where are they going?"

The members of the High Council had formed a wedge with Alexandra at the point. As a group, they marched toward the tall front doors of Capitol Tower. Out of the crowd, the yellow-uniformed guards reappeared and lined up behind them. A dozen Erasers stood guarding the entrance. At first, they stood firm. One of them shouted something about no one being allowed inside without the approval of Demos. Then a councilor dragged the collared emperor out of the transport, his hands bound. Alexandra stopped a few strides away from the Erasers. The other councilors flanked her. Behind them crowded hundreds of Atlanteans. Maybe more—Lewis wasn't very good at that sort of counting.

"We don't need the approval of your lying, scheming, traitorous leader," Alexandra proclaimed. "We have the support of the people of Atlantis."

Lewis raised his fists and whooped. His father joined him, and the Atlanteans cheered and chanted all around them. When Lewis pulled out his harmonica to play a few supportive notes, though, Hanna tried to snatch it away, so he returned it to his pocket.

The leader of the group of Erasers looked left at one line of agents, right at the other, and whistled to switch on his gravity suit. He sprang off the ground, and in the span of a few seconds, the rest of the Erasers launched into the air above Government Square. High above, on the top-floor balcony, the agents guarding the Council's meeting room leaped off and followed the others down into the side streets and alleyways, disappearing into the hidden corners of the city.

"How courageous of them," Rian remarked.

"A real bunch of heroes," Hanna added.

At the door, Alexandra turned and walked back to Lewis, Hanna, and Kaya. She squinted at Rian. "Who are you?"

"That's Rian. He's the kid who saved us," Hanna replied.

"Twice," Rian reminded her.

Twice? There was the scene at the mall in Evenor. Driving the drillship through the waterway was good, too, but that time he'd had help from this Dave guy Lewis still hadn't met. Plus, in Evenor, he'd kind of lost Lewis. So really, that balanced out to one save, right? Not that anyone was keeping score.

"Thank you, Rian, and each one of you, for all you've done."

Then Alexandra turned back to follow the others into the building.

"Wait!" Kaya shouted. "What are you doing? You're calling off the attack, right?"

Alexandra whispered something to one of her colleagues, then walked back to Kaya. "This news about Silver's messages is troubling. We've already received reports that several surface submarines are steering in our direction. We have to be certain Atlantis is secure, Kaya. I can only assure you that we will do what is best for our people."

Their small group turned silent.

Lewis felt like he'd been kneed in the chest.

"You can't be serious," Hanna said. "We're trying to avoid a war, not start one."

Without another word, Alexandra spun around and strode inside. The uniformed security guards, suddenly courageous again, formed a line in front of the entrance.

Quietly, Hanna asked, "Why should we trust them?"

"Right!" Kaya said. "Why should we believe they'll do the right thing?"

Kaya's father sighed heavily. He swept his long, silver-gray hair back over his shoulders. This wasn't the time to point it out to anyone, but Lewis decided he looked a little like an elf, only thicker and without the pointy ears. "The High Council has ruled Atlantis for more than a thousand years," Heron said. "This is the way things are done."

"Maybe it's time that changed," Rian suggested.

"Yes!" Hanna replied. "The way it's done isn't working."

Naxos inhaled slowly through his nose. He tilted back his head and gazed up at the top of the building. "The children have a point, Heron."

With a dramatic clap of his hands, Lewis's dad signaled his agreement. "We should demand an audience with the High Council immediately. You deserve to be heard."

"Alexandra didn't think so," Hanna noted.

Kaya was strangely quiet. She was looking down at the ground, thinking. "What is it, Kaya?" Lewis asked.

The question pulled her out of her thoughts. Her wide eyes brightened. "We need to talk," Kaya muttered. Then, louder, she added, "Not us and the council, though. Our leaders— Atlantis and the surface need to talk. That's what my mom was trying to do, right? And Demos's son? That's why they went on that mission?"

Her dad paused, considering the idea seriously before responding. "We also wanted to learn more about them, but ultimately, yes, that was the goal—to begin a conversation between our worlds."

"Right! And instead, we've been trapped in this quiet war for years. Why? The leaders of our civilizations need to talk this out before any more lives are lost"—she looked at Lewis and Hanna—"on either side of the fight."

The professor nodded along. "I suppose we could try to arrange a meeting at some point—"

"No," Kaya said. "You heard Alexandra. This can't wait."

How in the world were they supposed to arrange a last-minute conference?

"Lewis!" Hanna said, almost shouting. "Susan Silver's phone!"

The superphone was safely stowed in Wally. He pulled it out and tossed it to her.

"Susan Silver the billionaire?" his dad asked. "How did you get her phone?" The professor held up his hands. "No, let me guess. It's a long story, right?"

"Very," Lewis answered.

Hanna hurriedly scrolled, tapped, and typed. "It's still working."

"What are you thinking?" Kaya asked.

"I'm thinking this could be the way we start that conversation."

Their Atlantean friend didn't need to hear any more. Kaya marched them toward the door. The security guards blocked the entrance. One of them stepped forward with a sonic pistol. Kaya's dad pleaded with them, but they wouldn't relent.

Lewis couldn't believe it. Now these Atlanteans were tough? Their timing was terrible. They'd completely caved to the Erasers.

He remembered Hanna's unusual sweatshirt. "Karate?" he suggested.

She checked the control panel and shook her head. "Out of power."

Rian pointed up to the fifteenth-floor balcony. "The door isn't the only way inside."

Hanna nodded to the transport and the warship. Guards were blocking the doors to both. "Unfortunately, those rides aren't ours any longer."

The Atlantean boy looked at Lewis. Or not at him, exactly—at his gravity suit. "Got any power left in that?" Rian asked.

"Sure. Why?"

Lewis had barely finished uttering the question when he figured out Rian's plan. The girls understood immediately. Kaya started adjusting her gear, then helped Hanna with hers.

Rian was backing away when Hanna stopped him. "No," she said, "you're coming with us. We'll give you a lift."

Rian grabbed Hanna's right hand and Kaya's left.

Hanna pointed to the balcony. "Ready, Steelheart?"

No! Lewis wasn't ready at all. He was light-years from ready. He'd finally found his dad. And his heart was definitely not made of steel, or any other kind of metal. Couldn't he take a few minutes? They'd just dethroned an emperor and stopped a coup. He needed to digest these events. Maybe eat a snack, too. But Hanna, Kaya, and Rian were already rising, and the world still needed saving.

Lewis dialed up his suit. His body turned weightless, yet he was still anchored to the city floor because his father was holding his hand. Not too forcefully, but with enough strength that Lewis couldn't pull free. He didn't want to, either. He and his dad had never held hands before. Or not since he could remember. His dad's mitt was warm and kind of clammy. Calloused, too, and swollen. Yet Lewis didn't want to let go.

Not after all they'd been through.

His feet floated up over his head. "I'll be right back, Dad. We have to save the world."

Lewis squeezed his father's hand as the professor relaxed his grip, then slipped free, adjusted the dial at his waist, and followed his three friends up the side of the building. The added weight of Rian slowed Hanna and Kaya, so Lewis drifted past them, cruising up and over the railing. One of the councilors spotted them as they landed on the balcony. The robed man hurried over and slid open the glass door. "What are you doing back here?" he asked.

Shaking her head in frustration, Alexandra pushed away from the table. "Let me manage them," she said. "Children, I told you, this is beyond—"

"You have to let us send out a message," Kaya pleaded. "We have to let the Sun People know we're willing to talk."

"They will listen," Hanna insisted.

Alexandra took a quick breath, as if she'd just stopped herself from saying something. For an instant, she stared down at the floor. Or was she looking at Lewis's feet? His toes did look repulsive. They were so pale. He wriggled them, wishing he had his Jordans.

"I suppose if we could negotiate with someone in a position of power . . ."

Kaya spun around. Her face was strained with desperation. "Can we do that, Hanna?"

"Maybe we could reach my parents," Hanna started,

staring down at the brightly lit screen of the phone, "and they could try to get through to someone?"

Alexandra glanced at a few other councilors, then shook her head. "Not good enough. I wish we could be patient. Truly. But the surface submarines are moving ever closer to our borders. We need to prepare to defend ourselves."

Suddenly, Lewis remembered his new friend. "I've got it!"

"You have what, Lewis?" Hanna demanded.

Lewis reached into the pocket of his new Atlantean pants and pulled out his harmonica. Hanna covered her face with her hands. "No, don't worry," he said, "no music."

"No dancing, either?"

That was insulting. The grand tales of his dancing in Evenor had helped convince Alexandra that they weren't invaders. So his moves had helped save the world. He'd point that out later, though. For now, he removed a worn, wet piece of paper from his pocket. As Alexandra and the rest of the councilors watched, he unfolded it on the huge table. The letter had been soaked and dried out several times. The ink had run and bled into the paper, and the number . . .

The number was illegible.

No. This was not happening.

Hanna groaned. "That might have worked."

"What?" Alexandra asked.

"That," Hanna said, pointing at the paper, "was the direct number for the leader of one of the more powerful nations under the sun."

Lewis shrugged. "I was thinking you two could chat."

"Can you remember any of the number?" Kaya asked.

Maybe? Lewis wasn't some kind of genius like Hanna, but he had tried to memorize the number. The sequence started with a three. And then there was a twelve, which he remembered because that was the street address of a girl in his class named Ashley, whom he definitely didn't have a crush on. As he searched his brain for the rest of the numbers, Hanna kept talking to him. Kaya and Rian, too. His brain needed peace and quiet, though, and it didn't like to be pressured, either. Really, his brain was like a feral cat. You had to lure it gently, with bowls of warm milk, patience, maybe a soothing lullaby.

He held up his hands and closed his eyes, urging his friends to be quiet. He hummed a tune, tried to relax and ignore the pressure. Slowly, the numbers were coming back to him.

"Give me the phone!" he said. "I remember it!"

Lewis dialed, then waited an eternity before the old-fashioned ring of a phone sounded.

The remaining members of the High Council waited anxiously.

Hanna tapped the screen, switching the device to speaker mode.

Lewis couldn't believe the superphone was working. And that he'd actually remembered the number.

Next there was a click and a low buzzing sound.

A woman answered. "Stella's Pizza, what's your order?"

Lewis tapped the screen, ending the call.

"What was that?" Alexandra asked.

"And what is pizza?" one of the other councilors asked.

An important question, but one he couldn't answer right now. A wrong number was only natural on the first try. Lewis ran through the sequence again in his head. The first digit, he realized, wasn't actually a three. He dialed again. The councilors stared at the device with a mix of skepticism and wonder.

Another series of rings, a click, and then a different woman answered. "Hello?"

This voice was familiar. He'd heard it countless times on the radio, in videos and announcements. His mom had made them all watch her inauguration speech about seventeen times. Hanna recognized her voice, too. Her eyes widened and glowed. She elbowed him encouragingly.

This was his show.

His response caught in his throat. He coughed. "Laura," he said at last, "is that you?"

"This is President Moffat. Who is this?"

"It's me, Lewis."

Another pause. Then: "Lewis who?"

The councilors glared at him.

"Lewis Gates," he answered. "The kid who discovered Atlantis? With a little help. But mostly on his own."

Hanna leaned forward. "Hanna Barkley, too, Madam President. My mom and I are big fans."

This time, the president's response came faster. "Thank you for calling, Lewis. You, too, Hanna. May I ask, where are you right now?"

"Well, that's the thing," Lewis began.

"Atlantis," Hanna answered.

"You're calling me from Atlantis?"

"Yes," Lewis said, "and before I forget, could you tell my mom—and Hanna's parents, too—that we're all okay?"

The pause that followed was long and uncomfortable. Lewis thought he heard whispering in the background.

"Don't hang up!" Hanna urged her. "We're not lying. You have to listen to us."

Another pause. "Very well, Hanna, and yes, I'll inform your parents. Could you please tell me exactly why you are calling?"

Kaya, Rian, and the councilors were watching expectantly. Hanna was biting her lower lip. They were going to let him run with this one? Okay.

Lewis looked around the room. "There are a bunch of people here you really need to talk to, Madam President," he started, switching to her formal title. "They're kind of the leaders of Atlantis. They all wear robes. Maybe that's not important, but it's true. Anyway, all these Atlanteans are worried—actually, we're all a little worried—that some kind of war is going to break out. So, before that happens, we were thinking everyone should kind of get together and . . . well . . . talk?"

Silence.

They waited.

Lewis checked the signal. They hadn't lost her, but the president was being really quiet. Maybe she didn't like the meeting idea? His mom always complained about all the meetings she had to attend for work. "We could have a party instead," he suggested. "Not with balloons or anything. Or cake. Or I guess there could be cake—"

"Yes."

Hanna leaned forward. "Excuse me?" she asked.

"Yes," the president replied. "To the meeting, not the cake. I think it's about time the leaders of our two worlds sat down and had a long, difficult conversation."

At Hanna's urging, Lewis set the phone down on the table. Hanna introduced Alexandra, and soon there were solemn promises from both sides that there would be no attacks or acts of war. For now, they both added—this wasn't a peace agreement so much as a pause. The president assured Alexandra and the High Council that she would prevent the other nations on the surface from carrying out any aggressive actions, too. Then the two of them said something about women leaders not needing to behave like little boys, whatever that meant. One of the old, robed men growled and rolled his eyes. Rian and Lewis exchanged puzzled looks, but Hanna and Kaya both smiled.

Now that his work was finished, Lewis moved back out to the balcony. The floor was warm underfoot. A warm breeze flowed past the tower. Tapping a button at his waist, he loosened his clothes, then leaned over the railing and stared down at the crowd. Rian joined him. Far below, Lewis could see his father, Heron, Finkleman, and Naxos staring up. Waiting for news, he guessed. Lewis raised his fists, and his dad and the others cheered triumphantly in response. Rian slapped him on the back a little harder than he would've liked, and Lewis took a deep, satisfying breath. He was a hero. Right? His bravery, his dancing, his finely tuned whistling—he'd used all these talents and more to help save the world. The Erasers were finished. His father was safe. The war was on hold. And sure, the deal with Silver was off, so he wasn't going to be a gazillionaire, but at least he wasn't a thief.

Hanna and Kaya approached, sliding the door closed behind them.

The sight of their gravity gear and the thought of Silver made him want to shed the gloves, ankle straps, and chest plate as quickly as possible. Hanna draped her arm around his shoulders as he unbuckled the harness. "Well? What are you thinking?" she asked.

"We kind of saved the world," he said, slipping off the gloves.

"Not the whole world," Hanna replied.

"Almost," Lewis countered.

"Definitely a big part of it," Rian added.

Kaya stood on the other side of him. "An important part, too," she noted.

Bundling up his gravity gear, Lewis tried to hand her the equipment.

"Keep it," Kaya said. "I trust you."

"I'll take it," Rian said, grabbing the gear.

"Of course you will," Kaya replied, shaking her head.

As Rian started trying on the suit, Kaya turned to Lewis and Hanna. She swept her silver hair behind her ears. Any traces of tension on her face were gone. Lewis hadn't seen her this happy since . . . well, ever. The three of them stood there quietly. Lewis didn't know what his friends were thinking, but he was marveling at everything they'd been through over the last few weeks. The waves, the subsphere, discovering Atlantis, their escape and return—it all sped through his mind like the world's fastest movie. Hanna elbowed him affectionately as their friend turned serious.

"Thank you both," Kaya said. "Thank you for showing me your world and for helping me get back to mine." She ran her hand along the railing. "I couldn't have returned to Atlantis without you."

"I know," Lewis replied.

This time, Hanna's elbow wasn't quite so affectionate. "Thank you, Kaya," Hanna added. "We wouldn't have survived down here without you. Now, on to more important matters. Are you going to visit us again?"

"Definitely," Kaya answered. "But maybe not right away."

"How about you?" Lewis asked Rian.

Their new friend was already strapped into his gravity gear. "Absolutely!" he said.

A sequence of cheers drew their attention back to the crowd below. Lewis leaned on the railing beside his friends. Together, they'd halted a revolution, thwarted a billionaire, prevented a war, and—hopefully, if all went well—kickstarted a lasting peace between their worlds. They deserved a parade. Gifts, too. At that moment, though, Lewis didn't need new Jordans or showers of confetti thrown by adoring, appreciative fans or even epic songs composed and sung in his honor. Later? Sure. But simply standing there on the balcony with his friends was reward enough for now.

He looked to his left, where Rian was drifting off the floor with a huge smile stretched across his face. Next to Lewis, Kaya beamed as she stared out at the city—her city. She placed her hand on his shoulder, and Lewis nudged Hanna on his other side. Hanna didn't even notice. She was silently marveling at the wonders of Atlantis—the brightly colored buildings, the rushing, flowing water, the gravity-defying vehicles floating through the thick, humid air. Convincing Hanna to leave Atlantis was going to be difficult. Talking his dad into departing would be impossible.

But Lewis was ready to go home.

From: Porter Winfield

To: President Laura Moffat

Madam President,

Please accept this letter as notice of my resignation from the position of director of the National Security Agency, effective immediately. As we discussed, I wholeheartedly disagree with your decision to engage in diplomacy with the Atlanteans. You and your advisory team are endangering the lives of tens of millions of Americans. Furthermore, I deny any and all accusations regarding my alleged relationship with the executive leadership of the Sunshine Corporation and its admittedly charming founder. Finally, you borrowed my favorite pen during a meeting several months ago—my initials are on the cap—and never gave it back. Just because you're president doesn't mean you can take someone's stuff.

Sincerely,

Porter Winfield

Dear Mrs. Haney,

While I'm truly honored that you have chosen to publish my cookbook and greatly appreciate the editorial notes you've provided, especially with regard to my kelp pesto dish, I'm still not sure about your proposed title. I understand that *The Merman Diet* is catchy. Your assertion that this could launch an entire lifestyle brand might have merit. But there are no mermen in Atlantis! No mermaids, either! I honestly don't understand why people continue to hold on to that fantasy.

Regards,

Richard Gates

MAP OF NORTHERN ATLANTIS

2 EVENOR

3 CLEITO

4

5 RIDGE CITY

WEST TO
THE RIFT &
COLLAPSED
WESTERN
CITIES

PELLA

ACHERON

KEY #2

 Collapsed City

Vacuum Tunnel

 Waterway / Tunnel

Aquafarm

THE SCIENCE OF
THE BRINK OF WAR

An aquatic city like Atlantis—even an underground version like the one depicted in this book and its predecessor—would be very tricky to build and maintain. We humans aren't set up to live underwater. When Kaya, Lewis, and Hanna visit Evenor, for example, they swim down a hundred meters without much trouble, using diving weights and breathers to help. But in reality, the pressure of all the water above them would be far too intense; a real-life Lewis wouldn't make it very far. While I tried to be as scientifically accurate as possible, I stretched and bent reality sometimes, too. Here are a few of the cool technologies featured in the story that are based on real research, plus a brief description of what a merman or mermaid would actually look like, according to a biologist.

Invisible Esmerelda

So many stories and movies, from Harry Potter to *The Lord of the Rings*, feature magical invisibility cloaks. This book includes an electronic version that scientists have been speculating about for years. The idea, as explained in the book, is to cover an object with flexible screens and miniature cameras. If you were to stand in front of an object like Esmerelda, the cameras on the far side would record the scene behind the ship, then livestream that video on your side, where it would be projected as one giant image. You wouldn't see the ship—you'd see what's behind the ship—so it would basically be invisible.

This idea gets a little tricky when you introduce multiple viewers standing in different positions or when the object starts moving. But it's still possible. So why don't you see this technology at work today? Why isn't your family's car invisible? Well, maybe it is, and you just don't know it. Maybe there's an Atlantean ship outside your window right now. I know I'm safe from invisible invaders because I just threw my shoe out the window, and it didn't hit anything except my neighbor. She's fine, though.

Kung Fu Hoodie

Martial arts are very, very difficult to master. I have been studying kung fu movies for years, and I dreamed of being a ninja when I was younger, but I'm still only a rainbow belt, which is the one below the white belt. But Hanna's hoodie is based on another real concept. The robotics and computer science expert Daniela Rus of the Massachusetts Institute of Technology told me about her idea for helping people learn to swing a tennis racket or shoot a basketball like the pros.

The shirt—a hoodie, in the story—would be made of soft electronic materials, including flexible artificial muscles, and a miniature computer. An expert in a given field—say, a tennis pro—would train while wearing the shirt, and the shirt would remember how they moved their arms and torso. Then a regular person like you would pull on the shirt and activate the tennis training program, and the artificial muscles in the sleeves would nudge you through the same motions as the pro. Trained by enough experts, the same shirt could be used to teach someone a variety of sports and physical activities. Rus isn't looking to create a self-defense sweatshirt, which is how Hanna uses it in the book, but I couldn't really envision our heroic engineer beating back all those agents with a tennis racket.

Superphone

Susan Silver brings an unusual phone on her trip to Atlantis, and her tech connects with people above the water. How would that work? In 2017, the North Atlantic Treaty Organization, or NATO, an alliance of European and North American countries, announced the development of a new underwater communications technology called JANUS. The radio waves we use to communicate up here on the surface don't travel that well underwater, which is why you couldn't just text someone from Atlantis using your regular phone. This new approach uses a network of underwater robots, sensors, and floating communications buoys to transmit messages between the surface and the bottom of the sea. I can imagine Susan Silver hacking into that system and using it for herself. Streaming videos on Mars, though? That would be a little more difficult, unless someone stored a digital library of movies on an orbiting spaceship.

The Ugliest Merfolk

Okay, we have to talk about mermaids and mermen again. Most of the time, when we see mermaids on film or in comics, they are, to quote the philosopher Derek Zoolander, "really, really good-looking." When I spoke with a biologist named Frank Fish—yep, that's his real name—he explained that if merpeople really did exist, they'd look very, very different from what we'd expect. First of all, they wouldn't have long, flowing hair. If you had evolved to move quickly and efficiently through the water, you'd be as slick as possible. Second, they'd need undulating, flexible, dolphin-like tails. But these tails would stretch all the way up to their chests, since great swimmers use their entire body to kick, not just the lower half. Actual mermaids would probably have a pretty thick layer of blubber to keep them warm in cold water. They'd need gills, too, and would probably have large eyes to manage in the low light. Their ears would need to be very different from ours, too, in part because sound moves much faster through water than it does through air. Overall, Fish explained, a real merperson wouldn't look much like Ariel or Aquaman. They'd be plump, hairless, and alien in appearance. I swim as often as possible in open water, but if I ever meet a hideous creature like that, I'm pretty sure I'll kick the other way.

ACKNOWLEDGMENTS

Nika, Clare, Eleanor, Dylan. Toby. (Wait, did you see what Dad did? He mentioned Toby in his book! Do you think we'll get another dog? No.) Big Blue and Ludwig. Starburst. Nasuni. Momo & Poppy. (Matt, did he put us after the dog?) 509 Press and its clients. McCoy Tyner. Art Blakey. Max Roach. Mingus and Monk. Trad. Writing pants. Kate Campbell. Janet Zade. Jennifer Carlson. Howard Reeves! And Andrew, Jody, Jessica, Brenda, Megan, Hallie, Trish, Jenny, Sara, Kim, and the rest of the awesome crew at Abrams. Thank you all.